SNATCHED

A Selection of Recent Titles by Bill James from Severn House

DOUBLE JEOPARDY
FORGET IT
FULL OF MONEY
HEAR ME TALKING TO YOU
KING'S FRIENDS
THE LAST ENEMY
LETTERS FROM CARTHAGE
MAKING STUFF UP
NOOSE
OFF-STREET PARKING
THE SIXTH MAN and other stories
SNATCHED
TIP TOP
WORLD WAR TWO WILL NOT TAKE PLACE

The Harpur and Iles Series

VACUUM
UNDERCOVER
PLAY DEAD

SNATCHED

Bill James

This first world edition published 2014
in Great Britain and the USA by
SEVERN HOUSE PUBLISHERS LTD of
19 Cedar Road, Sutton, Surrey, England, SM2 5DA.
Trade paperback edition first published
in Great Britain and the USA 2014 by
SEVERN HOUSE PUBLISHERS LTD

British Library Cataloguing in Publication Data

James, Bill, 1929- author.
  Snatched.
  1. Museums–Fiction. 2. Black humor.
  I. Title
  823.9'14-dc23

ISBN-13: 978-0-7278-8379-7 (cased)
ISBN-13: 978-1-84751-511-7 (trade paper)

All Severn House titles are printed on acid-free paper.

Severn House Publishers support the Forest Stewardship Council™ [FSC™],
the leading international forest certification organisation. All our titles that
are printed on

Typeset by Pal...
Falkirk, Stirling...
Printed and bou...
TJ Internationa...

One

In the chair as Director, George Lepage considered this weekly session of the museum's management board to be getting along unusually well: some argument, yes, some insults, but nothing actually barbaric or even inhumane. And then, as if to kick Lepage's guarded smugness to death, the door was shoved hard open and, from the corridor outside, Keith Jervis stuck his head and short, thick, blondish pigtail a few inches into the Octagon Room. Alarmed, Lepage saw what appeared to be a broad streak of blood across his brow and more of it staining the lapels of his azure uniform jacket.

In a throaty, not quite panic-driven voice, Jervis, one of the economy-measure, hourly paid, part-time porters, said: 'Ladies and gentlemen officers of the Hulliborn Regional Museum and Gallery, we got what could be designated in my opinion a fucking riot at the Folk Department, pardon the demotic. Well, *starting* at the Folk. Ongoing. Now it's reached Coins, Badges, Medals and Smaller Artefacts. What I'm reporting for here, now, is to be given orders, really. This kind of incident – outside my parameters, especially not being promoted to established, salaried staff, despite representations. I'll accept lip from visitors and even assault, up to a point, but thereafter through channels – such as this door into the Octagon, yes – thereafter, through channels, reference must be made to my superiors, to the policy makers, as it were. That's only fair. Noblesse-o-what-they-call.'

'A disturbance in the Folk Hall spreading to Coins?' Lepage said. He stood.

'It's nasty, no getting away from it,' Jervis said. 'We was outnumbered. Withdrawal seemed the only feasible. "Regrouping" is the term, I believe. It's chaos, though. In the rush I stumble and knock against a glass showcase of specie, and suffer the wound.' He pointed to his forehead but didn't touch it, so as not to get his hand bloody. 'They got dangerous edges, some of them display stands. The public safety authorities wouldn't like them. But, then again, I got to admit there wouldn't normally be someone, such as self, falling over in the museum owing to a galloping fracas.'

'Quite,' Lepage said, 'but you've done admirably, and I'm distressed to see you're hurt.' Jervis had come a few steps into the room now. 'Please give us the details, Keith.'

'What's that terrible noise?' Pirie asked, very tense.

Lepage had heard it, too. From behind Jervis through the open door came the distant sound of an angry, possibly violent, crowd. The word 'baying' entered George's head to describe the din, but this he quashed at once: crowds in the museum was a difficult enough idea, but a *baying* crowd? 'We must go there at once,' Lepage said. He was in charge.

Two

Some might ask how come he was in charge. Possibly, they'd consider him too young for his post as Director of a major museum, like the Hulliborn, especially at a time when museums and their finances had begun to suffer increasingly unpleasant problems. Perhaps the last time they heard of George he was only head of a department here (Archaeology), among a barrelful of other department heads. However, George had moved up on the death of Flounce last September, 'Flounce' being the unaffectionately used nickname of Sir Eric Butler-Minton, former Director.

Anyway, now here was George Lepage, kingpin of the Hulliborn. He did look reasonably, though not outrageously, young: that is reasonably, not outrageously, young for such a job – forty-eight. He kept himself decently spry. Or in that area. His face was long and bony, though not cadaverous, in his judgement. He had good fair skin and was clean shaven – very efficiently clean-shaven: no missed stubble nests. His hair was straight – mousy to straw – and, to date, as full as it had ever been, with an impertinent, boyish cowlick that needed pushing back off his forehead now and then, but not so far that it didn't fall into position again soon. His brown eyes were keen and lively, not absolutely unsly but not ruthless or egomaniac, either: nobody could run a museum without at least a sliver of slyness.

Just before Jervis's incursion George had been wondering whether he could award himself some credit for the prevailing, moderately polite, generally civilized atmosphere of the management meetings, following his replacement of Flounce. Possibly. The orderliness of today's proceedings had pleased but also scared George. Wasn't it eerie to look down the big, leather-padded, mahogany table and see for a long stretch of consecutive seconds definite smiles and contentment on these customarily contempt-filled, arid, avid faces? This afternoon, no voice had employed yet that high-pitched, enraged snottiness, dubbed throughout the trade 'curator's retch', in which so much major business was traditionally done in premier division museums, here and overseas.

Lepage returned to the notion that perhaps some of his colleagues' apparent happiness derived from seeing him, George Lepage, actually there in the Director's chair, sturdy, unarguable evidence that Flounce really had been screwed down in that long, fake-oak box, garnished with a pair of foxgloves and burned at the crem: no question of a vigorous, slavering return, in one of his unbelievable Dominican Republic suits, to slag them off as cock-sucking subscribers to the *Independent*.

This didn't mean everything was peachy. The Hulliborn had enemies. Which museum worth its grant didn't? Sadly, several of Hulliborn's had previously been distinguished members of the staff, but now nursed festering psychological injuries after being flung out in the recent cutback programme implemented by Butler-Minton as one of his last duties, though enforced from Downing Street. For some, the Hulliborn's vast halls of preserved death and the past had been life. Deprived of them, they grew evil. Some went mad.

George had decided he would deal with this trouble as well as he could, but not for ever; not even for very long. He calculated that, with his improved pension entitlement, he could take extremely early retirement from the episodes of vividly-expressed, engulfing, bureaucratic flimflam, such as today's, and every other bit of this grand, tricky post. At fifty-four, or, with skill and luck, maybe before that – say 1993, when he'd be fifty-two – he might be able to quit and make a shapely, non-poverty-line go of things, granted, as he surely would be, a little flints and shards consultancy; plus whatever Julia made at her 'Spud-O'-My-Life' jacket potato kiosk near the rail station, if Julia were still interested then. He recognized, though, that he must not go before he got the Hulliborn's future properly established. Or had clearly failed, and would just as clearly go on failing, to get the Hulliborn's future properly established.

The Director loved Julia and her body and so on, and he loved the Prime Minister, also, though not in that way.

Thatcherism decreed among other things that the young should do the work, while the marginally less young in the public sector took whacking redundough pay-offs and precocious pensions and were deemed old and spent, although almost everything about them – knees, bowels, sassiness, feet, self-esteem, appetite, genitalia – particularly these last three – said 'get stuffed' to that. Just for now, as newly risen Supremo of the Hulliborn Regional Museum and Gallery, George had to be numbered among the trapped, working young, but he and Time should be able to rectify that, thanks very much. Time was something museum people knew about, and if anyone could get it by the short and curlies they could. At present, Time was unquestionably the Director's bread, butter and official Volvo, but soon it might be transubstantiated into an ejection seat.

He hoped that by then he would have totally wiped out most of the dire results of Flounce's period as Director. People who knew Flounce normally had very down-and-up reactions to him. In a million and a half ways, he had been a prime and towering shit, yet some did feel sympathy that he failed to live quite long enough to see the collapse of the Berlin Wall in November. So many of Flounce's shady, mysterious afflictions, which did the Hulliborn no good at all, seemed to stem from behind the Curtain under the old regime: maybe in East Berlin itself, but Rostock also was mentioned. The ripple of terrible, and terribly vague, rumours about the haversack straps and a whippet appeared to start in one or both locations, the geographical uncertainty part of that overall vagueness. But, however nauseating and absurd Butler-Minton had been, he'd surely deserved his personal fragment of Europe's grand triumph last year when that chunky, dangerous, check-pointed barrier came down. However, Butler-Minton had died just ahead of that. And so, Director George.

'Hulliborn will undoubtedly emerge from the impending post-cuts appraisal and audit as a Grade One-A centre of excellence, to use the admin wallahs' own jejune, schoolmarm terms,' Simberdy, bulky, emphatic, focused, (Asiatic Antiquities), had said early in today's proceedings. 'Naturally, it is crucial that we should, since under the current philistine political crew

there will be next to no cash for the also-rans. Hulliborn, as
we have known it, and know it, would be extinguished. Plainly,
we will not let this occur.'

'Never,' Angus Beresford (Entomology) said.

'We must snatch all opportunities for betterment. The way
museums are treated tells us the state of culture and learning
in a country,' Simberdy said. 'Think of the Victoria and Albert.
And, certainly, one way to help towards the highest rating is
to ensure no slip-ups – ABSOLUTELY NO SLIP-UPS – in
our efforts to attract the Japanese Ancient Surgical Skills exhibition, against all competition.'

'Absolutely,' Beresford had said. 'The Tokyo show that proves
they could yank kidney stones and appendixes from – from
the year dot?'

'And far far more than that, including transplants,' Simberdy
said. 'These instruments are a wonder, and their number and
variety astounding. Well, there'd be no JASS exhibition otherwise. This goes far beyond the trumpeted discovery recently
– 1988? – of that comparatively primitive Roman medical gear.'

'Do we know if the people lived?' Lepage had said.

'Director? Which people? The people of those ancient civ-
ilizations? Oh, certainly. Plenty of indisputable evidence,'
Simberdy said with exceptional mildness, surprising restraint.
Normally, Lepage might have expected impatience, perhaps
irritation, because his question hinted at doubt.

'The people who were operated on with this equipment,'
Lepage said. 'Did they survive?'

'We must assume so, Director,' Simberdy said, 'or would they
have persisted with the manufacture of these things? The people
were not called Japanese then, you'll understand, but native to
those islands. This would be the Yayoi period, or even earlier,
the Jomon era, perhaps around the time of the Iron Age. Some
sort of advanced civilization long before Christ – the very point
of the exhibition. It has astonishing implications. For instance,
some medics say tonsils only developed recently, coincident,
apparently, with extended use of the "i" vowel sound owing to
the growth of the middle classes and trade – "dividend", "profit",
"impecunious", "invest", "increase", "interest", "discount",
"insolvency", "rich", "business".

'But the exhibition makes such time-fixing very question-able, since instruments found were obviously intended for tonsils' excision. This is a world-acclaimed collection. It's been everywhere – the States, New Zealand, Sweden – and I feel sure that we at the Hulliborn are not going to stint in our efforts to attract it here. Our style is gloriously different from that, thank God – particularly now, if I may say, Director, under your leadership. And the dear Japanese can be so touchy. They were reluctant that these unique relics should leave Tokyo at all, but have been persuaded. What I know we all wish to avoid is any appearance of, one, churlishness, and two, insta-bility, which could lose everything. The grapevine tells me that we are virtually sure to be selected for the only British showing of these wonders. Not even London or Glasgow will get a sniff. It would be a clincher, a life-saver, a real boost to our image, Director.'

'Well, image is important, but not *all*-important,' D.Q. Youde (Art) had said.

Lepage felt a momentary shift in the meeting's mood, not a helpful shift.

Simberdy said: 'Yes, a real boost to the Hulliborn's image, despite our recent purchase for unbelievable money of the disputed quote "El Grecos" unquote.'

'I'll stake my reputation they are genuine!' Youde said, the articulation big but nervy, his fine pallor enhanced by rage. He had on that black leather blouson: mutton dressed as cow, to quote Julia.

'Well, you *have* staked it, Quentin,' Simberdy replied. 'And ours. But I say that, despite such shadows, the Hulliborn would stand high and benefit immeasurably from JASS. No further threats to our grant and status or, indeed, existence could be contemplated, not even by the present vandals in power.'

'Obviously, we're in your hands on this, Vince,' Lepage said. 'You're the expert, and a very considerable expert.'

'We must devote all our efforts into winning the exhibition,' Pirie, Museum and Galleries Secretary, said. 'It will put even Tutankhamen and the Dinosaurs into the shade.'

'Admirable shows in themselves, but ultimately gimmicky and concerned with comparative trivia,' Simberdy said. 'Nothing must be allowed to shake our reputation at this important stage. We should be particularly on guard against attacks, in whatever form they might take, from people who have lost their posts here during what we would all admit were painful rationalization measures, and whose chief purpose now is to wreak revenge by bringing contumely upon the Hulliborn. Yes, contumely. I need only mention one name and you will understand my point – Neville Falldew, formerly Palaeontology. I can tell you – or perhaps I don't need to tell you – but, for those who haven't heard, he's been seen loitering, possibly disguised, in the vicinity of the museum grounds, day and night, his purpose unknown. This is impeccable info.'

'Scheming, embittered, crazed swine,' Beresford said.

'Oh, Nev's not wholly bad, even now,' Wex (History of Urban Development) said.

'Ursula, we are aware of your former, possibly continuing, feelings in that direction,' Simberdy said. 'Neville certainly had a way with him. But the rest of us can only judge as we see and hear now, following his enforced departure. Poisonous intimations. Threats. Lethal envy of those of us who were *not* let go. He reads some reflection on his work and reputation in this. He is a very strange case, of course, in that he continues to worship – indeed idolize – Butler-Minton, who actually made him redundant.'

'Butler-Minton fought for him,' Ursula Wex said, 'but was overruled by the politicians. Nev is eternally grateful for his efforts, sees them as a noble failure.'

Simberdy had stood up to make his later points and, very wearied by the tiny effort, tried to arrange himself so that his great, buff-cardiganed gut was supported by the edge of the table, like Humpty Dumpty on the wall. His ample cheeks glowed puce. 'We must not forget Falldew and should try to counter him, pre-empt his malevolent plans, whatever they may be, and look to the future. The local Press, in commending us recently, rightly said our management group was now lean and fit and strong. "Bracingly lean" was the phrase, I recall,' he said, bracingly leaning his belly on the fine old timber, 'and—'

Three

But this was the moment that Keith Jervis erupted into the Octagon Room with his news and stains.

Simberdy, still on his feet, radiating delight from Press praise, stared at Jervis and said, mildly: 'You speak of channels, Keith, but I'm not sure this is the way to approach your Director and his Keepers, Curators, and Museum Secretary. This *is* our Hebdomadal Conclave, you know.'

'Never fear, this is a ructions that can still be kept in bounds,' Jervis replied.

'You spoke of the withdrawal of the museum staff,' Simberdy said. 'Withdrawal to where?' He was seated again now, panting slightly.

'I was cut off,' Jervis said. 'Was involved at the earliest, then couldn't reach the refuge. Became separated from the other porters. Cornered, like a cop at a Millwall game, such as in the papers. Hence, the personal damage.'

'My God, yes, the Press,' Simberdy whispered, as though a reporter might be under the table. 'This disaster, whatever it is, must not get out. It could ruin the previous good publicity, and the Japanese might turn extremely inscrutable.'

Pirie mentioned the noise.

'We must go to them,' Ursula Wex said very loudly, perhaps eager to emphasize her loyalty to the new, slimmer Hulliborn, after her possibly unpopular defence of Neville Falldew. She picked up the full water carafe, a modern, worthless thing, and held it by the neck like a club, drops of the liquid dribbling out down her sleeve and on to her shoes. She was small, slightly built, brilliant, off-and-on combative, mostly gentle.

'Which refuge, Jervis?' Simberdy asked.

'Like I mentioned, Coins and so on,' Jervis said. 'The Secure Room? The Chief Porter – staff – pulled the grille down after them, self-locking.'

'Presence of mind,' Beresford said. 'Good for Hamilton. Some of these NCO types – remarkable leadership qualities.'

'They're like animals in a cage,' Jervis said. 'Or the Black Hole. I mean, four in that tiny place, only intended for historic moolah: shekels, doubloons, ducats.'

'We should go to them,' Ursula Wex shouted, waving the carafe.

'I was trapped,' Jervis replied. 'Caught in the killing fields between Urban Development, History of, and *Draped Snatch*.'

'Vintag's *Serenity* statue,' Quentin Youde said.

'Obviously, I knew I had to get an account of the incident through to management, regardless—'

'Sterling,' Beresford said.

'—Regardless of not being staff. To date,' Jervis replied.

Ursula went to the door and pushed past Jervis. She listened for a second, then turned her head back and snarled to the meeting, 'Yes, downstairs, bloody *sans culottes*.'

'How it all started,' Jervis said.

'What do you mean?' Simberdy said.

'*Sans culottes*?' Jervis asked. 'French Revo term for the republican poor. Literally, no trousers. Supposed not to be able to afford them.'

'I know that, you self-educated, ungrammatical ponce,' Simberdy said. 'But why did you say "how it all started"?'

'A lady's modesty given fleshly outrage,' Jervis said.

'Which lady?' Ursula said.

'Then friends and relatives ran to her defence. A coach full, from Kidderminster.'

'Outraged how?' Lepage asked.

Jervis said: 'I have to piece things together from all the screaming, howling, bellowing, but as I hear it, she was by herself in that cosy ancient peasant room off the Folk Hall—'

'Middle Ages Domestic Scene, yes,' Lepage said.

'Wax models of some early-century yokels and their kids having the much-missed traditional Old English breakfast – a couple of swedes, some dandelion leaves and an acorn, you know. Suddenly, the Dad figure stands up from his tree stump – yes, this dummy gets to his feet and offers the solitary, lady visitor a big, inviting grin from behind the medieval moustache and whiskers, then drops his trousers and gives her a full meat and potatoes frontal. This was a pre-boxer-shorts epoch. She screeches and passes out. Well, who wouldn't? This is a meaningful tableau! I heard her cries, and visitors heard, and we all came rushing. She stirs a bit on the floor and does something of an explanation – "the patriarch, a flasher" was how she finished. Friends of hers go berserk and start attacking the models, pulling garments awry, looking for any more working vitals, but they're all just models, nothing there but seams. He's gone, scarpered, while she lay out for the count. So they turn on Mr Hamilton and me and the other porters who've arrived because of the din. I mean, these visitors have come to believe this is what the Hulliborn stages as the normal thing, and they're upset, belligerent.'

Simberdy boomed: 'Don't you see, all of you, it's someone who aims to sabotage our standing with the Museums Inspectorate, and destroy our chance of hosting JASS? I've dreaded something of this sort.'

'Falldew,' Beresford hissed. 'Neville's name is written all over it.'

'She didn't mention no tattoo,' Jervis replied.

From the door, Ursula said: 'As to that, is there a description of the perpetrator at all?'

'Well, he's covered in hair, isn't he?' Jervis said. 'Couldn't see much face, most probably. But tall, I understand, thin, and the woman said glassy blue eyes; glassy, mad blue eyes.'

'And?' Ursula said.

'Dr Wex?' Jervis asked.

Ursula stared towards his crotch.

'Oh, I get it,' Jervis said. 'Your special knowledge. But all the woman said was it seemed very present-day and alive, not a prop.'

Four

So, Lepage, in charge, hurried excitedly towards the door and
Ursula. Perhaps if the job was going to be like this he wouldn't
want early retirement after all. As he stepped into the corridor,
he heard Simberdy call: 'Director, nothing extreme, I beg.
No police. Don't invite media interest. TV! Christ, think of
it. Something unkind, satiric from Bernard Levin! Remember
JASS.'

Simberdy was right to detect overtones. The Hulliborn's
fight for status might typify many a similar fight in Britain's
menaced cultural bodies. Although his views about his own
future might vary, Lepage would never deny a strong love and
admiration for the Hulliborn. After all, he had been here for
fifteen years and was fond of its big, ugly buildings and its
galleries smelling of floor polish and school groups. He wished
the Hulliborn only good, more or less.

Another factor: Julia wanted him to collect a knighthood
for his time at the top of the Hulliborn, in line with Flounce's
and the previous Director's. It had to be admitted that Julia
could be a bit of a snob. It had to be admitted, too, that there
were times when this side of her came near to turning him
fatally off. Julia liked being live-in partner to the Director of
the Hulliborn, and if he quit early she wanted something to
replace that rank and cachet: a knighthood would suit very
nicely. Julia did not visualize their future social ranking as
dependent solely upon her ownership of the Spud-O'-My-Life
kiosk, or even upon a chain of kiosks, if things took off. But
a knighthood for George, possibly marriage, and so, Lady
Lepage, renowned head of a food combine – that might add
up to something decently eminent.

And so, because George Lepage for most of his time did
want to hang on to Julia, and because he had a soft spot for
the Hulliborn, its good repute was doubly vital to him. The
JASS exhibition seemed the best way on offer to lift its rating

and impress those who gave out gongs. He must do all he could to further Vince Simberdy's campaign – *snatch* all helpful openings, in Vince's term – particularly as very destructive, knowledgeable flak could start flying any day about Quentin Youde's expensive 'El Greco' deal, which would have to be diverted and offset. So far, the insurers and auditors had the paintings as assets slightly above the price the Hulliborn paid, but some troublesome questions had begun to circulate.

Now, Lepage went ahead, descending at a rush the iron spiral staircase from the Octagon Room level to the public Reception area. He was aware of Ursula and Jervis clattering after him, and perhaps a couple of others from the Hebdomadal following them. As he reached the bottom and stood gazing about, a chill column of water from Ursula's flask speared down alongside the spiral's central pillar and struck him on the head with a spattering thump, like that sounding cataract in some poem, and then slipped down inside his collar, went the length of his spine, and continued on between his buttocks as if a new strain of big, fast-moving slug wanted to show off its pace and dauntlessness.

Dripping moderately, he made his way across Reception and towards Coins. As Jervis had suggested, this was where most of the noise originated. Lepage thought he could distinguish five kinds of sound. There were angry men's voices, angry women's voices, and frightened men's voices, these latter presumably Hamilton's and some of the other porters'. He heard fierce rattling of metalwork, which must be visitors trying to break down the Secure Room grille to get at those inside, plus the deep, possibly hysterical wailing of a woman. He went past the *Serenity* nude, on through the Raybould Gallery, where the 'El Grecos', with their bet-hedging caption sheets bravely hung, and then took the short cut via Early Industrial.

Suddenly, some distance ahead of him, he saw the tall, skinny figure of a man crossing the arched entrance to Coins and seemingly making his way towards the museum's main exit. At the same time, from a few steps behind him, came a brief, anxious gasp. Ursula must also have seen this man and recognized him as Falldew. He was dressed in his own modern-day clothes now, not medieval costume, and seemed properly zipped up. Although he appeared to be taking his time, ambling in the style of most museum visitors, he actually managed swift, long-legged progress. It looked as though he wanted to guard against getting conspicuous by hurrying, but planned to be out and clear very fast, just the same. Falldew would know all the odd corners of the Hulliborn, and must have used somewhere hidden away to change his gear. So, had Simberdy's reported sightings been correct? 'Neville,' Lepage called. 'Neville Falldew, please wait.'

For half a second, Neville paused and looked back. Deeply unwise. He stood framed by the entrance to Coins and as he turned, his features were momentarily fully on view to the people in there. It seemed enough, although Falldew's face was so thin that at times it appeared to be nothing but profile. The wailing from the woman stopped, or, rather, switched to a scream, a scream composed of mixed horror and rage. She shouted something. Lepage could not be sure exactly what, but he thought it something like, 'Him! Him! Glassy eyes!'

Almost immediately afterwards, Ursula yelled: 'Nev, darling, make a dash, for God's sake. They've got you marked. Evade! Evade!'

It was too far for Lepage to see, but the avenging crowd in Coins must be adjusting to this new development; perhaps turning away from the Secure Room grille and the trapped staff, to register the woman's information and fix their purpose on Falldew. The noise stopped. Ursula, too, had grown silent, gripped by disabling tension, maybe, as she watched to see if Nev would snatch the chance in this hiatus to escape. Another scream from the woman broke the sudden, disturbing soundlessness, and then more words: 'It's the prick-proud special exhibit! Don't let him do a runner!'

Immediately, a great, ferocious roar arose in Coins. Lepage heard the beat of many feet galloping over the boarded floor, like a rain squall on a roof. Obviously, Falldew saw the crowd belting towards him and did what Ursula had urged. Abandoning all pretence at casualness, he pulled his suit jacket tight about him, as a woman might gather her skirt, and gave it all he had in a sprint towards the main door, knees pumping up near his chin, arms flailing ungovernably. Lepage had never seen him in a suit before. Invariably, he wore a scruffy old suede jerkin and, summer or winter, a lengthy blue Oxford college scarf. The present outfit was disguise. It didn't work.

When Falldew had gone about twenty metres, the leader of the mob from Coins appeared, hurtling after him; then, in a straggle, about twenty people, men, women and children, all of them shouting abuse at Neville and calling on him to stop. Uninvolved visitors in the Hulliborn watched fascinated, possibly thinking it some sort of organized Happening, to illustrate a hue-and-cry from the good old days. The revolving door sped around as Falldew burst out on to the street. Although pensioned and gangly, he seemed to be leaving his younger pursuers. Whatever had happened in the peasant home did not seem to have taken much out of him. But Lepage had better have a proper look there later.

When he reached Coins, Medals, Badges and Smaller Artefacts, he found the section almost empty, except for Hamilton and the other porters. Lepage had a master key, and he opened the grille. The porters emerged in a rush. They appeared strained and battle-chastened, like pictures of troops back from Dunkirk. A woman lay on one of Coins' sofas sobbing quietly. Lepage went to her. 'Are you the lady who—?'

'Oh, this outing was to have been so educational and uplifting,' she replied. 'But you are wet. Is that part of it?'

'I'm sorry,' Lepage said. 'Please try to think only of the worthwhile elements of your Hulliborn visit. You had no comparable trouble in Entomology?'

'I've brought you some water,' Ursula told her. The carafe had a few centimetres left.

'If only he'd said something – communicated, explained, put matters in context,' the woman moaned. Lepage thought she must be a teacher. 'But he just stood there, seeming so undiffident and display-prone,' she said.

'Yes, that's got to be Neville,' Ursula replied.

Five

'A commotion?' Olive Simberdy said. 'Neville Falldew?'

'We think Nev. They couldn't catch him, so we're not totally sure,' Simberdy said. They were in the living room of their four-storey Edwardian house, not far from the Hulliborn.

'How?' she asked.

'How what?'

'Well, what happened?'

'Shall we say a private showing? Neville – we think Neville – historicized himself in Folk and double-shocked a visitor. That kind of incident could be bad for the museum as things are at present, Olive. Luckily, Lepage realized that at once – he'll make a good Director. He was on the scene immediately. He took her off to recover properly, as soon as she seemed over the worst.'

'Took her off where?'

'You know, I'm not sure. To his room, I suppose. Important to make our apology really tell.'

'Alone?' Olive had a round, friendly-looking, even jolly, face, but it could be speedily adjusted to display out-and-out suspicion. It did that now.

'Ursula was with them at first. She gave the woman water from a carafe. She might have wanted to find Nev instead. They had, have, that *tendresse*, don't they?'

'What age?'

'The woman?'

'Yes, the woman,' Olive snapped.

'Late twenties.'

'Nice looking? Tits?'

'Anguished at the time. My main thought, and George's, probably, was damage containment. Something like this could be disastrous, disastrous. That kind of publicity – catastrophic re the Japanese thing. Of course, Nev Falldew realizes that. It's why he chose to act now. The Folk Hall crisis must be seen as very much a test of George's new regime. He had to seem decisive. Whatever one thinks of Flounce, he was certainly that.' A fit of trembling hit him for a moment.

'Darling, the Hulliborn's beginning to get you down, make you ill.' With her palm she felt her husband's brow for a while. Then she resumed cutting her toenails. A large, curved shiny trimming arced across the over-furnished, almost cluttered room like a jet fighter on TV news, and struck one of their few real china cups, producing a delicate, pure, continuing sound that made her pause for a moment and smile excitedly. The jolliness returned to her face, or more than jolliness: the gorgeous china-chime made her look exultant, like a surfer who'd just come in on a huge wave. Sometimes, when listing Olive's assets, Simberdy would say she had a supreme ear. She went on snipping but had no repeat of the luck.

They were both dressed in black, and on the coffee table three black woollen balaclava helmets lay ready. When finished with her feet, she pulled on black silk socks, and then a pair of black plimsolls.

'I'm sure Falldew will try something else,' Simberdy said, stretching out on the *chaise longue*. 'He cultivates hate and revenge like plants. We'll just lurk about in the Hulliborn grounds for a few nights – deal with this "in house", as it were. We don't want the police concerned and, above all, not the Press and broadcasters. We must try to surprise him. It's shadowy. These outfits should do it.'

Stuffed into his, he looked like a parked VW Beetle, Olive thought.

'I have my main door key, but I don't think we should wait inside. We're more likely to get close to him unobserved if we use the natural cover in the grounds. As to keys, I suppose Nev still has his for the main door. He's clever and devious enough. Flounce might have been decisive in his prime, but he became doddery, forgetful and careless at the end: that East German stuff – the haversack straps, Mrs Cray, and the friend of his shot dead from the Wall trying to escape to the West, etcetera. All this was bound ultimately to get to his mind.'

'I never understand. What about the haversack straps and so on?'

'Nobody's completely clear, but that stuff's important.' He sighed. 'I aim to give Nev only a forceful talking to, no brutality. I'll use shame: appeal to the undoubted good in him and his basic love for the Hulliborn. I know it's there, temporarily soured, that's all. I'll ask him why he's siding with the new vandals.' He gave her some gaze. 'It's sweet of you to say you'll come.'

She tried on one of the balaclavas before the mirror. Her voice became muffled, but Simberdy thought she said: 'Could we let you undertake something like this alone, Vince? He might turn nasty. You, too, love that museum, and *I* love *you*. We must act as a team. It will inspire us.'

Simberdy considered that the almost total black sheen of Olive's outfit – only her eyes breaking it, now she had the balaclava on – made her look overwhelmingly desirable. As well as the wonderful ear, she had a sumptuous arse, somehow tonight given additional ripeness and mystery by those dark, conspiratorial trousers. Would there be time to get all these clothes off, and his own cripplingly tight garments, before they set out? But, if her uniform was what had given him special excitement, perhaps he didn't want it off, beyond the necessary. Ignoring exceptional cases such as working Eskimos, he'd bet not many men had given it to a woman wearing a balaclava.

He put an arm around Olive's waist and, turning her towards him, kissed lightly through the gap on both eyelids and the top of her nose. She responded, as she always responded when he touched her, clinging hard to his bulk and thrusting her face up towards his. Behind the thick wool he could just make out her lips, soft, warm, open. But he didn't care for what they said.

'Darling, Vince, you do realize that Nothing Known will be here in a couple of minutes?' she murmured.

'What? Oh, him.'

'He'll expect us to be ready, and looking professional. He's meticulous.'

Olive was a solicitor and, in case of physical aggravation from Falldew, had recruited one of her firm's most gifted clients to help tonight, as bodyguard – bodies' guard: Wayne Passow, noted burglar and general criminal, often prosecuted, never convicted and, as his nickname told, with no police record.

Simberdy released her, and she pulled off the balaclava.

'Wayne can only stay a few hours,' she said. 'He's going on to a late-night date.'

'Lucky lad.'

'He seems to have something really nice under way,' she replied. 'He's very keen.'

Simberdy put on black silk gloves to go with his black trousers and black, roll-top sweater. He felt very committed and effective. This adventure was turning out to be a tonic, as Olive had said it would. Optimism had always come easily to him, like weight.

Passow arrived. He was short, gymnast-wiry, about thirty, in a dark three-piece suit, blue bobble hat, black lace-up shoes, burgundy open-necked shirt. His features were small, neat, would-be-winsome.

In the car, Simberdy said: 'We want no violence, Wayne, unless Falldew becomes rough himself. We – I mean museum folk – we have our own ways, conditioned by a respect for others and for the gentle beneficence of Time; and we do these things by force of words and logic, nothing cruder.'

Passow said: 'Lovely evening for it. Don't like that obstreperous moon, though. I'm taking risks for you, Ol, if he does turn heavy. And not a sausage in it for Wayne boy at all.'

Olive's chummy face now took on a prosecutor's sharpness. She could move with ease through her many personas. 'Think of what you're doing as repayment,' she said.

'For what?' Nothing Known said.

'For the practice getting you off so often,' Olive said.

'That's what lawyers are for, isn't it?' Passow replied.

'Some lawyers are fussy about whom they take on,' Olive said.

'Fussy how?' Nothing Known said.

'They're careful,' Olive said.

'I hope so,' he said.

'Have you come across the word "recidivist" at all?' Olive asked.

'I'm always amazed at how many words there are around,' Nothing Known replied.

'It means someone who's been convicted and then reoffends and reoffends,' Olive said.

'This don't apply to me because I never been convicted,' he

said. Passow spoke this casually, no argumentative bite, as if
what he said was so obvious and indisputable that it didn't
need reinforcement.

'I know – thanks to the practice,' she answered.

'Just police trying to frame me non-stop,' he said. 'All you
got to do is show the truth. Innocence can sometimes speak
for itself, but sometimes requires a lawyer or two. Innocence
is powerful. This is famed. It's in *The Song Of Sullivan* in the
actual Bible. A tip for tonight? Leave the car open and the keys
in for a fast exit. You never know with this kind of sortie. Half
seconds can be important. Crucial.'

'Is that in *The Song Of Sullivan*, too?' Simberdy replied.

In the museum grounds, they stood together for a while
under a larch, watching for any movement near the great spread
of dark Hulliborn buildings. 'What kind of trouble from him
would you expect?' Passow asked.

'Graffiti daubings – insults in quick-drying, very luminous
paint, yellow or red. Breakages,' Simberdy said.

'I never took much notice of museums,' Nothing Known
said. 'Yet I hear they got paintings in some of them worth a
stack of noughts. Is that so, Vince?'

'You're here for a specific task, Wayne,' Olive told him.

'Sure, sure,' he said. 'Only using this waiting time to learn
– art's quite a topic, nobody can deny it.'

'Yes, a stack of noughts, but only if they're the right pictures,
or, alternatively, if the Art wallah in the museum is a cunt and
shells out daft when buying,' Simberdy said.

'Who says what's right?' Wayne replied. 'How do you tell?'

'The big, big question,' Simberdy said. 'Some *can't* tell. Ask
Dr D.Q. Youde.'

'Who's he?' Nothing Known replied.

'It doesn't matter,' Simberdy said.

'It sounds like he makes you ratty, though,' Passow said, 'but
in an artistic fashion.'

'We don't get ratty – not museum folk. Disappointed,
perhaps,' Simberdy said.

'Let down,' Olive said.

'But if the doctors of art and that can't get it right, what
chance the rest of us?' Nothing Known said. 'Just pot luck?'

'Probably,' Simberdy said. 'Fine art's nine-tenths auctioneers' bullshit, and the rest leg-pull.'

'Is this him?' Olive whispered, and they all drew their balaclavas close. But it was only the wind spinning some dumped porno mags across the grass.

'I'll do a bit of a recce,' Passow replied. 'Make the most of our forces.'

'Reassemble in ten,' Olive said.

'*Jawohl mein Kapitan*,' Nothing Known said.

After half an hour, he had not returned. Off-and-on clouds covered the moon, and light rain fell. Simberdy said: 'If he runs into poor Nev when we're not there to insist on restraint . . . My God, what's that?' They'd both heard the sound of glass shattering on the far side of the buildings, what could be a large window. All the Hulliborn's alarms started to scream.

'Vincent, we should get out. I mean, dressed like this, how will it look?' Although he heard this through two layers of balaclava, his and hers, fright made him get her message very well.

'Exactly,' he said. 'This is uncatered for.'

They ran back across the grounds towards the car, Olive holding his arm to help him keep going. Above the alarms' din, Simberdy thought he caught the blare of police sirens. There seemed to be flashing blue lights as well, but he felt these might be internal only, springing from his terror and blood pressure.

'Not far now, darling,' Olive said. He groaned. 'There's the car,' she added. Simberdy muttered two prayers of thanks: one, because they had almost reached it, and two, for Nothing Known's back-alley wisdom in making sure there'd be no delay messing about with keys. But what about Nothing Known? Where was he? Nothing was known. Well, they couldn't wait for him. He would have to look after himself. He'd broken the arrangement. Maybe broken more than that. Now, it had to be *sauve qui peut*.

They'd almost reached the gates of the grounds and the road when Olive shrieked, 'Bastard! Recidivist bastard.' It would be easy to forget she ever looked inoffensive. Again Simberdy heard with the foul clarity of crisis. His head had fallen forward

in exhaustion as he staggered on, but when he forced it half
up off his chest for a second he saw their Vauxhall suddenly
pull out ahead, lightless, tyres screeching, and race away from
them. There seemed to be only the driver in it, probably a
man, crouched forward and possibly wearing a black balaclava.
Simberdy's brain was not in a state to do much with these
facts, half facts. But he felt a vast gratitude that further running
for the car must be hopeless.

He stopped and clung to the perimeter railings. His legs felt
filleted, his chest alight. The balaclava obstructed his breathing,
and he tore at it with weak fingers, striving to clear an air
route. Olive had run a few useless steps after the car, waving
her black-clad arms furiously and still yelling curses. Simberdy
thought he had seen something like it in Wagner – *The Ring*?
He considered she appeared wonderfully demonic and *maudite*
and would have loved to stand with her and yell, too, but he
needed his strength to fight the fucking wool and wipe away
sweat and slobber, which had begun to course down under
the helmet's neck piece and soak his roll-top.

In a while, Olive returned and helped him take off the balaclava. She removed hers, too, and threw them both into the
bushes. 'We ought to vamoose from the area, love,' she said.
'You're doing fine.'

'Am I honestly, Ol?'

'Fine.'

'It's a bit of derring-do, anyway.'

'Of course it is. Wouldn't have missed it,' she said. Even in
the dark he could see her face was back to sweetness and
empathy.

'He'll get to his date on time, I suppose – in our car. And
if he's pinched anything from the Hulliborn he can hide it, or
them, in the boot.'

'He's very cautious. And so, nothing's known about Nothing
Known,' Olive replied.

Six

George Lepage also heard the sound of breaking glass, followed by the alarms. If anything, he felt even more troubled than Olive and Vincent Simberdy. The noises reached him with greater force because he was on museum premises at the time, seated alone in his office, waiting for a personal telephone call on the direct, non-switchboard line.

Instinctively, he stood and faced towards where the noise had seemed to come from, like a dog pointing. Art? The Raybould Gallery? There was no repetition, and after a few minutes he decided he'd have to go and investigate. For a reasonably quiet approach over the board floors, he took off his shoes and socks, then left the Director's suite and hurried towards the spiral staircase. A few dim security lights shone. God, was this Falldew again? How deep could injury and the thirst for vengeance go?

As he made his way, he wondered how Flounce would have dealt with the intriguing, apparently growing trickiness of this situation. More than once lately Lepage had tried to invoke the memory of Butler-Minton. Although he might feel only very limited admiration for his predecessor, he would concede that Butler-Minton never panicked. There was, for instance, the famous tale from early in his career when he walked naked into a Meknes restaurant and demanded couscous and barley water, after being jumped by a gang of robbers as he left an excavation. More recently, Flounce had still managed to land that knighthood, despite the *vol-au-vents* tainted with Stain-Out! and fed to the Minister and his entourage on Founding Day in the Octagon Room during Flounce's Directorship; despite, too, the unsettling rumours about Mrs Cray, the haversack straps and so on.

Lepage had met nobody yet and seen nothing extraordinary, although the alarms still clanged and whined. Because of this noise and his lack of shoes, he could not hear his footsteps and seemed to progress silently, effortlessly, like dreaming.

Further, the urgency, plus the feel of the fine old timbers on his soles, strangely exhilarated him. There was something invigorating about striding barefoot and fast through these chambers of eternally motionless antiquities, and for a moment he even experienced a little sympathy for Neville's performance in the Folk. Mightn't that have been only another fleshly assertion of vibrant life, and of the thrillingly pressure-filled present? Again, Lepage wondered whether he really did want early retirement. Apart from this sudden plunge into rich tension tonight, what chance would he have, if he left this job, of meeting and talking on quite intimate terms with someone as lovely as Kate Avis, the targeted lady from Kidderminster? This was important because it could be lonely and very demoralizing sometimes at home, now Julia stayed out late to grab a quota of the post-pub trade at Spud-O'-My-Life, and sometimes *exceptionally* late, as though the night's goings-on did not end when she shut up shop. Julia might offer vague explanations – a club turning out well after midnight and people wanting a snack – and Lepage was not the sort to quiz and interrogate.

He entered the Raybould Gallery and realized straight away that his early placing of the broken-glass noise had been correct. First evidence of something wrong was a wave of much colder air on his feet: cold and possibly touched with moisture. Looking to the end of the Raybould, he saw that one of the lower panes in the window had almost totally gone. The wind rattled a few jagged remnants of glass sticking up at the bottom, and carried rain in, scattering drops across the gallery. Lepage stood for a little while, doing an assessment. He was confused. The space where the three 'El Grecos' had hung was empty, except for the caption sheet, with its carefully ambiguous, agonizingly hatched words about their provenance. On the opposite gallery wall he saw another gap and felt virtually sure that the museum's most valuable, unquestionably genuine Monet normally occupied that spot: *L'Isolement*, a mostly blue, mauve and shimmeringly silver job, plus all the usual Monetian frigging about with light and shade. What baffled Lepage as he gazed around was that a thief, or thieves, smart enough to snatch the Monet should also bother to cart off Quentin Youde's triptych of likely duds.

He hurried towards the window but could not get very close for fear of cutting his feet on the glass splinters littering the floor. Staring out, he thought he saw disappearing among the trees on the south side of the grounds a running, agile man wearing some sort of mask or balaclava helmet and carrying under his two arms what might be four or five framed pictures. Lepage turned and did another inventory of the Raybould. So, *four* pictures. The galloping figure could be Neville Falldew, but he hoped not. Things had become a little grave. Above the sound of the alarms, he thought he heard a car start somewhere and then drive off fast. A moment afterwards he certainly made out approaching police sirens and glimpsed flashing blue lights.

Although he had not wanted it known that he was in the building so late, waiting for his call, he remained at the broken window until Security arrived. He told them what he'd seen and heard. One of the guards went to let the police in and to kill the alarms. Lepage returned to his suite. His phone was ringing as he arrived. 'Kate?' he said, putting his shoes and socks back on.

'I haven't been able to call earlier, Dr Lepage.'

'Please, we did agree on "George", didn't we?'

'Thanks . . . George. But isn't it a bore for you, waiting there? Wouldn't it be better if I phoned you at home?'

'Probably not.' Most bloody assuredly not. He never knew when Julia was going to pop in from the kiosk. She wouldn't understand. Yes, she *would* understand. '*I* can't ring *you*, can I?' he said.

'The phones here don't take incomings.'

Someone knocked on Lepage's door. He covered the mouthpiece and said, 'Yes?'

A uniformed police inspector and sergeant appeared. He waved them to chairs.

'George, I'm still very troubled by what happened,' Kate Avis said.

'Of course.'

'I don't want to sound precious, unduly sheltered. I'm not a child. But it was the setting, George. The abuse, not so much of me, but of history. A slur on scholarship. This is bound to disturb me.'

She was doing a postgraduate degree at Worcester on something medieval and lived at present in a student block. 'Why he did it, I'm afraid, Kate. He hates us all.'

'You were so kind to me following. The spiral staircase. Sherry.'

'The least I could do, in the circumstances.'

'You have a lovely room. That stuffed creature.'

'The duck-billed platypus. It belonged to my predecessor. Sometimes I need to feel I'm still in touch with him. The platypus does help. He could be difficult and mysterious, but capable, all the same.'

'I've been thinking about your suggestion. I said I'd call about it.'

'Yes?' Yes!

Kate said: 'That I should go back into the peasant breakfast room, see it in its normal state, exorcize the unpleasant experience and show I've come through it whole.'

'Wise: the way pilots in the war went straight up after a crash, before their nerve was affected.'

The police inspector cut in: 'Excuse me, sir, but we ought to make some moves. We have a possible offence to look at. Will you be long?'

Lepage waved a hand reassuringly.

'Who's there Dr Le— Who's there, George?'

'Police.'

'Police? About that?'

'No. We have some bother.'

'So, not the incident?'

'No, different, quite different.'

'At night? It seems a very . . . a very, well, *active* place. I mean, for a museum.'

'Thank you.'

'Look, George, perhaps I'd be willing to go back into the room, but would you accompany me – at first, anyway?'

'Oh.' Yes, yes, yes. 'If you think it necessary.'

'I would like it.'

'Well, certainly.' Certainly, certainly, certainly.

'Is it all normal there now?' Kate said. 'I mean, the old peasant is the real old peasant. Or rather, not real, but a real model, if you understand. Not live.'

'Yes, totally real,' he said. 'One hundred per cent genuine wax. Don't agitate yourself.'

'But how? Have you made a new one, or did you find the original somewhere?'

The police inspector shifted on his chair.

'He'd been flung into a preservative cupboard in the Avian section,' Lepage replied, 'the clothes obviously taken off for the masquerade, and then thrown in with him afterwards. As we've all thought from the start, it's someone who knows the Hulliborn well.'

'This to do with the art?' the inspector asked.

Lepage covered the mouthpiece again. 'No, another matter.'

'Masquerade?' the sergeant said.

'That kind of thing,' Lepage said.

'A cupboard?' Kate said. 'You found him there, just plain wax? It sounds horrible. Unfeeling.'

Lepage freed the mouthpiece. 'Yes, but he's re-dressed and tidied now and put back in position with his nice little family, "blithely breakfasting all".'

'That's Hardy, isn't it?' the sergeant said. '*During Wind and Rain.*'

'They've smoothed out bumps to his head and face, caused by being chucked into the cupboard among the preservatives.'

'Who?' the inspector said.

'Nobody could tell there's been anything wrong,' Lepage said. 'You'll see.'

'I'm trying to visualize it,' Kate said.

'The display is just as it appeared when you first walked into the room,' Lepage replied.

'No, what I mean is, trying to visualize this poor, shiny, uncovered wax object in a cupboard full of those cans and application brushes. Was he up the right way? It's hurtful to think of him shoved in there on his head, or thoughtlessly crumpled. So degrading and chaotic. It's only an imitation, I know, but . . . do you see what I mean, George?'

'Jervis, a porter, found him. I didn't hear the details.'

'George, when I go back into the . . . the Folk room – do you know, I can hardly force myself to speak the words, I'm so shaken by it still? But when I go in there, I'd like it, really, to be when there are no visitors about at all. I don't think I could bear that – others in the vicinity.'

'I do understand.'

The inspector said: 'Dr Lepage. Please.'

Kate said: 'Do you think you could take me in there one evening when the museum is closed? I need to feel very relaxed if I'm going to do this, George, and I know I *must* do it to rid myself of a memory that could become a complex.'

'Evening? Well, yes, that could be organized. Would you drive here?'

'Perhaps I can return hospitality and buy you a drink afterwards.'

'Why not?'

'It will be such a relief, George. I've always loved museums, and I don't want to develop a block because of – well, because of the merely untoward. It's important for my work that I should feel comfortable in museums.'

'Yes, untoward, you're right.'

When Lepage had rung off, the inspector said: 'Nice, the bit about communicating through the platypus. It does look very knowing. Now, sir, I've read the maybe-maybe statement on the wall about the three supposed "El Grecos" that seem to have gone. We've got cars out and put road blocks in place, of course, so your little chat on the telephone won't set things back too much.'

'I assumed that,' Lepage said.

'If I get correctly what the caption sheet says, as far as the "El Grecos" are concerned, and leaving aside the Monet for a moment, we could be looking for stuff worth millions or three pounds ninety-nine pence.'

'Along those lines, yes,' Lepage replied. 'I didn't think it necessary to cut my conversation.'

'Was that why you were on the premises so late?' the inspector said.

'Was what why I was on the premises?' Lepage replied.

'To take that call,' the inspector said.

'If someone rings late I feel obliged to give proper attention,'

Lepage said. 'I reason that they wouldn't do something so unusual if they didn't consider it important.'

'A man gets his clothes taken and then hurled back at him in a cupboard?' the sergeant asked.

'A place like the Hulliborn has all kinds of unexpected nooks, niches and recesses,' Lepage said.

Seven

'So, what the hell's this?' Julia hissed.

'What's what?' Lepage grunted.

'I'm going to tell you. Oh, am I going to tell you, George!' she said.

For the immediate present, Lepage kept his eyes shut, though he judged from Julia's voice that this would not give long-term, all-round protection. Saturday: they had both slept on. Last night was one of those very late ones for her, and he had been in bed and blotto by the time she arrived home, despite all the trouble at the Hulliborn. As usual, though, she awoke first and must have gone down to pick up the newspapers. When he did open one eye he saw she was holding the local *Morning Messenger*, Final Edition, in front of her and away from her, like something foul and incriminating found in a waste bin.

She was doing her hair auburn-to-flame these days, a successful choice, he thought, and he would have liked to tell her now how much it suited her and brought out the excellent lines of her profile. But she would probably regard this as an attempt to flatter and placate her. He stayed quiet. In any case, she had on that cream housecoat, never a favourite with George, a thing of padded rectangles, lacking shape and style, which might have been made from a discarded judo fall mat. Yet it was her knack at choosing outfits marvellously right for herself which had helped attract Lepage, and it amazed him that she never realized this one was so totally off. He closed the eye again.

'Here we go, then,' she said in a vile and threatening mock-merry tone, beginning to read the headlines aloud: '"Hulliborn in multimillion art treasure raid. Brave, barefoot Director surprises thieves at midnight. International gang suspected. Who is 'The Fatman'?"'

Lepage opened both eyes and sat up. 'They've decorated things a bit.'

'Yes?' She sat down at the dressing table and moved to the text. '"Three priceless El Grecos – secured only recently in a sensational deal by world-renowned art ace, Dr Quentin Youde – were taken in a daring, brilliantly organized robbery at the Hulliborn Regional Museum And Gallery late last night. The three paintings – *The Awakening, Vision of Malachi*, and *The Stricken Fig Tree* – cost the Hulliborn undisclosed millions three months ago, but this is thought among art-world experts to have been a bargain, and informed sources say they are probably worth at least twice as much today."'

'Bollocks,' Lepage said. 'They must have rung Quentin Youde in the small hours and he's been doing some advertising of himself. Is that the lot?'

'I'm only just starting,' Julia snarled, and her voice continued at about that flavour as she went on. Her profile was still splendid: her nose straight, noble, non retroussé. But, on account of something Julia did with her jaw now – a kind of long-lasting thrust forward – her lower lip moved up a bit, engulfing some of the top one. But she had to relax it all when she spoke. 'Front page, and then on to four.' She read: '"A Monet is also missing." Now, Georgy, here comes the nicest slice.'

He got back down in the bed. He would have liked to whimper because of what he sensed was coming, but Directors of the Hulliborn did not whimper. They were masterful, like Flounce.

'"By a fortunate coincidence, newly promoted Director of the Hulliborn, forty-eight-year-old, divorced Dr George Lepage was in the museum at the time of the raid, working late, and taking telephone calls."' She rattled the paper, like a town crier with a handbell. 'You were what? Since when have you been going to the Hulliborn at midnight? Flounce used to take girls there, didn't he? That a recognized perk of the job, then? What telephone calls? Why do they say divorced?'

'Well, I *am* divorced.'

'Yes, but— What kind of telephone calls?'

'What kind? Well, museum business, obviously.'

'At midnight?'

'From abroad. It wasn't midnight everywhere, love. Consider

Japan. We're in important contact with Tokyo about a possible
future exhibition.'

'How does their time zone relate to ours, then?'

'We have to be as tactful and positive as we can,' Lepage
replied. 'The situation is quite sensitive. Frequent conversations.
The very future of the Hulliborn is involved.'

'So why couldn't you take the calls here?' She read on, not
waiting for an answer to this, thank God. Instead, she sing-
song, sarcastically read: '"Lepage – his name derives from a
proud line of fifteenth-century fighting men in the Auvergne
region of France – although alone in the Central Wing of the
Hulliborn, stalked the gang in his bare feet through the corri-
dors, spurning broken glass, Security sources told the *Messenger*,
but was unable to apprehend them. Police say he showed great
courage and presence of mind. It is not known whether any
of the robbers was armed. None of them had been arrested as
we went to press."'

'Armed? They're crazy,' Lepage said.

'There's a dinky pen-portrait of you, part from cuttings, part
from what you told the police last night. Presumably, the
fighting men from the Auvergne must have come from the
stuff you gave them when appointed. "A distinguished scholar
in his own right, whose hobbies include cooking and real
tennis, Dr Lepage is regarded as something of an eccentric and
keeps a stuffed duck-billed platypus (a furry, egg-laying, Eastern
Australian creature) on his desk to remind him of his predecessor in the post, Sir Eric Butler-Minton, and to maintain a
kind of contact with him."'

Jesus. Lepage dug himself further into the bed and used the
top of the sheet to wipe sweat from around his mouth.

'George, you actually told this rag that you communicated
with the spirit of Flounce through a web-footed mammal?
And that's not what I heard got stuffed on his desk.'

'I've said nothing to them. We're ex-directory, aren't we,
and they wouldn't have had time to come out here for an
interview. Police were in the room while I was on the phone.
I might have mentioned the duck-billed platypus to Japan.'

'Why? Was it relevant to the exhibition that might come?'

'Not directly, no.'

'How, then?'

'It just came up.'

'In what way?'

'I suppose you'd call it a kind of aside,' Lepage said.

'You just said to this caller from Tokyo, "Oh, incidentally, I've got a duck-billed platypus on my desk handed down by Flounce Butler-Minton and which is handy for getting in touch with him, although dead. This will be very useful in our dealings about the exhibition."'

'I don't know that I would have said anything as specific as that,' Lepage replied. 'I wouldn't call him Flounce, not to Japan. They are a very undemonstrative people. Even good English speakers there might not know the word "flounce".'

'What *un*specific comment did you make to them, then, about the platypus?'

'It would have been a sort of ambience thing.'

'*Which* sort?'

Julia could be like this, disgustingly relentless. She reverted every now and then to her Hapsburg-jaw mode. 'Incidental to the main subject of the conversation, yet helping to establish a friendly basis for talks.'

'Via dead Flounce, whose nickname must not be mentioned to the Far East, and a very dead animal?'

'This would be a museum talking to a museum,' Lepage said.

'So?'

'We are people with a particular style. It's true worldwide.'

'Has Tokyo heard about those behind-the-Wall rumours affecting Flounce – the whippet and Mrs Cray, etcetera? Is that how the matter of the platypus came up?'

Lepage snatched at this ludicrous, donated explanation. 'It might have been something like that. The newspaper stuff is very garbled. They must have produced the article in a hell of a rush. I remember a while back its editor telling me their final edition is printed at four a.m.'

'This is a big story for them – the barefoot hero.' She began reading again. '"Dr Lepage occupies a luxury home at King Cottages, with his beautiful companion, Mrs Julia Chakely, in her thirties –" thanks very much: in her thirties always sounds

like a lifetime – "who is a business woman in her own right."
They like people who exist in their own right, don't they?
And what's this "companion" crap?'

'They'd have difficulty categorizing our relationship, darling.'

'Captain Scott had "companions" on his polar trip.'

'It's a term covering some ground, yes.'

"'Mrs Chakely is sole proprietoress of the Spud-O'-My-Life
kiosk in Bray Square,'" she quoted.

'Would you quarrel with that description?'

"'Museum sources spoken to by the *Messenger* said the Director
saw one member of the gang, possibly masked, running through
the grounds at Hulliborn carrying pictures,'" she replied. "'It is
believed that at least three people took part in the extremely
bold raid. Police searching the grounds found almost at once
two black balaclava helmets casually hidden in bushes in the
museum grounds, and these will be sent for forensic analysis.
Security guards report hearing a car being driven off very fast
just after the museum alarms sounded. Police said a householder
near the Hulliborn telephoned them at 23.52 because he saw
two people behaving suspiciously in the museum grounds. Both
were dressed in black. One was very heavily built – like Sydney
Greenstreet in *Casablanca* on TV, the neighbour apparently said.
This man seemed to be either wounded or exhausted. The
neighbour had heard no gunfire. The other one seemed to be
helping him. This other person might have been a woman.
She, if it *was* a she, seemed to be in charge and was waving
her arms about like a leader, reminding the neighbour of George
C. Scott playing General Patton in the film of that name. Road
blocks set up by police were unsuccessful.'"

'The neighbour seemed to be a cinema buff,' Lepage said
tritely. Safe triteness was what he yearned for.

"'Keeper of Art at the Hulliborn, Dr Youde, told our reporter
that international criminals were always on the lookout for
especially attractive and valuable works. 'The El Grecos would
be an obvious draw for well-informed gangs all over the world,'
he stated. 'We have always known this, yet it is the inescapable
duty – and, indeed, privilege – of a museum such as ours to
display great treasures for the public's pleasure, despite risk.
Why else do we exist?' Dr Youde also said there were many

of these gangs and that one might have a 'Fatman' as a member. He pointed out that thieves were known to wear black so they would be less obvious at night. He stated that thieves interested in art would naturally appreciate the uses of colour. 'I don't know how many were in this particular gang,' Dr Youde said, 'but there are normally at least eight. It is not uncommon for a woman to be included, and these can be as ruthless as any of the men, often more so. A woman might even be the leader,' he concluded.'"

'Perhaps it will be in *The Times* and we'll get something a bit more accurate,' Lepage said.

'Of course it won't be in *The Times*. It all happened too late at night for the nationals. Anyway, what's inaccurate in the *Messenger*? You were in the museum late, yea, doing . . . well, doing whatever you are supposed to have been doing. That's right, isn't it?'

He rolled out of bed. She'd use anti-educated pronunciations like that 'yea' sometimes to show she knew low life and considered Lepage part of it. Julia gave him another extract from the *Messenger*: '"Dr Youde said it was significant that the thieves had taken only the El Grecos and the Monet, which were 'easily the most valuable works in the museum'. He declared that this 'gave the lie' to those who had 'malevolently' raised doubts about the authenticity of the El Grecos. 'Thieves of this status and experience don't steal rubbish,' he said."'

The bedroom telephone rang. Penelope Butler-Minton, Flounce's widow, spoke: 'George, I found your number in Eric's old address book. I just wanted to say how touched I was by the reference in the *Messenger* this morning to your continuing feelings of contact with him. It's something I understand so well. Those fool journalists refer to it as an eccentricity, because that is the first damn cliché they come to in their mean little workaday store. But we know differently.'

'So true, Penny.'

Julia heard the name, performed a little bow and left – to make the breakfast tea, he hoped.

Lady Butler-Minton said: 'I feel continuously in touch with dear Eric – am ever aware of his damned festering nosiness and strength.'

'Exactly,' Lepage replied.

'You, too? Yes, you, too, look for help? Eric would have known how to deal with your troubles now.'

'I'm sure of it.'

'He never knuckled under. For instance, I mention that creepy Mrs Cray and the haversack straps.'

'True.'

'He would have seen the perils that touch the Hulliborn – the government's fluorescent contempt for its greatness and standards. And for *all* greatness and standards, save those of commerce. "A pox on cost-effectiveness," Eric would have cried. Oh, a rampaging idiot and jerk at times, yes, but he would not allow problems to crack him. He reckoned there was an ancestral line between him and that indomitable Norseman Eric the Red, though, of course, he disliked what had happened to the word "Red" in our time.'

'"Indomitable" is so correct, though.'

'A rare, unconscionable man, George. As I read the *Messenger* just now, I was inevitably reminded of the occasion when he, too, was working very late at the Hulliborn, and some young woman's father and mother arrived with a quite large and angry posse of supporters, several carrying baseball bats and flails, claiming Eric had done a Svengali on the girl and had her in the building at that moment. She was a research assistant of some sort, and Eric had helped her along in that patient, painstakingly libidinous fashion of his – you know the process. Well, clearly you do. But Eric was able to turn that quite unpleasant, in fact, potentially ugly, incident to glorious advantage for the Hulliborn.

'It was always his belief that a difficulty could be transmuted into a plus. In almost the best sense he was an opportunist. He'd mention that situation in the Old Testament where people couldn't get in or out of Jericho because of its terrific wall, and then, on the seventh day of walking around it blowing trumpets, and now, also, shouting, the wall fell down flat because of noise-assault. And the besiege group were able to walk in and kill everyone, man, woman, young, old, plus ox, sheep and donkeys. So, where you'd had an impasse because of the wall, you not only had a solution when it fell down, but also the extra boon of all the slaughter. He had a fascination with walls, didn't he, and he'd have loved to see the Berlin one taken apart.'

'I do vaguely recall that baseball bat situation,' Lepage replied. Yes, there was Flounce's own account often told by him with many a chuckle in the executive dining room. Security had managed to keep that group of avengers at the Hulliborn main door, but after a while Flounce, disturbed by their shouting, had come down from his suite and invited them in. After his denials of polluting the girl, he had insisted they all search the museum for her together. Gradually, he had turned the occasion into a kind of educational tour, graced by his personal commentary. This had lasted five hours and took them almost until morning opening time. Certainly, it was daylight before the party escaped, and by then some men had worried about being seen with offensive weapons. The girl was not found.

Her mother had grown so fascinated by Flounce that she persuaded her husband to make a heavy contribution to the Hulliborn Building Fund. Flounce's gorgeous arrogance, learning, charm and sombre handsomeness, despite the scar near his eye – or, possibly, that handsomeness augmented and made more interesting by the scar – all these no doubt helped captivate the woman. At the conclusion of the trek, Butler-Minton had urged them to come with him for a repeat saunter through Geology, because he'd missed out a few pre-Mesozoic rocks, but had grudgingly consented to their leaving once he had the cheque.

This was probably the first time the Preservatives cupboard in Birds had been turned to emergency use, and probably Nev had remembered it from Flounce's account, accounts, of the night. Flounce had hidden the girl in there and then marched the seekers everywhere else in the building. While he and the rest were immersed in a forty-minute, two-part video on ancient tombs, the baseball bats and flails laid aside, the girl had let herself out of the cupboard, dodged Security, and got a taxi home to bed. Flounce said that as she dressed in the dark she accidentally knocked over a bottle of dye on one of the shelves and was splashed by its contents. As a result, the colour of some body hair was permanently changed to that of the Arctic tern's plumage: grey-white, but a *lively* grey-white, not an age sign.

The girl's mother, obviously still impressed by him, had telephoned Flounce several times over the next few months, suggesting a meeting to discuss the Mesozoic rocks, but he had been able to discourage her, without in the least giving offence, or so he maintained, citing pressure of work and a 1957 loin injury received in Ethiopia. 'Get this, Lepage: one should always strive not to be rude or cold to people, and especially not to frantic, sex-starved old boots,' Flounce had said. 'It was a *Lolita* situation, wasn't it – the mother assuming in her need and foolishness that I could be interested in her, rather than the daughter?'

'Victory out of seeming setbacks,' Lady Butler-Minton said on the phone now. 'Opportunism, yes, but occasionally a justi-fied, worthwhile opportunism, not something cheap, shallow, and furtive – though he could certainly do it that way, too. An all-rounder. I know you have learned and will learn from him. He had a great belief in you. Always said you were . . . what was the word? Ah, yes, *sturdy*. I'm sure that was it – sturdy.'

This wasn't the term that Lepage remembered as most often on Flounce's lips to describe him, though the core sound came close. 'Thank you so much, Penny,' he said.

Julia returned with the tea tray.

'I still talk to Eric every night,' Lady Butler-Minton murmured, 'usually in the gym. I do a couple of snatch episodes with the weights, then rest and perhaps ask his views on matters general, discuss old times – topics such as those absurd Harvard people in 1971, or the dear Wolverhampton rat trainer, or Mrs Cray and the windsock. It's nice to realize I might not be the only one in touch with him like that, George.'

'Indeed you're not.'

'The past is alive, though I'm sure I don't need to say this to a museum Director.'

'Sometimes I forget. Sometimes I even try to deny it.'

'You mustn't, George. You can't. It's part of us. It activates us. Eric always used to maintain that Henry Ford was misheard when he supposedly said, "History is bunk." The actual words were, "History is spunk."'

That might have some bearing on Neville's flourish in the medieval tableau. 'So thoughtful of you to call at this tricky time, Penny.'

'What was all that about?' Julia asked when Lady Butler-Minton had rung off. She discarded the ghastly housecoat on a chair and began to dress.

Lepage poured the tea. 'Just encouragement, commiserations, triumph out of setbacks,' he said. As if accidentally, he stumbled over the telephone extension cable while replacing the phone on the dressing table and spilled most of his tea on the housecoat. 'Oh, Lord, Julia, so sorry. And it might not come out. I'll have to get you another.' He poured himself some more. 'Yes, Lady B-M was talking about opportunism.'

Eight

Dr Kanda said: 'Oh, not the least bearing, I sincerely assure you.'

'You're kind,' Lepage said.

'Not the least bearing on whether the JASS comes to your museum, pray believe me. Please do not fret yourself even in minor fashion over this, Dr Lepage. We must all expect such occasional acts of outrage,' Dr Kanda said.

'Sure,' Dr Itagaki added. 'These thefts are a plague of our time, nothing more, nothing less. This is unquestionable. All, yes, all are vulnerable to them. Why, perhaps this very gang will be at its monstrous work soon in Japan itself. Who knows? I would not be surprised at all to see news of the mysterious "Fatman" and the woman with extremely strong leadership qualities like General Patton, as I believe she has been described by an onlooker. But perhaps we Japanese would say like General MacArthur, though it does not greatly matter: I would not be surprised in the least to hear of them in dire operation in my homeland. Certainly not.'

'Unfortunately, only too possible,' Dr Kanda agreed. He and Dr Itagaki were on an official assessment visit to the Hulliborn from the Japanese Arts and Culture Council in Tokyo and London, and were seated with Lepage and Vincent Simberdy in the Director's suite. Kanda, who looked very fit and cheery, went on: 'Perhaps, indeed, it was this "Fatman's" predatory outfit that got clean away – yes, clean – with the Gauguins and Rembrandts from the Tokyo Hall of Fame last year, despite unparalleled security. Unquestionably unparalleled. As a matter of fact, I think I have it at the back of my head that a Fatman was mentioned, though this might be auto-suggestion.'

'Yes, we could be said to be hot stuff on security in Japan, yet we still lose treasures. On the other hand, it is the way of the British, and such an admirable way in many respects, not to be deeply strict about security,' Itagaki said. She was a little too bony, with large, blue-framed spectacles and, like Kanda, looked full of high spirits. Maybe culture and museums were fun things in Japan. Lepage had been there, but hadn't noticed those qualities then. He felt rather envious of their exuberance now. She continued: 'You are a freedom-loving people, with a great tradition of what is referred to by the British themselves, a mite self-disparagingly I deem, as "mucking through". Some phrase that, by heaven, and not at all akin to "mucking out" or "mucking up". Or, indeed, "mucking nuisance", where the "mucking" is, in fact, a squeamish sonic euphemism for the expletive "fucking". We Japanese do not always manage that quality of "mucking through", but we recognize it, understand it. Your museums are not fortresses. Perhaps they are the better for that.'

Lepage thought Simberdy looked very tense, compared with the visitors. 'We're extremely grateful for your attitude to the theft,' Simberdy said. 'I'll be frank, we—'

'Something else to admire in the British – their frankness,' Kanda cried delightedly. 'Even bluffness at times. It is still appealing. An all-consuming contempt for duplicity.'

'True,' Simberdy replied, his voice still strained and nervous. 'Yes, above all, one loathes duplicity. But, you see, the Director and I did fear that publicity associated with the incident might mean the Hulliborn stood no further chance of hosting the medical and surgery exhibition, because you would report that the relics could not be safe here. And the exhibition is crucial to us.'

'To, as it were, the *health* of the Hulliborn,' Kanda said with a chortle. 'A medical exhibition equals health!'

'The exhibition is vital in the long-run to the safeguarding of scholarship and learning in our country: the Hulliborn is a symbol, a paradigm,' Simberdy said.

'A very worthwhile paradigm, a very grand symbol,' Dr Itagaki cried.

Kanda laughed in a style loaded with large-minded tolerance: 'Absolutely no danger to the Hulliborn's prospects as recipients of JASS. As Dr Itagaki and I understand matters – though, of course, this is mere hearsay – but as we understand things, the "Fatman" goes only for the best – hence the Hulliborn and the El Grecos and the Monet. One could say, I venture, though a little wryly, perhaps, that, if anything, it is possibly a privilege to receive the attention of him and his people: a jolly testament to excellence, albeit a bruising testament. Oh, no, rest assured that his activities here will not count crucially against the Hulliborn, in this regard.'

'A way with a rounded phrase, hasn't he?' Itagaki said.

'Oh, forbear your mucking bile and envy, will you?' Kanda replied.

Lepage thought both scholars must have been in Britain for quite a while. They seemed to have picked up some of that Western brusqueness, even belligerence, and now and then lost at least a little of that celebrated Japanese politeness.

'From the published plans of the Hulliborn buildings, we have been able to study its facilities very thoroughly, which are excellent, and we know all about its history since the founding by Lord Hulliborn of Nadle-and-Colm in the 1830s,' Kanda said, 'Sir Eric Butler-Minton, previous Director, of course, was a great friend of museums in our country. I have wondered whether his sobriquet, "Flounce", indicated a liking for frills and transvestitism, though this would be of no great significance.'

'I'm surprised you know the word "flounce",' Lepage said.

'Oh, we have our flouncers, too. Think of all the snorting and pirouetting in that film, *The Seven Samurai*. Anyway, Butler-Minton's foibles are hardly a museums-policy concern! His wife, now widow, Lady Butler-Minton, we admire, too. She has borne matters with splendid phlegm, oh, definitely, splendidly redoubtable phlegm. The Hulliborn has a wonderful reputation for scholarship through Sir Eric and many others, including your good selves, of course – certainly your good selves. It is regarded by my Council and, yes, Government, as an honour that you wish to provide a setting for our little exhibition.'

'Little exhibition!' Simberdy said.

Itagaki smiled. 'I'd say it was not inappropriate to ask at this juncture whether the "Fatman" or any other thieves would be interested in running off with some very old Yayoi or possibly Jomon tonsil-removers. Correct me if I'm awry, do, but I don't believe these would be up the "Fatman's" street at all. Hardly in a league with the El Grecos or Monet. How would he unload such commodities, for God's sake, and where find a fence interested in an ancient scalpel for gall bladder removals? I believe "fence" is the correct word for someone who middle-mans stolen goods – not, obviously, to do with "a fence" as barrier, or "to fence" with swords.'

Simberdy said: 'It's most heartening and amusing of you to be so modest about such a magnificent collection, isn't it, Director?'

'Indeed, yes,' Lepage said.

'We would like to assure you, and your Government, that we most earnestly wish to provide a worthy temporary home for the so-distinguished JASS wonders,' Simberdy crooned. He seemed to have fallen into their rococo way of doing English. Perhaps out of good manners he was thinking in Japanese and translating, though Simberdy was not famed for good manners. 'We cannot exaggerate our hopes,' he added.

Dr Kanda, still almost laughing, said: 'You will understand, gentlemen, that, in our rather tiresome, ultra-methodical Japanese way – I do believe we could give even the Germans a fine pasting in that respect nowadays – I say that, in our gradualist way, we shall be visiting all the museums considered to be front-runners for the JASS show and making our report on each. We Japanese – always reports. We are God's gift to bureaucracy, I do believe! I imagine you might be quite fed up at the prospect of another report. I believe your Government and the museums authority here are doing some scrutinizing, and this will also entail reports. It is like a series of embarrassing and inconvenient medical examinations: the Hulliborn required to drop its trousers.'

'What did you say?' Simberdy gasped.

'Just a metaphor, a sally,' Kanda said.

'We see the need for these things, Dr Kanda,' Lepage said.

'The Japanese and the British are both stoical races,' Dr Itagaki said, 'though occasionally, perhaps, we can both go over the bloody top.'

'I fear so,' Simberdy said. He sounded slightly more relaxed now. 'It was such affinities that drew me to Asiatic studies in the first place. Yes, "over the top" is certainly fair enough.'

'Butler-Minton – so strong on stoicism,' Itagaki said. 'In the matter of Mrs Cray, for instance, and the Wall.'

'You heard about Mrs Cray?' Simberdy said, less relaxed again. He spoke as if he had assumed they'd heard but hoped they hadn't.

'We do a small saunter into backgrounds when this kind of thing, the JASS thing, comes up,' she said. '"Vetting", as I believe you call it, in the British way of animalizing so many important matters and items: "pussy", for instance.'

'This is very much a preliminary, path-finding visit,' Kanda said. 'I expect you know how it works – the whole elaborate shebang. We do an initial appraisal for our masters in the first instance. They chew over these findings in their supposedly wise, Oriental way and produce a shortlist. Three? Four? I'm not privy to their procedures in detail, I fear.'

'"Fear" is rather to overstate, surely,' Itagaki replied. 'Aren't you talking out of your arse?'

Lepage felt she'd devoted a lot of work to informal language.

'It's a usage in English. It does not mean I am afraid,' Kanda said. 'It is merely a kind of apology.'

'Such usages should be used only when the usage is in tune with the general tone of the conversation, I hold,' she answered.

Kanda said: 'Then, for those selected, a further visit, this time by the real cultural heavyweights. Another survey: the tough one. Further reports for Tokyo. And so, the final decision is made. It's a crummy sort of bore, I know, but there are no short-cuts, I fear.'

'Fear?' she said.

'Due processes, due processes,' Kanda said.

'However, it's all quite swift,' she said. 'It will be concluded long before your government's and the Museum Board's evaluation.'

'We certainly want no favours, do we, Director?' Simberdy said.

'So, this is the much cherished duck-billed platypus,' she replied.

'What I would propose is that Vincent and I take you around the buildings now, and perhaps we could discuss which areas would be most suitable for JASS.'

'That seems a first-rate idea,' Kanda said.

In the Folk Hall, Dr Itagaki said excitedly: 'Oh, but here is fine light and space. Of course, we knew from the plans, but to see it in actuality is most helpful. It would be brilliantly suitable.'

'Best not to get your knickers in a mix-up as to which leg goes where owing to excess enthusiasm at this stage, I believe,' Kanda said.

'There are rooms off, you see, in case one wanted specialized, subsidiary exhibitions,' Simberdy said.

'True,' Kanda said, and led the way into the Middle Ages Domestic Scene exhibit. Even so many days after the event, Lepage felt a tremor as he followed. All was decently in place and peasant trousers, though.

'Moving,' Dr Itagaki said.

'Bloody what?' Simberdy screamed, volume suddenly back to normal-plus.

'So moving. So redolent of the British spirit,' she replied. 'The father figure so stalwart and erect.'

'Oh, right,' Simberdy said.

Nine

Olive Simberdy had her legs wrapped around him. She said: 'Give it to me now, Fatman. Give it to me. Now.' They were in bed.

'I deal in antiquity not in now,' Simberdy replied. 'But I'll stretch a point for you.' He kissed her breasts.

'Yes, stretch your point for me,' Olive said.

They began to giggle, but not fatally. 'God, but we're a pair of rogues,' Simberdy said. 'Supposed to have done half the art thefts in the world, including Japan. It's flattering, but I felt damn twitchy with those two and George at the Hulliborn.'

'You don't feel twitchy now.'

'I've never had a gang moll before.'

But he saw that Olive had left jokiness and fantasy behind and was concentrating on reality. And why not? The realities were pretty fine.

Afterwards, when they were lying quietly, (Simberdy, a little anxiously, trying to bring down his heartbeat by willpower to at least below 300 a minute), they heard a car draw up near the house. A door slammed, and then there came the sound of running feet, approaching and later receding out of earshot. Simberdy left the bed and went to peer around the edge of the curtain into the street. 'It's the Vauxhall,' he said.

They dressed and hurried down to it. The keys were on the dashboard. Simberdy saw a large, stiff-edged parcel on the back seat, done up in several sheets of fancy wrapping paper, and tied with blue ribbon, knotted at the centre into a bold, ornamental bow.

'Oh, Wayne Passow's undoubtedly a swine,' Olive said, 'but he's always had a streak of niceness. This is his way of apologizing for the other night – the car pinched, but then returned to the doorstep this morning, with a big pressie.'

'Don't open it yet,' Simberdy hissed. 'Let's get inside.' He

garaged the car and brought the parcel to the living room.
They removed some of the paper.

'The El Grecos!' Olive said. 'You see what I mean, Vince.
There's an element of decency in him, always liable to shine
through. He knows he's done something out of his league.'

'So where's the fucking Monet?' Simberdy replied.

They went back to the car and searched it, but did not find
L'Isolement.

In the living room again, they took off the rest of the wrapping from the paintings. 'There's a note,' Olive said. She handed
it to him.

He read aloud: 'This is your cut, oh, Fatman. Till the next
caper.' It was not signed.

'Well, this is crazy, obviously, Vince, but thoughtful.'

'He's heard the "El Grecos" are probably shit,' he said.

'But—'

'I don't want the bloody things here. The police. All that
mad "Fatman" stuff, for God's sake. I could be on their list
already. Both of us. In their book we might be a black-garbed,
big-time team.'

Olive arranged the pictures on their sideboard, then stood
back and viewed them. 'Who says they're rubbish, anyway? I
love this one. What's it called?' She bent down and read the
plate: *The Stricken Fig Tree*. 'It reaches out to one, don't you
think, Vince? Isn't that the mark of truly great art?'

'Ol, how would I know? I'm Asiatics.'

'The title even – spot-on. I can feel real empathy with that
fig tree, although it's so long ago and in a different country.
As a matter of fact, I see it as a fig tree for all ages, an envi-
ronmental emblem, in a way. Like for the Green Movement?
In those days, too, they might have had pollution. I mean,
when was El Greco? Not pre-soot?'

'I told you, I'm Asiatics.'

'Stricken by a plague, or a curse. It might be a Bible fig
tree. Didn't God take it out on trees sometimes in the OT
when He was having a wrath?'

'Anyway, this "El Greco" could be 1986.'

'Does it matter? Does it really matter, if the message is there?
It's a stricken fig tree, just as stricken, I mean, whenever. How

many ways are there for a fig tree to look stricken, after all? Does that change through the ages?' She looked at the other captions. '*Vision of Malachi*. Ochre, black, livid white. Something like this – supernatural, other-worldly, fears of hell, maybe: isn't that the same for all of us, everywhere, no matter what the period? You see what I'm getting at, Vincent? Actually, I feel it really thrilling, deep down. I wouldn't mind going back to bed.'

She did look warm and eager and very beautiful, more beautiful than anything in the *Vision of* sodding *Malachi*, though with its clutch of barmy and wino faces that wasn't saying much. Might it be a characteristic of art that it turned women on, even phoney art? Or could Olive be turned on by almost anything? At one time, an old 78 of Peter Dawson singing 'Shipmates o' Mine' used to get her unbelievably juicy and urgent, and it was a record he'd never heard the end of without a hard-on. Confusing, really, because it could seem as though the shipmates of his had got the desire going.

Briefly, they did return to bed, and she was wonderfully sweet and tender. His heart would just have to put up with it.

Downstairs again, he'd concede that with the morning sun on them the pictures did add something to the sideboard. Ol had set them out exactly right. She could give Quent Youde lessons in display. Most people could give Quent lessons in some aspects of art. Even breakfast assumed a special quality because the pictures stood in the way of the cheap crockery they generally used, and Olive took the real china. 'Well, obviously, you'll have to return them at once,' she said sadly.

'Think of the questions that will be asked.'

'Couldn't you just dump them where they'll be discovered?'

He drank some coffee and thought he felt a slab of toenail tear at his tonsils as it went down, reminding him of the JASS exhibition. 'Anyway, I'm not sure the Hulliborn wants them back.'

'Don't get it, Vince.'

'As long as they're missing they could be genuine. Robbers don't bother with duds.'

'Oh that again,' she said. 'I thought we'd decided it didn't really matter whether they were so-called genuine, or not.

Isn't it . . . well . . . isn't it the inherent worth that matters
– what it does to the viewer?'

'There's no such thing as inherent worth where art's
concerned. It's fixed by the opinions of a gang of influential
people. Value is belief in value. So, all that shit about provenance and attribution might not signify to you and me, but
it signifies to the museums board in London, and to its inspectorate. And it signifies to the insurers: as things stand, they
owe the Hulliborn many millions because the "El Grecos" are
in the policy as genuine, and authenticity can't be effectively
queried if they are unavailable for re-scrutiny. Above all, the
status of the pictures matters to the Japanese. At the moment,
they have an equation in their tidy, systematic minds: it says
that if the Monet is real and precious, then the "El Grecos"
must be, too, because the famous Fatman does not make
mistakes. You've heard of guilt by association? This is worth
by association. The Hulliborn enjoys some of that worth, even
though the paintings have been stolen. This is a museum
distinguished enough for their exhibition. But, if the triptych
goes back on the wall, and half a dozen El Greco experts fly
for a gaze and pronounce Quentin Youde a fool for buying
them, then all of us at the Hulliborn – every department,
including Asian Antiquities – partake of that foolishness. We've
failed the pay-your-way test, and this is the only one that
counts these days.'

Ten

Through the massed blades of plastic straw, Kate Avis commanded in his ear with lovely warmth, 'Give it to me now, Modern-Man. Give it me now, now, now, Now-Man.'

'Is it what you needed?' Lepage grunted solicitously.

'What I needed? What I *need*, for God's sake. Present tense. Future, too.'

'I mean, a total therapy.'

'Everything. You're bringing me back from limbo to the living. But not too quick, George, OK? Twentieth-century pace is frantic, but, please. Please.'

Quite a few times tonight he had thought of Julia, though admittedly not at this moment. Obviously, it wasn't wholly right to be here on the floor of the Hulliborn's medieval breakfast tableau room with Kate Avis, he naked except for socks, passably comfortable, thanks to the mock straw, and stirred to the marrow, while Julia, in her Bray Square kiosk, struggled to convince half the piss-artists and ragtag boulevardiers of the city that their revelry fell quaintly short if they didn't buy a scooped-out potato stuffed with Zappy-Tang sauces.

Kate seemed to get this crude word from him by telepathy: 'Yes, stuff me, stuff me until there's no room for pain or dread or poisoned recollections,' she told him.

'I love the things you say, Kate, but can you do it quieter, darling?' he whispered. 'Additional security since the break-in.' They had given Keith Jervis and others some extra night duties to go with their part-time portering.

This was not the first occasion in his museum career that Lepage had noticed the way the words 'stuff', 'stuffed' could take on very opposed meanings: one so bristling with life and extremely coarse vigour; the other to do only with death and sad imitation. Hadn't Julia used this distinction the other day when talking about the platypus? Julia could be very harsh, and if Lepage carefully listed all the matters for which she might refuse to show tolerance, having it off with Kate Avis in front of old wax peasants and their brood might come out near the top. She would be unable to accept that what was happening here amounted to no more than essential, philanthropic repairs to Kate's psyche: just a kind of *in situ* cure. Wouldn't it have been monstrously cruel and untypically callous of Lepage to reject Kate's tacit appeal for comforting? He thought so. But Julia would never see it like this, whatever the mysteries of her own private life.

She was unlikely to be impressed by the argument that, as Director, he always had an unavoidable, if occasionally tiresome, responsibility to compensate for deep offence given by the museum, and in the most simple, suitable and effective method to hand. Sometimes, Lepage thought he spent too much time wondering how other people might view a situation – for instance, what would Julia think; what would Flounce do? It was weak. It was pitiable. Didn't he have a self?

'Do you feel it, too?' she said.

'Yes. What, exactly?'

'Just how wonderful it is to have the patriarch watching us, a kind of blessing, a union of past and present.' For a second she glanced up at the glossy-cheeked, ever empty-eyed father of the model family; all his face craters and lumps smoothed out now, after that rough treatment in the Birds cupboard. 'This assertion of living love in a dead place, or a place where love was mocked, abused.'

After a while, Kate's movements under him became exceptionally strong and telling, and she flung out her arms on each side, fingers clutching and unclutching, mangling some of the indestructible straw, which Lepage had commandeered from the tableau's cottage floor. Her body squirmed appreciatively. He felt proud to have helped in her recovery. She was making a noise, but only a small, blissful, gentle, fairly safe mixture of humming and speaking in which gibberish words featured now and then, utterly unintelligible, but almost definitely to do with fulfilment, not *angst* or any of those other dark matters she'd mentioned.

Yes, Lepage could assure himself that something worthwhile was being achieved here: nothing less than restoration of a

lovely woman's faith in one of life's core celebrations. In a few
months there might be changes and this room filled with the
primordial Japanese equipment, and this was fine by Lepage.
He would certainly never disparage the splendid, thrilling
distinction of the exhibition, even though he might seem to
think and speak lightly of it now and then. One could recognize its qualities and still enjoy the sound of Kate Avis's buttocks
bouncing sweetly and regularly on the Hulliborn boards and
mock straw, and to feel her thrusting tirelessly back at him, in
glorious proof of brave progress towards a complete mental
rehabilitation. Scholarship and heritage were not everything.
Neither Time, nor the two of them here now, could stay still.
No, he certainly could not.

Kate's eyes were closed and her head turned to one side, as
she softly half sang and mumbled and savouringly gasped, so
she did not seem to notice when a third figure joined them
on the floor. Her feet, thrashing out as an adjunct of her joy,
must have caught the patriarch, causing him to tumble sideways
and finish up alongside them, the sound of his fall muted by
the straw. His face lay near Kate's, and one of his legs rested
on Lepage's right. The patriarch's arm, which was stretched
out in the tableau to point invitingly at the excellent, full old-
English breakfast, now reached across Lepage's shoulders, in a
sort of comradely embrace, as with bonding soccer players.

Although Lepage recognized at once what had happened,
he decided to ignore it. In fact, he was quite swiftly, so swiftly
– he was quite swiftly approaching a point when ignoring
almost everything would become easy. He did try to shove the
effigy away before Kate saw it, afraid that the intrusion might
wipe out all the improvements in her state, but they had little
space around them and the patriarch kept rolling back, nudged
by a wall or one of the other models, like a piece of flotsam
carried gently in and out and in again by the tide. To Lepage,
dazingly preoccupied, the peasant's face looked terribly hurt,
as if conscious of rejection but determined to fight it. Maybe
troilism was quite a thing in his times. During difficult and,
yes, painful early days with Julia, Lepage had sometimes seen
that look of rejection on his own face in the shaving mirror.
He found it not very pleasant to be gazing down at Kate, so

obviously enclosed in contentment, and at the same time have this whiskery, reproachful set of features next to her.

'Darling,' she whispered, 'now?'

'Yes.'

'Oh, yes, yes.' Her responses grew even more powerful, and the humming more intense and happy, like a slice from one of the least unbearable operas. But then, suddenly, she asked: 'What's wrong?'

He did not know how she had detected a snag. Perhaps he sounded tense, or her flailing hands had touched some part of the patriarch. Anyway, she opened her eyes and saw the model, snuggled sweetly against Lepage, moving up and down with him, and seeming to hold Lepage fondly with one arm. 'I'll put him back,' he said.

'No, George.'

Lepage was surprised to see her smile grow larger, happier still. 'He's joined us. Perfect. How it should be.' She reached up and languorously ran her hand over the wax face and gross, manufactured hair. Under Lepage, her body still responded with magnificent strength and concentration. 'The past and present together,' she muttered. 'Oh, yes, yes, yes.' She brought her own arms into play and squeezed the two of them hard to her, Lepage and the pushy yokel, hugging both around the neck, chanting softly to each, and moving her face and mouth rhythmically, gently, democratically, between one of Lepage's ears and the vile, token blobs that were supposed to be the peasant-in-chief's. Christ, but what did it mean? To her, did he and the puppet rate equally? She had decided, had she, that as long as she knew this model was only a model, and not a present day dick-swinger, she could give it affection? If symbolism of some sort was being enacted, what sodding sort was it? Behaviour like Kate's could cause deep wilt.

And then Lepage's worries soared even higher. Although one of his ears was against the figure's sacking smock, and the other being crooned into on rota at this point, he thought he heard the door of the tableau room pushed open behind them, then, some time afterwards, quietly re-closed. In terror for a moment, Lepage wanted to turn and look, but Kate held him too firmly. Maybe it was better like this, anyway – not to show his face: an intruder would have trouble identifying him from a rear view only. The socks, after all, were Marks and Spencer, plain navy, two of a million. He recalled, as a comforting example from years ago – long before the Birds cupboard girl – that Neville Falldew had surprised someone, almost certainly Flounce, stripped on the floor of the religious icons room with one of the secretaries. Although Nev could identify the woman because she was face-up, he could never be sure about the man: Nev had only the bare back and so on to judge from.

In any case, for Lepage now, every one of these anxieties disappeared: fear, worry, guilt, confusion, each gloriously relegated, each gloriously displaced. Her odd reactions had not knocked the power out of him, after all, thank God, and the standard machinery did its gorgeous, agonizingly short-lived, age-old, ever-fresh, supreme job for both of them.

'Oh, yes, such sweet therapy,' Kate said, chortling, 'worth every minute on the motorway from Kidderminster.'

'It will always be like this, I promise,' Lepage said, trying to free his leg from under Wax-Man's.

'Nobody can promise anything about life,' she said. 'Life is change, and change is life.'

'Ah,' he said. To his disappointment, Lepage had never heard Julia attempt an epigram. She could be terse – very often was – but did not really go for style. Lepage realized that since meeting Kate, he had found himself thinking about Julia with rather more detachment, rather less affection, than before. It was something that confused and troubled him, as those lousy, traditional post-love blues took hold. Where had it gone, that previous unswerving devotion to her? But, as Kate so effortlessly put it, 'life is change and change is life'. People and their thinking and ways did shift, he'd admit: he didn't much object to her correcting him about promises. Constancy was for museums; for the exhibits in museums.

Eleven

Lady Butler-Minton spoke to her late husband. 'Well, Lip,' she began, 'how say you now? Still think what you had was only a touch of hay fever?' Working on weights in the gym that he had designed for the old barn on their grounds, she wore red, knee-length shorts, like footballers in the 1950s, a red string vest, red suede desert boots, and a red and blue check sweatband around her bouffant grey hair. At the moment she was lying on her back, pushing the bar up above her face in sequences of four and, as she'd told Lepage, addressing Flounce aloud during rest spells. Understandably, she, herself, never liked that nickname but had devised one or two others for him. 'Lip' was the most humane, a jolly testament to his rudeness. He had tended to call her 'Incisor', commemorating a frenzied and bloody incident years ago when she bit him near the eye during a rough squabble in the street over how to rate Woody Allen films, or it might have been something to do with the cat. On the whole, Flounce had been very good about that bite, telling the people who mentioned the open wound – or, later, its rather vast, complex scar – a number of yarns, one being that he was attacked by a seagull while foraging on the local tip. Nobody could gainsay there had been quite a few decent aspects to Eric, and now and then, or even oftener, she did half miss him.

'But you went at a good time, darling,' she said. 'The Hulliborn chaos and that gut you were getting, almost Vince Simberdy class. Well, aren't we all? Never send to know for whom the belt holes won't do any more, they won't do for thee.' She spread a hand over her own slightly spreading stomach and resumed the exercises, her normally square, comfortable face twisted gravely with effort. 'I know of several people who were upset when you died, Lip. Certainly several. Or something like that. I wouldn't exaggerate. I've got one calling here today. Yes. Remember that little postgrad – the bird in the Bird cupboard? Due in an hour.'

She began working again, raising the sequence to six. How much more pleasant things were in the gym without Eric showing off and staggering about hazardously under weight overloads, eyes protruding like hot cross buns, legs buckling, mouth cursing quietly in that ostentatiously non-panicking style as he tried too much. And he'd risked conversation while carrying – all that methodically repeated tosh about needing to prove himself mentally and physically, then prove himself again and again in what he called 'the fierce hierarchy of the gifted', because his mother's aunt had known the poet Walter de la Mare. A shorter name would have suited better because Eric couldn't afford the breath. Penelope had sometimes felt he might die during these compulsive exertions, and had never been able to make up her mind whether she wanted to be there when it happened, or not. He would certainly have put on a show and a half once he realized he was going, particularly if he had been struggling with dumbbells at the time.

In fact, it hadn't happened like that, and he'd died in bed without either a whimper or the bang, thud and clang of cascading metal. Apparently, he muttered something, though the nurse who was in the private room with him did not hear it properly. A couple of minutes earlier he had seemed all right, and Lady Butler-Minton had just slipped out of the hospital to place some bets in the shop across the road. When she returned they were pulling the sheet up. The nurse had heard the gargle go in his throat and was probably rushing about, trying to keep him breathing, so hadn't listened too carefully for words. And, in any case, it was obvious she felt embarrassed. 'I think some of it was about . . . well . . . about a woman, Lady Butler-Minton.'

'Oh?'

'Well, not a woman, if you understand me, not like that, but a *Mrs* Something.'

'Not Mrs Ubiquitous Cray?'

'Cray? Cray: yes, it could have been Cray. You know her, then?' The nurse sounded relieved.

'You said "some of it". What else was there?' Lady Butler-Minton replied.

'East Germany? Is there a town called Rostock?'

'Haversack straps? Part of an air-sock used as a tablecloth? He was still on about all that, was he?'

'A dog?'

'Whippet?'

'Yes.'

'Look, are you sure he's dead, nurse? People will want it very definite, especially colleagues. They're a scholarly crew. They nit-pick and haggle about every damn thing.'

'He was a great man, wasn't he?'

'Yes, that's fair,' Lady Butler-Minton said. And it was, wasn't it? Eric really had something, originally.

In the gym now, Penelope stood up and, before going for a spell of snatch and lift, leaned against the wall-bars, trying to recall what Lip had looked like when at his best − a good while before she started calling him Lip. Today she failed to free herself from more recent memories of him, crimson in the face, fighting with appalling, total calm incompetence to keep the bar above his dear head, and occasionally whispering disjointedly that some enemy had somehow doctored the weights, secretly doubling the poundage to rupture him.

'Yes, Eric, this one-time-researcher is deeply cut-up and talks about a biographical article for *Archaeology* or *Museums Monthly*, to preserve your name. Nice, considerate thought? In a way. Informs me she already has a couple of "basic" approaches in mind. I nearly said I already knew that was her speciality, but let it go now.'

Penelope took hold of the bar, steadied herself in the desert boots and brought the load up to shoulder height, then ramrodded her arms and put the lot above her hairdo for a full three seconds. There was a wall mirror opposite, for watching points of style, and she thought she might not be Atlas but looked pretty reasonable all the same: the uncompromising, by no means over-trendy outfit, the balanced stand, and only a minor line of sweat across her upper lip. Anyway, hadn't she done more than any of the world's most eminent and powerful schemers accomplished and seen Eric off? She could queen it here now. Bringing the bar down in a controlled, single movement, she muttered: 'Remember how you used to handle that one, Lip? All the beauty and system of scaffolding ripped from its building in a storm.'

Penelope did a couple more snatch and lifts, then stripped and went and sat in the sauna before showering. 'Lip, I liked the sound of this girl on the phone,' she said. 'Trudy. Sensitive. Considerate. You'll know that already, though, won't you, given your *droit du seigneur* carry-on? But, a biography? She says it will be a full account, warts and all. She'd be familiar with those, of course. Could be tricky, however. I believe in some honesty. Not sure I should cooperate, just the same.' She sat hunched forward on the bench, letting the steam well up around her, breathing slowly, enjoying the slight burn in her throat and lungs. It was in the sauna that she missed Eric most. He loved the heat and would invariably pretend the bench was a small boat, and sing what he swore were Egyptian watermen's working shanties in words that might indeed have been Arabic, or possibly some made-up, nonsense language, while pretending to paddle his craft across the harbour at Alexandria.

The paddle still stood there, in a corner of the sauna. It always made her feel sad and contemptuous; just a crudely shaped lump of wood, since Egyptian watermen could not afford anything fancy. He liked it when she joined in the singing, and she used to try nasalling away with him, in frenzied, whining, rubbish words, occasionally putting a hand up to shade her eyes from the Middle Eastern sun, and ensure they weren't run down by a dhow as sport. 'Now, all together in the chorus,' he would bark. She considered that sometimes during this playful, inane ritual they had been at their closest.

Not invariably: now and then, unable to take any more of the temperature or the nut music, she used to leave early, and he would turn and look dolorously, as if hardened to deep betrayal and desertion, then resume his paddling and intensify the trill. But it had been he who deserted her finally and, really, she would have liked the chance to wave goodbye to him and signal regret. No question, she'd delayed her trip to the betting shop for as long as she could, and only just made it before the Off. She'd had a win and a third place, so her absence from his bedside when he chose to pass away seemed to her not wholly unjustified and inconsiderate.

Only once had Eric stayed in the sauna too long even for him and, realizing the loony singing had stopped, she went to see what was wrong, dragged Lip clear and left him to come round at his own pace in the vegetable area of the grounds, screened from the road by a fine hedge. This might have been the time when Enteritis, the cat, did whatever it did to him and caused the flare up later in the street between her and Lip, if it *was* about the cat and not Woody Allen. 'Re this proposed biog, Eric, I'm not convinced it's for the best. I don't mean the Bird cupboard, all that – no, I'm talking about the international aspect: the haversack straps, the windsock, the Wall, and so on. Are such revelations going to be advantageous? All right, what went on then – Berlin, Rostock – isn't totally clear, isn't clear at all. Christ, Lip, what *did* happen then? Why haven't you ever told me in full? Too late now, evidently. I don't know whether you come out of it smelling bad or good. Can they take away a knighthood posthumously? Might I get returned to the ranks? Quent Youde reckons it was completely different with me from the time I became a Lady. He still finds it incredibly exciting to give one to a title, like taking the Bastille, and I don't want him upset at the moment, what with the "El Grecos" and those slobbering, wildebeest kids of his: he *would* send them to a church school.

'Is it going to do the Hulliborn any good if Trudy's biography is picked up by *The Sunday Times*, say, for serialization, and we get all that Mrs Cray stuff retailed? It's known about – part known about – here and there already. That's not the same as having these things all over a newspaper supplement, and probably followed up by others. If there's a stink side to those episodes, this bloody government would instantly look for vengeance on you, dead or not, and they'd do it in one of the few areas possible: by stopping or fiercely cutting the Hulliborn's grant. Any excuse will do them for kicking learning and culture in the balls. Then again, although they might not be able to cancel your title, and mine, that little jerk, Lepage, would never get his, this is certain, and how would Julia react to that? All right, she can be a living pain, but one has to be thoughtful.

'The fact is, Lepage has taken your mantle and, as it were,

become Hulliborn, and Hulliborn would be nothing if battered by reprisals. Besides, he talks to you via the platypus, Eric. There'd be many – some with hefty power – who would resent that: it would be beyond their understanding. So, the biog is a very complicated issue, isn't it? Part of me, as ever, says Truth. The other part says tell this intrusive Trudy to get lost.'

Twelve

Always first downstairs on Sundays to get breakfast, Simberdy, mostly covered by his purple and white kimono, screamed: 'My God, they've gone.'

'What?' Olive replied from above, in bed.

'Bloody gone. You heard.'

'Yes, but what?'

'The "El Grecos",' Simberdy said.

'What!'

'The "El Grecos".'

'Yes, I know.'

'What?'

'You already said.'

'Oh hell,' Simberdy replied. He heard Olive's feet hit the floor and after a moment she came down at a rush wearing only the football shirt she slept in and gazed with agonized wonder at the space on the sideboard where the pictures had stood. Immediately afterwards, she turned methodical and began to examine the windows.

'You're showing the world your snatch,' Simberdy said.

She pulled the shirt marginally lower. 'Wayne Passow never breaks in through doors,' she replied. In a moment she said: 'Here we are – the force marks. In at windows, out through doors. Police call it "The Passower".'

'Nothing Known has taken them? Why?'

'Who else?'

'But he made all that effort to give them to us.'

'Some change of mind. Wayne boy has a temperament.'

'What the hell does he want with that fake trio anyway?'

'I liked them,' she said.

'Oh, excuse me. A matter of taste, you think? Passow's turned arty? Wants to build a collection?'

'Vince, maybe we should have returned them to the Hulliborn.'

'And we would have. Of course we bloody would have. Am I an art thief? Am I the unstoppable "Fatman"? But I told you, Ol, the museum might not be all that keen to get them back just now. Their absence suggests authenticity and worth. The Hulliborn's status remains undamaged.'

The phone rang, and Simberdy answered.

'Is this the big-time Fatman speaking?'

'That you, Wayne, you bastard?' Simberdy replied.

'Don't fret.'

'I could throttle—'

'So, I been able to do you a terrific favour. I don't ask for no gratitude. We're a team, so it's only natural that we help one another.'

'Let me talk to him,' Olive said. 'I can scare the shit out of Nothing Known.'

But Simberdy waved her away.

'Tell me this, Fatman – you got a bit of a library in your place?'

'What? What library?'

'You know – like books.'

'Yes, some books. So?'

'You got a book called . . . hang on, I got the name written down here. I made a note. Oh, that's it: the *Bible*. Familiar with that book at all?'

'Yes, there's a Bible here somewhere.'

'Not just somewhere, Fatman. You need to know exactly where that book is. You got another book called – here we go – *Westward Hot*?'

'Ho! It's an exclamation mark.'

'That right? Ho like in ho-ho?'

'Get on with it, Wayne, will you. Where are the works?'

'What comes between the Bible and that Ho! then, Fatman?'

'What? Well, the Bible translation is seventeenth century and *Westward Ho!* nineteenth. So, half the literature of the world's between, I should think. What's that to do with the paintings?'

'On the shelves, Fatman. Between on the shelves.'

Simberdy covered the mouthpiece and spoke to Olive: 'The Bible?'

'What?'

'Where do we keep the Bible?'

'Is this to do with *The Vision of Malachi*? He's in the Bible,' Olive said. 'Last book of the OT.'

'Find it, please, would you?'

'Have you got to swear on it or something?'

'Swear? No, just find the fucking Bible, will you, Ol?'

'You still there, Fatman?'

Simberdy removed his hand. 'Yes, of course.' He watched Olive as she began to scan their bookshelves. 'We're searching.'

'Olive there too? Good. You're going to love this, both of you. This is for the whole posse, Olive, you, Fatman, and me.'

'Here,' Olive said. She pulled out a pink-covered Gideon job that Simberdy must have taken from some hotel. She opened it and found the end of the Old Testament.

'Not that,' Simberdy snarled.

'You said the Bible,' she snarled back.

'Something near,' Simberdy said.

'Near? So, the *Prayer Book*? The TUC Constitution?'

He put the receiver down, crossed the room and reached into the space left by the volume. On one side of it was *Westward Ho!* and on the other *From A View To A Death*. He pulled out a package wrapped in the same sort of festive paper as had covered the paintings, but minus the bow. This parcel was, in any case, smaller and felt less rigid. He handed it to Olive and went back to the phone. She tore the paper away and he watched her place on the kitchen table ten packets of what looked to Simberdy like fifty-pound notes.

'Where we at then, Fatman?'

'What the hell is it, Passow?'

'What the hell it is is twenty thou real ones. You can count it. I'll wait. Wayne Passow likes things right.'

'From where?'

'From where what?'

'Where does it come from?' Simberdy said.

'From me, of course. From Wayne Passow.'

'Where did you get it? What's it doing here?'

'Obvious. It's waiting for you. You deserve it.'

'Where does it come from?' Simberdy stuck at it.

'Have I got news for you!'

Olive had broken the band on one packet of notes and was counting.

'This is an unknown country for me, Fatman,' he said.

'What is?'

'Art and that. Something I never wandered into previous. Well, I already told you.'

Simberdy felt weak and pulled a chair under himself with his foot.

'But I found what you could refer to as an adviser – a business adviser, relating to art, that sort of matter,' Passow said. 'Someone who knows this scene perfect, and who's straight, too. You know what I mean, Fatman?'

'What advice?' Simberdy replied.

'If you remember, them three paintings you had was not the only ones that happened to go from the museum during the said operation.'

'There was a Monet,' Simberdy said. 'Of course I remember. Nothing Known, where is it? This is serious, *L'Isolement* is unique. It must go back to the Hulliborn. And it must be intact.'

'You said it, Fatman!'

'You've returned it?' Momentarily, Simberdy's voice sang. Perhaps, after all, Olive was right and Passow did have fragments of decency at the centre.

'Yes, it's serious – seriously valuable.'

'Have you any idea of how seriously valuable seriously valuable is?'

'That's it, what I mean – this adviser.'

'He told you how much it was worth?' Simberdy said.

'He did more than that.'

This, Simberdy could have guessed. 'Yes?' Oh, God.

'Are you all right?' Olive asked. She went to the kitchen and brought him a glass of water. He spilled a lot on the way to his mouth.

'He took it off your hands, did he?' Simberdy asked.

'You're the smart one, aren't you? Yes, he said he'd like to buy it from me. I felt glad. I mean, to be frank, did I know how to market such an item? I could learn, for sure, but just now I'm at the very threshold of this new career. Nothing Known is never too proud to know he needs help on stuff he don't know.' He was silent for a moment. 'You think they might be on to you, Fatman?' he asked. 'This line could be tapped. Have you noticed anything like that? And here I am using my real name more than once, and you using it as well. Too late now, though. It's done.'

'Which adviser?' Simberdy replied.

'This is someone London way. Oh, very much London way. They got all sorts of art spots, true class there, and proper experts. This is somebody who really got to grips with art from way back. He've heard of them all. You say any painter, all the foreign names, he'll know it — in his head, just like that, he got it. Michael Angelo, he can tell you everything about him up on church ceilings. The *Mona Lisa*? He could inform you of the size straight off. If there's only a certain space on the wall, the measurements become very important, don't they? Paris — all them galleries — he been there, and paying attention, giving scrutiny, not just a culture stroll. He loves it — art. He knew about Monet, straight off of his own bat. I never told him one thing because he knew it all already. I got a book on art from the library. Monet, in France, painting away there, big beard, well, just like a painter, and into water lilies, he couldn't get enough. First thing in someone's garden, he'd ask, "Any water lilies?" and if no, the day was a washout for him. Really great.'

Simberdy said: 'What did this sod pay you, Wayne? What's this money about?'

'Pay? You know what he paid, Fatman. You can work that out easy enough.'

'Wayne, how the hell would I know? How much?'

'One thing about Wayne Passow, he looks after his friends right. He splits fair with his partners. Wayne Passow is famed for this,' Wayne Passow said. 'So, you get twenty grand there for two of you. Ten each. And exactly similar for self.'

'He paid you thirty thousand?'

'Beautiful, yes? Surprise? But, like we was saying, this is a very special painting, and he thought the frame pretty good,

also: so a bit of a bonus. That Monet, he's what's referred to
in art circles as "much sought after", meaning people collect
him. He's called an Impressionist because he sees things – usually
lilies – and gets an impression from them, or that's my impression, anyway. This kind of operation – paintings – is a long
way up from nicking televisions and cars.'

Simberdy covered the mouthpiece again and half sobbed to
Olive: 'He's sold *L'Isolement* for thirty grand. It's worth how
many millions?'

'And he's ready to help further,' Nothing Known said. 'I'm
real well in with this guy.'

'Of course. It's why you came back and took the "El Grecos",'
Simberdy said.

'There'll be another nice little packet for you soon, Fatman.
I reckon I have a duty to do what I can for you and Olive.
Again I say it – this is a team. All for one and one for all, like.
All right, I'm doing most of the actual work, but that don't
mean special treatment as regards my share. Straight split. Maybe
next time it will be up to you, Vincent, and Olive, to do the
selling. So, don't you worry about it at all. Wayne's going to
handle the deal. Wayne got it under control. All right, I heard
them three might be phoney. Only might. Worth a try?
Obvious. This could be an even nicer package – three times
as nice. This adviser, he'll know about the other painter for
sure. Yes, you can bet he've heard of old El. OK, it's not
Monet and so not quite so tip-top, but Monet's not the only
big painter in the world. Art spreads itself all ways. This is the
great thing re art. No limit.'

'Where is he, Wayne? What's his name, your fence?'

'London way.'

'Yes, you said. But where, exactly?'

'Art is life to him,' Passow replied. 'I love to hear him talking
about tints and palettes. An eye-opener.'

'What's his name, Wayne? Look, we're partners. There
shouldn't be secrets.'

'Although most artists have what's called an easel to work
on, Michael Angelo obviously wouldn't of been able to use an
easel when he was up there painting a chapel's ceiling,' Wayne
said.

Thirteen

Legs dangling, wearing her tangerine and blue gear today, Lady Butler-Minton was seated on a roof beam near the gymnasium ceiling, resting before her sauna, when she saw the door from the garden swing slowly open and Neville Falldew, once Palaeontology at the Hulliborn, stand for a second gazing in, then hesitantly enter. Penelope had been idling after a couple of climbs on the hanging rope, chatting to Lip again and explaining why she had decided after all to be fairly expansive in her first meeting with the Butler-Minton biog girl. 'I can see what it is about Trudy that would activate your juices, Eric. Yet it only came late in your life, didn't it, this taste for big chins?' She stopped talking and watched Falldew. In the old days, when Eric was Director, Falldew and other Keepers and Curators would occasionally turn up, looking for him in the gym to discuss some urgent point of Hulliborn business. She recalled there was even an occasion when Falldew had been conscripted to join with her and Eric in carolling the Egyptian boatmen's shanty.

Falldew had obviously failed to notice her now. He did not look too good, she thought. Had he ever? That eternal, tatty Davy Crockett suede jerkin, with all the greasy, knotted, trailing bits and discoloured zips, plus a college scarf, regardless of weather. It wasn't just his clothes. Penelope had always thought Neville's face seemed to have been squeezed in a vice – the solitary vice, Lip used to allege, despite that long on-off affair with Ursula Wex, Urban Development. The narrowness of Falldew's head made it appear only two dimensional, as though he'd just stepped out from a placard. At parties, Penelope had seen people meeting Nev for the first time actually walk around to the other side of him, checking he *had* another side and didn't depend on *trompe l'oeil*, as in sculpture shows she'd visited. When worried or sad he would lean forward, nursing his head in both hands, like someone carefully holding a rare

LP. Recurrent anxieties seemed to have weakened muscles in key regions of the body, so he could often give the impression he might crumple and break up, the way a newspaper did in the bath, though she'd heard he could now and then force his long legs into quite a gallop. His moustache and beard were brave and well-intentioned but a terrible error: meagre, struggling, dark elements clinging to this angular surface, resembling Marmite on a kitchen knife.

Today, he appeared abnormally bad, special worries digging shallow tracks in what there was of his cheeks: desperate plough marks on a stony field. For a while, he stared about, tugging convulsively at a couple of the rat-tails on his jacket, like a tumbling parachutist searching for the rip cord. He went forward and tapped on the door of the sauna. He waited, then knocked again, harder. Finally, he pulled it open and, crouching, peered in, speaking her name through the clouds of escaping steam. In a while, he gave up and let the door swing shut. Penelope was about to descend on the rope when he seemed to change his mind and, turning back, violently pulled the sauna door open again. Squinting in, he this time began to call not Penelope but Butler-Minton himself, in a low, intense, suddenly joy-filled whisper that only just reached her on the beam. She had begun to shiver a little, partly on account of cooling, but also a reaction to the eeriness of what was happening. All the same, she decided now she must stay and observe.

'Sir Eric? It's Neville. Neville Falldew, Palaeontology. All right, you were a glistening bastard, but a Hulliborn glistening bastard. That's what counts. I've always known as a certainty you weren't gone for ever. Wonderful to see you there in the Folk the other night, nearly starkers on the floor and in beautifully traditional form. Thank heavens I'd hung on to my museum keys, although thrown out. I'd recognize you anywhere, even from behind, as it were, even in the half dark and wearing those little navy socks. Well, didn't I have that earlier similar occasion as a prompt – the one in the icons room?

'But the other night in the Folk! Oh, for me such an encounter is a kind of revelation, indeed, an epiphany. And those two people with you, splendidly tumultuous in the straw, so close and chummy. I think I knew them, too – people from their very different centuries, yet so mystically fused, thanks to you, Sir Eric. This was a brilliant demonstration of what museums are for: that fusing of apparently, and *only* apparently, discrete areas of Time. I have to tell you that there have been long hours since the Hulliborn spurned me when I felt sickened, almost deranged by anger, and the need for revenge. Yes, madness came very, very close: a man craves his work, and a museum man craves his contact with the fruitful past. These were torn away from me. But now I know all will be fine, because you are with us still. And stay with us, Sir Eric, please.'

It was a supplication, yet spoken in a voice alight with happiness and confidence. Above all, confidence. Nev grew silent for a minute or two, continuing to look into the sauna. Then he said: 'Ah, old boatman, still plying your humble but noble trade, I see. Still singing in honour of simple labour and the beauties of creation.' He paused, as though listening – listening and revelling in what he heard. '"All together in the chorus," you jovially command. So be it.' Falldew leant against the sauna doorframe and instantly began at full volume a classic, tuneless, meandering, gobbledegook lyric in would-be Arabic, beating monstrously irrelevant time with one hand and smiling barmily.

It lasted for seven or eight minutes and, at the end, he waved slowly and supremely meaningfully into the sauna with large, sweeping movements, as though across a great spread of water, and closed the door. 'We shall meet again, venerable harbour person,' he said. Then, after one more glance around the gym, he readjusted his scarf with a considerable flourish and left, his steps now more positive, his body strangely stronger looking.

Lady Butler-Minton slid down the rope, pulled on her Mr Universe sweatshirt, and did some undemanding weights work until the sauna heated up again. 'Well, Lip, I accept you were a "bastard", but a "glistening bastard"? Nev was always a bit purple, wasn't he, and now he's flipped. So, what the hell does he think he saw in the Folk? And who was it?'

Fourteen

It was George Lepage's first Founder's Day ball as Director, and, standing in the minstrels' gallery, looking down a bit tensely at the dancers, he wished he could have avoided inviting Neville Falldew. There were others he would willingly have done without, too, but Neville effortlessly claimed top spot as potential supreme master of aggro. His presence meant a chillingly heightened chance of messy public crisis. Lepage dearly wanted to dodge anything of that sort, especially as he had also felt obliged to ask Dr Itagaki and Dr Kanda from the Japanese Arts and Culture Council, as well as the chairman of the local authority, two newspaper editors and several important broadcasting people. Any Hulliborn catastrophe tonight was sure of a good show.

Itagaki and Kanda stood with him now, also gazing down. 'Here is harmony, here is vibrancy!' Kanda delightedly cried. 'Could it be surpassed, could it even be paralleled in any other museum? One substantially doubts it.'

'Oh, yes, one substantially does,' Itagaki said. Her big, blue-framed spectacles twinkled life-lovingly under the revolving coloured lights, brought in for the Ball. 'Among the Hulliborn's precious artefacts we see cheerful concord and general amity.'

Maybe. The trouble was, revered tradition dictated that, along with all current staff, retired Keepers and Curators should be sent Ball tickets, to commemorate Lord Hulliborn of Nadle-and-Colm, creator of the museum in the nineteenth century. Since nothing had actually been proved against Nev, he could not be excluded. Naturally, an unpleasant debate had erupted about this at a Hebdomadal Conclave, with Angus Beresford, Entomology, sounding off so threateningly and coarsely, plus graphic stiff-arm mime, about Falldew's alleged indiscretion in the Folk. Eventually, a request by Lepage for tolerance and customary Hulliborn saneness of outlook, made entirely against his better judgement, helped get Beresford's case rejected.

Ursula had willingly undertaken to police Neville from start to finish. Ursula was resourceful and tough, but could she really manage it?

George had to hope so. As he watched the two of them now dancing together with full, funky energy in the marble surrounds of the Hulliborn Central Hall, he felt for several minutes that things might just turn out OK. Possibly, that warmth between Ursula and Nev would pick up yet again and provide him with some theme to life once more: a healthy and fruitful link with the Hulliborn, not that vile, crazed enmity. It had to be a heartening sign that Nev seemed to have taken the trouble to rent a reasonable tuxedo and mauve cummerbund. Studying Nev's scant face, George Lepage could read no hint of planned mischief and violence against the museum. Perhaps Nev had come to realize that although he might have a grievance, it was not against the Hulliborn but against the philistine political view that the only organizations entitled to helpful treatment were those contributing in a measurable, concrete way to the country's Gross Domestic Product. That was why the Hulliborn had to reduce expenditure. That was why Nev had been flung out of his job early.

George waved and smiled to Nev in a way he hoped said that Hulliborn friendship still meant a bucketful. Falldew ignored this, as though too deeply immersed in private reverie or in the grisly music. Lepage took no offence and would have settled for nothing but private reverie from Nev all night, just as he would settle for the tuxedo and cummerbund, although the occasion was always white tie.

'I see below Lady Butler-Minton, I think,' Itagaki said, 'unceasingly elegant and goodly.'

'Oh, yes,' Lepage replied. 'All those with distinguished links to the Hulliborn are welcome on Founder's Day.'

'We are greatly honoured to be in such a category, having, so far at least, not earned that accolade,' Kanda said. 'This is British generosity, this is *politesse.*'

'Dear Lady Butler-Minton,' Itagaki said. 'And are D.Q. Youde, Art, and James Pirie, Museum Secretary, still stoking her boiler turn and turn about, as during Sir Eric's lifetime, and squabbling over her so feverishly, so wonderfully waspishly?'

She gave a little excited tremor and her black gown, trimmed with gold, rustled ungovernably.

'We understand this rivalry *d'amour* was always an inspiration to witness, a stirring matter,' Kanda said. 'Such deeply competitive devotion. Here something more was involved – and maybe still is – than mere leg-over. Was she not earnestly searching for consolation, in view of so many stresses in her life?'

'Penelope has recovered from her husband's passing very well,' Lepage replied.

Anxieties extra to those about Falldew nagged George. It had been at a Founder's Day Ball that Sam Vaux, the Arts Minister, and his party, were fed the *vol-au-vents* accidentally smeared with flecks of Stain-Out! True, Butler-Minton's knighthood had come through afterwards, regardless, but this year neither the current Arts Minister nor any of his senior officials had accepted an invitation. Lepage was unnerved by this. It seemed the kind of blatant snub Itagaki and Kanda would undoubtedly notice and make their possibly harmful deductions about. Lepage did not blame himself for any aspect of the *vol-au-vent* untidiness, though. It had been a different regime, a different period. In any case, he knew as fact that nobody suffered serious illness or disability through the slip-up. Butler-Minton had maintained that museum *vol-au-vents* were so bland that they needed something like Stain-Out! to perk them up.

And then came what was probably his chief worry. It concerned lovely Kate Avis from Kidderminster. He felt an abiding tenderness for her and had tried to help her eliminate bad memories of the Hulliborn by providing wholehearted affection. She surely deserved it. But there had been tearful arguments about the Ball right up until yesterday. When Lepage had first mentioned it to her a while ago she seemed to recognize there could be no question of her attending, what with Falldew certain to be present and likely to recognize her, and what, also, with Julia present and watchful. As the event grew nearer, though, Kate had begun to question this thinking, saying she ought to be close to George on one of the most important occasions in his calendar. Given what had happened between them, and was still regularly happening, she believed she possessed rights. And Lepage had to accept some of this, damn it. She stated that she felt a complex bond with the Hulliborn, one which should take in its glamorous, festive moments, such as a Founder's Ball, as well as the impertinent flash in Folk, plus, of course, those subsequent sessions on the mock straw with George, benignly, comfortingly audienced by dummy yokels. She said she'd bought a new turquoise, silver and white gown. She had some savings from a legacy.

Kate had obviously come to feel that some indication of the way Lepage rated her was involved. And he would hate her to think it only something casual to him. Surely, it wasn't, was it? But the Founder's Ball? Tricky. Kate did grudgingly admit that Julia probably had the prime claim on him, and she promised that, if she came, she would remain among the crowd of guests and make no approach to George, content merely to be on museum premises and able to see him on such a special evening. If he somehow signalled that he wanted something more than that, she would respond. As cover, she would hire a male escort from an agency. Lepage didn't like the sound of this and, in any case, thought the whole plan foolishly risky. For a long time he resisted.

Finally, though, worried at the extent of her distress, and unwilling to hurt her by a curt, absolute refusal, he had given Kate two tickets, but pleaded with her to use them only if she found it intolerable not to be present. Now, looking down from the gallery on the horde of dancers, he searched for a turquoise, silver and white gown, but didn't find one. He allowed himself to think *thank God*, though he realized that this could be regarded as cruel and cowardly. Kate's tempers were sometimes a high-flying pain, yet had, too, a childlike charm about them, something Lepage didn't see much of these days.

'Are there any indications about Hulliborn's chances of the exhibition?' he asked the two Japanese. 'It's so important for us, perhaps even the difference between life and death for the Hulliborn.'

'Shop!' Itagaki said. 'It must not be talked, you know, not on such a social occasion.'

'We love the Hulliborn,' Kanda said. 'The fine intimacies it achieves with the local community and further afield, too. There will certainly be a decision in good time, rest assured.'

He laughed a little. 'We can't have those anatomical tools with no settled destination, adrift for ever, endlessly roaming the world, like the Wandering Jew or *The Flying Dutchman*.'

'I adore whimsy,' Itagaki replied.

'Which museums beside the Hulliborn are you looking at?' Lepage said. 'What's the opposition? The Victoria and Albert? Others? Well, of course.'

'Tokyo always does its sad little nut to build what's called "a good field",' Itagaki said. 'A nice long shortlist! Those bigwigs get a feeling of power from that – so many organizations waiting on their word. Pathetic, really; the result of much self-doubt, since we have no Eton or Winchester. Those frowsty idiots back home derive as much of a kick out of telling someone "No" as in saying who has won. This is so unBritish that I fear you might not comprehend it.'

Hurriedly, Kanda said: 'But please do not conclude from this that the Hulliborn is to be told "No". All remains totally indeterminate. Totally.'

'A veritable fucking melting pot,' Itagaki said.

'It's just that I have to give a speech tonight,' Lepage said. 'Obviously, I would not wish to make premature, confidential disclosures. But I feel very much in the dark as to what tone I should take.'

'Ah, tone,' Kanda remarked excitedly. 'Could anything be more crucial? This is where the English language is so famously subtle. You are very lucky. But, no, I must take that back. It is not luck that has produced such splendid sensitivity in your language. It is time, it is answered need, it is imagination.'

'Oh, yes indeed, "tone",' Itagaki said. 'This is where irony comes in and such matters as understatement, or "litotes", to give it the Greek via Latin term. If there is one thing I can never get my fill of it's litotes. Among colleagues I am notorious for this. Upon being posted to Britain I declared that what I most looked forward to were real ale and litotes.'

As the music stopped and people began leaving the floor, Lepage thought he glimpsed for a moment a gorgeous turquoise, silver and white dress on a woman who might be Kate. Then she was obscured by the crowd. He watched keenly for her to emerge, but there was no reappearance.

Itagaki said: 'Continuing our theme, there were, I believe, "ditties of no tone" in a poem by John Keats, but this is a very difficult concept. What a ditty must have, surely, above all else, is tone – namely, the specific tone of a ditty, otherwise we could be in the realm of the roundelay or barcarole.'

'I don't know whether to sound optimistic in my speech about the Hulliborn's prospects, or guarded, or depressed,' Lepage replied.

'Do not be ashamed of your uncertainties, Dr Lepage,' Itagaki said. 'They are the very stuff of life. Doubt can be a right old bastard, but also a stimulant.'

The music restarted, and people came out to dance again. 'There now is Quentin Youde, partnering his wife, Laura,' Kanda said. 'That is very charming and wholesome, in the circs.'

'Decent,' Itagaki said.

Lepage could see Julia partnering one of the BBC people. Although he scoured the faces once more he still didn't see Kate. He left Kanda and Itagaki and went down to the bar. He waited for Julia to join him. But when the music ended again, it was Ursula who touched his arm. 'George,' she said, 'you'll have noticed that, as agreed, I've been taking close care of Nev.'

'Yes, good.'

'But now he's given me the slip. I'm sorry.'

'It could be nothing,' Lepage said. 'He seemed happy.'

'Yes, he did. But what about?'

'Being with you? Memories revived?'

'It was calculated.'

'What?'

'Escaping from me. Very deliberate and crafty, and to hell with memories. It's worrying, isn't it, George?'

Yes, bloody worrying. 'I expect he'll turn up,' he said.

'Where, though?'

True. They went to the edge of the dance floor together and looked for Falldew. No success. 'It should be easy to spot him – that head which is almost not a head, and the cummerbund. Keep searching here, will you, Ursula?'

Lepage followed instinct – absurd instinct? – and made his way quickly towards the Folk gallery. Reaching there, though, he found the door to the medieval breakfast tableau safely

locked and no sign of Nev. Lepage was about to return to the
dancing when instinct – super-absurd, atavistic instinct? –
pushed him again, and with his master key he opened the
door, switched on the non-medieval light and went in. Here,
too, everything looked normal. He stood in the doorway and
stared very thoroughly around the room: possibly Falldew
owned duplicates of all Hulliborn keys. Although nothing
seemed wrong, Lepage could not rest. As if merely pacing
aimlessly, he crossed the room towards the old patriarch,
humming with emphatic nonchalance, and, when close, very
suddenly turned and grabbed its raised arm, the one pointing
so proudly at the table spread with its prop breakfast. 'Better
come quietly, dear Nev,' he cooed. 'You won't be sporting
your oak in here any more, will you?'

But, of course, of course, under the sack jacket its arm was
unmistakable wax: thin and pipe-like, and not the thinness and
pipe-likeness that might come from undernourishment, and an
attempt to harmonize with Falldew's flimsy head, but the thinness and pipe-likeness of artificiality. Lepage felt ashamed of his
suspicion and stupidity. What would have been in it for Nev
tonight with no public present to witness any personal display?
God, Lepage thought, perhaps he – he, Lepage – did need early
retirement after all. Had some of Falldew's mania rubbed off
on to him? Was the job too big? Once more he found himself
asking what Butler-Minton would have done about all this;
found himself, in fact, actually preparing the words to be used
in a plea. At the same time, he had a vision of himself all
ponced up in tails and shiny black shoes, official host at a notable
function, and yet about to address the definitely dead, implore
the definitely dead flouncer for help.

Then, while he continued to hold the effigy very firmly,
paralysed for the moment by guilt and confusion, Lepage heard
someone move swiftly behind him at the door, and, turning,
full of panic, he gasped: 'Flounce? I mean, Sir Eric? Thank God.
Aid. But no, no, how could it be?' It was, instead, the squat,
energetic untentative frame of Angus Beresford, Entomology,
that Lepage saw entering at a fierce rush, eyes full of rage and
hatred above his excellent, obviously custom-made tails. 'What?'
he said. 'What the hell are you talking about, Director?'

'I—'

But Beresford was not interested. 'Is it Falldew again? I've said all along he shouldn't be asked. But, anyway, we've got the creature this time, before he can start further disgrace and trouble. Hang on to him. Oh, yes, hang on to him. I saw the door was open, knew something must be up. Yes, something must be up. Great work, George.' He pushed the door shut. 'Now, together, we can beat the shit out of him. Nobody will hear the screams above the band. Let's use the bumkins' medieval hoes and pitch-forks, yes?' He more or less sprinted across the room and, before Lepage could say anything, threw a heavy left-hand punch that landed square in the middle of the patriarch's face, and followed it with a swinging right to the stomach. The model was torn from Lepage's grip, spun around and dropped once more on to the straw. The closed door kept the band noise out, and Beresford would have heard the particular, almost negligible sound when the dummy hit the floor. It had nothing like the solidity and weight of a human body falling. It settled at their feet with not much more than a mild, rustling crackle. 'My God,' Beresford said, 'it's not Neville. What the hell are you doing in here, Director, holding a nothing's arm and talking to Flounce?'

'We should get out,' Lepage replied. 'There's been a slight error. It might all be difficult to explain. I'll try to do repairs tomorrow.'

Beresford went and picked up the patriarch. He lifted him very gently, as though to compensate for the ferocity of his attack. Because of the first punch, the model's features were wrecked, with both glass eyes and the nose now on one side of the face, like a tilted fruit salad; and the body seemed twisted and unnaturally bent on account of the later blow. 'Can we really put him back to rights, George?' Beresford said.

'I don't want to hang about in here. I have a bridge-building speech to make.'

Beresford tried to get the figure propped up safely against a big piece of tree trunk that was there as its chair, but all balance and poise seemed to have gone, and it slumped forward into Lepage's arms like a drunk. Its own arm still pointed forwards in what could be mistaken for a warm and moving attempt to embrace George.

'We'll just have to leave it, Angus. Say it was vandals, or the room temperature too high, causing selective meltdown.'

Hand-brushing his tails, Beresford said doggedly: 'Director, I don't regard myself as blameworthy. Why, almost any man with the Hulliborn's interests at heart might have done the same. I still mean to catch up with Falldew.'

Lepage had been so frequently in contact with the patriarch lately that he'd begun to develop a terrible feeling of nearness, as if their lives were unbreakably bound together, like Héloïse and Abelard. Now, while Beresford took the body of the old, beaten-up peasant and went to lay it out as neatly and humanely as possible on the mock-hovel floor, Lepage moved towards the door, ready to leave. As he neared it, though, it suddenly started to open gently and he caught sight of the skirt of a beautiful turquoise, silver and white evening dress. Kate looked happily around the door's edge at him.

'Darling,' she said, 'somehow I knew you'd come here and wait for me, despite that silly spat we had about the invitation. Oh, George, love, this is our own special place.'

'No, Kate, there's someone else here,' Lepage whispered. He stepped out from the room past her and pulled the door more or less closed In the passageway he spoke very *sotto* to Kate. 'There have been developments.'

'Someone else?' Thank God she whispered, too. 'Who? Who've you brought here now, you insatiable swine? That Japanese slag in black? You want everything in sight! So, where is she? She going to give you a bit of geisha? This your regular lech venue, is it, no matter who with?'

'A minor crisis,' Lepage replied.

'What?'

'The old father peasant was misunderstood, and some violence resulted.'

'Misunderstood? He's wax. How could he be misunderstood?'

'Misunderstood in the sense that his waxness wasn't recognized – not until too late. It's the opposite of what happened to you.'

'Damage?'

'Some.'

'Oh dear. I must see.'

'Well, all right.' Lepage pushed the door open. Beresford was still on the other side of the room with the peasant family, crouched very low over the dad, like someone giving the kiss of life, apparently trying to do some cosmetic repairs on its face with his thumb. He looked up as Kate and Lepage came further into the room.

'Good God, don't I know you?' he asked Kate. 'You're the affronted woman, surely. I saw you in the mêlée on that appalling day, didn't I?'

'What's the matter with that dummy?' Kate replied.

'It can all be put right,' Lepage said.

'Why are you here?' Beresford asked her.

'I believe Miss Avis has a fixation on this room, following the incident,' Lepage said. 'Something that compels her. It's sad, yet, perhaps, understandable.'

'And dressed up for it so beautifully,' Beresford said. 'I don't get it. You were invited, Miss Avis?'

'It seemed the decent thing to do,' Lepage said. 'A sort of apologetic gesture for what happened on these premises under different circumstances.'

'That bastard Falldew has done lasting psychological injury to her,' Beresford said.

'I felt an obligation to counter that,' Lepage said.

'You've been very wise and considerate, George,' Beresford said.

Kate crossed the room and stared down at the peasant. As far as Lepage could tell, Beresford's attempts to reconstruct a face for the model had not worked, and its nose had more or less disappeared. 'What's happened to him?' Kate asked. 'I hadn't realized he was damaged when he fell the other—'

'He's very fragile,' Lepage said.

'You mustn't be upset, Miss Avis,' Beresford said. 'I see that he might be of special significance to you, in however dark a fashion.'

'No, not dark,' she said. 'Not any longer. Not in his authentic form. I feel very fond of him, as a matter of fact.'

'Oh, that's rather beyond me. I'm only a Keeper of Entomology, not a psychologist.'

'We share certain memories, as it were, he and I,' she said.

Beresford considered this for a few moments. 'Ah!' Suddenly, he nodded in recognition. 'I see – think I see. You mean in the deepest sense: that of folk memories? You feel a link across the ages, perhaps. Our common humanity. He – it – can only *represent* humanity, being simply a model, but it works, just the same. Very fine. That's what museums are about in large measure, of course.'

'Most of the time, I think of him as "he" not "it".'

'Arthur will be gratified,' Beresford said.

'Who's Arthur?' she said.

'Hugh Arthur is Folk,' Lepage said.

'"Is folk"? I don't understand. Aren't we all folk?'

'That's what Angus means,' Lepage said. 'Linkage across the centuries: you, me, Angus and what the wax man stands for. Look, I think we should leave now and say nothing of this. It doesn't really fit in with the occasion.'

'Agreed,' Beresford said.

'But what did happen to his face?' Kate asked, bending over the patriarch, which lay on its back near the piece of tree trunk. 'This isn't the result of just a fall. It's as if he's been struck with something. What kind of loony would thump a waxwork, though?' She raised the figure a little by its shoulders, so she could examine the damage more closely. It was a bit like a tango movement, Lepage thought, when the man swings the woman towards the ground and pulls her up, though now Kate had the man's role, like Daphne with Osgood Fielding in *Some Like It Hot*.

Her remarks had made Beresford ratty. 'I'm not certain how one judges the cause of injuries in a dummy. Perhaps we should send for a medieval medic.'

'What did you say you were Keeper of?' Kate replied. 'Wit? You certainly keep all that to yourself.'

The door opened, fairly abruptly this time, and a youngish man unknown to Lepage stood there, his tails grand. 'Kate!' he cried. 'I've been looking all over. Saw the light under the door. Listen: there's something very strange going on in the ballroom. You *must* come and see. But why are you holding that ghastly thing?'

'Strange? "Very strange"?' Lepage asked, full of alarm. 'Strange how?'

'This rather bizarre looking guy out there.'

'"Bizarre"? So, the archbishop? The BBC Head of Programmes? The place is full of them.'

'But really bizarre. His head.'

'What about it? Who are you, anyway?'

'He's my escort,' Kate said. 'Adrian. From the agency. We hit it off at once, didn't we, Adrian?'

'His head?' Lepage said.

'So narrow,' Adrian replied. 'Like a fox's.'

'Falldew,' Angus Beresford said. 'What's he doing?'

'Now, wait a minute,' Lepage said. 'Let's be sure of our moves. Close the door, please, Adrian.' He found himself deliberately working for delay, scared of discovering more trouble.

'But what's going on in here?' Adrian replied. 'You ask who am I, and I ask who are you?' He did not shut the door, as if determined to have an exit available. 'Why is she holding that dreadful thing? I don't want to get involved in any . . . well, in any far-out behaviour, three men one girl, that sort of agenda, and all these bloody dolls. Is this some annual Founder's Day carry-on? People often expect too much from a hired escort. These tails belong to the agency, and I must keep them in good order; they stressed that. I'm new on their books. Can't risk any . . . well, unsavouriness. They're so keen on reputation. They very specifically told me, "We are not Rentaknob."'

'I have to go to Central Hall immediately,' Lepage said. He led the way swiftly from the tableau room and back towards the dancing. Kate hurried to keep up with him. Beresford and Adrian followed a little way behind. 'You were there for me, George, weren't you, and only because of me?'

'Of course, darling,' he said. 'But let's be circumspect.'

'Perhaps the peasant room later?' she replied.

'What about Adrian?'

'Look at the swine,' Beresford said as they came to the edge of the dance floor. He pointed up at the balcony. 'Yes, that's the one,' Adrian said. 'He's been there a while, capering about.'

'I think he's going to make a speech,' Beresford said.

'Yes,' Lepage said. 'Oh God.'

Dr Itagaki and Dr Kanda were still where Lepage had left

them on the balcony, talking now to one of the newspaper editors and his wife. All watched Falldew with sickening, amused interest as he came to the balcony rail and signalled to the band to stop playing, so he could be heard. He looked wonderfully serene.

'But I know this man,' Kate said. 'The glassy blue eyes.'

'You had more of his body bits to go on previously,' Beresford said.

'I might be able to get to him in time and limit the disaster,' Lepage said.

'I'll come,' Beresford said. 'We can pitch him over the rail if we're lucky. But he'll probably float down like a paper dart.'

'I'll go alone,' Lepage said. 'Dealing with this kind of thing is my sole responsibility as Director.'

'Which kind?' Beresford replied. 'You come up against such situations regularly – ex-Keepers going ape? There's a laid-down procedure?'

Lepage said: 'Well, the scale, the implications. Angus, I feel I have to take—'

But as he spoke the music came to a natural break, and at once Nev's waving grew more imperious and urgent. Except for Falldew's build, it reminded Lepage of Mussolini, also on a balcony, declaring the capture of Rome by his mob, or something similar. People below gazed up wonderingly, many waving back, a few shouting encouragement or rough, jolly insults. His smiling self-confidence shone even brighter, and soon he began to address the crowd on the dance floor and around the perimeter. 'Friends,' he said, 'yes, it is indeed I, Neville York Falldew, recently a part and a proud part of this famed institution, so rich in achievement and distinction: someone who, I believe, may reasonably claim to have added a quantum through scholarship, loyalty and diligence to that Hulliborn achievement and distinction.' For one so slight looking, his voice was remarkably big, hypnotic and commanding, and Lepage found himself compelled for the moment to stand and listen.

'I bring great news,' Falldew said. 'Yes, news that could transform all our lives. I'm sure you'll all remember that epigraph from Dante at the start of T.S. Eliot's *Prufrock* about Lazarus returning from the dead, with unprecedented wonders to describe. Well, Neville York Falldew does not pretend to have returned from the dead, but he can say he is the custodian of a marvellous revelation.'

'Oversell if it's going to be just another flash,' Beresford snarled.

Nev leaned forward on the balcony rail, thin face glowing like an illuminated address. 'Rest assured, this will be no disappointment, no anti-climax.' He seemed to hear something shouted from the crowd. 'No, not Mrs Cray or the haversack straps. Infinitely more important. Matters transcendental.' His eyes swept the audience, searching. 'But, first, I want to invite the lovely Lady Butler-Minton to join me on the balcony,' he continued, 'noble widow of our former world-renowned Director. For what I have to tell you concerns her more than anyone. Penelope, where are you? You must be part of this triumphal moment.'

'What the hell's he on about?' Beresford asked. Lepage had waited with him and the others, at first transfixed by the rhetoric and then reluctant to try to silence the sod in full view of this fascinated ground-floor gang. He saw Lady Butler-Minton, wearing yellow, begin to climb the marble stairs towards Falldew.

Julia joined Lepage and took his arm. 'Where've you been, George? You're the fucking host, yet you drop out of sight for an age.' Some harshnesses had invaded her language since she started the Spud-O'-My-Life kiosk and learned how to choke off troublesome late-night riff-raff.

'One or two problems, love,' he said. 'Nothing epic.'

'And who is the forever-panting piece in turquoise, white and silver you reappeared with?'

'Which is that?'

'The bird behind you who looks as if butter wouldn't melt in her mouth, but who'd prefer to get to work on something harder.'

'Oh, yes, she's here with Adrian.'

'Who's Adrian?'

'They're very much an item.'

'She gazes at you non-stop, George.'

'I want to catch what Neville says,' he replied.

'I think he's been driven half mad – or more than half – by what's happened to him. He'll talk nonsense.'

'Let's see, shall we?' Lepage said.

Falldew beamed to all sides. When his eyes reached the Japanese, Kanda gave a small, very understanding bow. Penny Butler-Minton was standing close to Falldew, and he reached out and put an arm around her shoulders, after the way the patriarch had seemed to embrace Lepage on the cottage floor. That look of contentment in Falldew's face had been definitely replaced by something more intense: he still seemed happy, but it was a radiant, throbbing happiness now. Again it was Il Duce that Lepage thought of – if only Falldew had more to his lips. 'I have been very downcast,' he told the crowd. 'Despite years of devoted service, despite the contributions I feel I might still have made to the Hulliborn, I was rejected by the institution I lived for. I am not alone in being spurned. Nor is the Hulliborn, and museums generally, the only area where this kind of Philistine brutality has been exercised. Nonetheless, it hurt me. There was even a time – I admit it, ladies and gentlemen, when I considered taking some form of revenge for my heinous treatment.'

'Here we go, then,' Beresford said. But he had it wrong.

'Fortunately, better sense prevailed,' Falldew went on. 'One rethought. One recalled the fine history of the Hulliborn. The damage would be gross – nay, heinous in its turn.'

'Right. Thank God he's come to see that.'

'He's a liar,' Beresford said.

'And I am here tonight to tell you all is well,' Nev said, 'indeed, to tell you something more than that. I want you to think of a quietly opened door and the lovely sight I saw before me. A lovely, rehabilitating sight. I must not become more specific than this. But I want you to believe it was a moment of healing, a moment of renewed hope, it stemmed from that transcendental area I have spoken of. There before me on the floor—'

Lepage was not altogether clear then or afterwards what happened at this point, except that it silenced Nev. He saw Lady Butler-Minton suddenly stoop and wriggle decisively to free herself from Falldew's arm. Then, remarkably quickly, she turned fully towards him, and lifted Nev aloft with total ease, gripping him by the seat of his dress trousers and a handful of the back of the tuxedo.

'Christ, Penny's going to chuck him over the balcony. She trains on weights, doesn't she? Fair enough, but I was only joking,' Beresford said.

'Which quietly opened door?' Julia said.

Lepage wondered whether he, in fact, knew which door. Perhaps he had provided that rehabilitating sight, without knowing it. Did Nev, in the grip of his vast mental turmoil, think he had seen a reincarnation of Flounce in the tableau room? Carrying Nev with some care in front of her at shoulder height, with no sweat, Lady Butler-Minton moved slowly away from the rail and took him towards the rear of the balcony as he yelled in protest and struggled uselessly. In her loose-sleeved gown, arms outstretched holding Nev, she looked like some superb, predatory, yellow insect, bearing off a mauve striped grub, as grub.

Lepage, listening as hard as he could to Falldew's cries, thought he heard, above the generalized yells, something about Flounce and 'a longed-for, now realized return', then, later, a jabbered string of words that contained what was almost a jingle: 'I saw reassertion of his person in vigorous, fleshly form.' Penelope might have been swinging him around a bit in the air, and his voice seemed to come and go, like from a faulty mike. A little later, there was nothing audible from Nev at all because the guests broke into loud spasms of outright laughter and applause, presumably at Penny's performance. Possibly, they imagined the whole thing was a piece of Founder's Day cabaret, sign of inventive new ways under Lepage's leadership. Itagaki and Kanda clapped with great enthusiasm, though decorously. Lepage felt damned annoyed at being spied on in the tableau room, and in being mistaken, though admittedly from the back, for a resurrected Flounce.

Lady Butler-Minton and Falldew disappeared from the balcony – Lepage imagined into one of the galleries behind. Lepage saw Ursula hare up the stairs to reclaim Neville. The band resumed with 'Teardrops'.

'So, what was that?' Julia said.

'Hard act to follow,' Lepage replied.

'He was screaming about Flounce, wasn't he, George?'

'I thought so, but what?'

'A "return". He spoke of a return. Gee.'

'He's deep into craziness.'

'I had the idea he said something about vigour and flesh. If that's to do with Flounce, it means only one thing, doesn't it?'

'He's dead, so what does it matter?' Lepage said.

'Yes, but Nev was so committed, so sure.'

'The mad are like that.'

'Did Penny carry him off so as to silence him? Had she heard something about Sir Eric's escapades and didn't want any awkward, public disclosures from Falldew?'

'Let's have a go at this one, shall we?' he replied, getting out on to the dance floor. It was a reasonably creaky foxtrot, put on for their age group. From there, he could glance back at Kate, but she was turned away, playing up full-steam to Adrian, fondling his grey waistcoat one hundred per cent, and rubbing an ear against his shoulder pad. 'See?' Lepage said. 'She's really stuck on him.'

'Who on whom?'

'The turquoise, silver and white girl and Adrian.'

'Why are you so interested?' she said.

'You asked about her, that's all.'

Julia watched Kate for a while, and then leaned closer as they danced and spoke loudly above the music: 'She's putting on a show, to niggle you through jealousy.'

He pretended not to hear. She yelled it again, and Simberdy, who was trundling about with Olive near them, mouthed a reply: 'Who wants to make whom jealous?'

'Having a good time?' she answered.

A little later, Lepage was circulating among guests, geniality in overdrive, when Keith Jervis, the part-time porter, approached urgently. He was on security duty tonight, looking extremely smart and purposeful in his neat blue Hulliborn uniform. 'Something undue in Art,' he said.

'"Undue" in which respect, Keith? Which "Art" did you have in mind?'

'I can understand that, as Director, you need the specifics.'

'That is the case,' Lepage said.

'The Raybould Gallery,' Jervis replied.

Lepage felt a huge rush of alarm. 'Not something else missing?'

'The opposite.'

'What's that mean?'

'An extra, as far as I can tell.'

'Christ, Keith, are we talking about a bomb? Have you told Dr Youde, the Keeper?'

'I think he's rather tied up.'

'"Tied up" how?'

'With Lady Butler-Minton. You probably know, there's a traditional element to this.'

'But Youde's wife is here with him, for God's sake.'

'Mrs Youde is also preoccupied, helping lay out the raffle prizes at present, I believe, sir.'

'Tied up where, the two of them? This could be – well, it could be embarrassing. I've enough of that already. Am I my Keepers' keeper?'

'If Dr James Pirie, Secretary, happened to light on them, you mean? Or Mrs Youde. Yes, Dr Pirie can get intemperate, I know. I did think of this, but it's not something I, as merely a part-time employee, can speak to Dr Youde, Art, about. Lady Butler-Minton is certainly conspicuous wearing that bright yellow, if this is still the case.'

'But she was with Falldew only a short time ago.'

'She did have Dr Falldew in her hands, yes. But I think Dr Ursula Wex, Urban Development, relieved her of that burden and is now seated in China and Glass pleading with Dr Falldew for sanity – well, no, not going that far, but asking for restraint, like. I wouldn't bet on it from him, though, would *you*, Director? We should go to Art.'

'Of course.'

They set off together, Lepage trying to keep the pace to a saunter, so as not to excite attention, but Jervis striding strongly like a sword of honour cadet on pass-out day leading the parade, except for the ponytail. Before they left the ballroom, though, Lepage was waylaid by Ivor Pinnevar, Zoology (Birds), standing on his own and looking agitated.

'Director, I must talk,' he said. 'I couldn't hear all of Falldew's address – too far away and a noisy group near me – but am I right to believe he spoke about Mrs Cray?'

'Not spoke about. Mentioned. He was replying to a shout from the crowd. The matter's closed.'

'My God, this is disturbing,' Pinnevar said. 'A nightmare. These echoes from another time.'

'Yes, another time. No longer relevant.'

'Awesome glimpses into the abyss.' Pinnevar shook that big, blond curly head and moved his hands about convulsively in the air. He had pinkish, very round cheeks, fine skin and light-blue eyes. Usually, the effect was of a large, cheerful, insubordinate young girl. Now, anxiety had screwed up all his face muscles, and with the spasmodic arm waving he still looked sort of feminine, but now more like a mature lady harpist going into the bit she knew she always fucked up rotten. His sufferings seemed even to have taken some colour from his eyes so that they looked slaty. 'The whippet and the tennis ball and the air-sock, too – he spoke of those?'

'Not at all,' Lepage replied. 'Do enjoy the Ball, Ivor.'

'You keep a brave front, I'll say that for you, Director.'

Jervis stood near them radiating impatience.

'I must go, Ivor,' Lepage said.

'Another crisis?' Pinnevar asked, appalled.

'Certainly not. A routine matter.'

'But Nev Falldew, once the most balanced of men, sent deranged like that,' Pinnevar replied. 'Is a job so crucial to people?'

'To me, it's balls,' Lepage said. 'But perhaps not to everyone. You know about Samuel Smiles and his so-called gospel of work? *Gospel*! Work as a means of salvation? Rubbish. But it does get to people, still.'

Lepage and Jervis moved on and in a while entered the Raybould. It was Hulliborn policy not to hang other paintings in the spaces left by the Monet and three 'El Grecos'. Youde had argued in Conclave that the areas of blank wall conveyed a tragic eloquence, signalling the museum's grief, and making their mute but telling protest about the theft. But Jervis now pointed to the spot which *L'Isolement* had once graced, and Lepage saw that a large brown envelope hung there, fixed to the wall by four drawing pins. There appeared to be one word hand-printed in capitals on the envelope and, as he went nearer, he thought at first it was 'MONET'. Closer, he saw it said 'MONEY'.

'I decided not to touch,' Jervis told him.

Lepage wondered whether he should handle the envelope himself, or leave it for the police.

Jervis had obviously done a pondering session. He said: 'Important, the way Monet and Money are like each other, like. Maybe it draws attention to that very shadowy line between the values of art and then of commerce.'

'What?' Lepage said. He didn't enjoy getting a lecture on aesthetics from a part-time porter. 'It doesn't look to me as if there's much money there. Not anything like enough for a Monet.'

'Just what I mean,' Jervis said.

'What?' Lepage asked.

'It's great art, and this tells us it's worth a fat packet.' Then Jervis said more sharply: 'I never infringed on it, Director.'

'No, no, of course not, Keith. I wasn't hinting at that. The envelope's still sealed, anyway.'

'I thought there might be questions – someone not on the permanent staff.'

'Nothing of the sort, Keith. No doubts of your integrity. Tell me, did you look into this gallery before the Ball began?'

'Every half hour, sir.'

'And, obviously, the envelope wasn't there then?'

'Correct.'

'So, in all probability, it's been placed by someone who is a guest.'

'I know what I observed, Director. Full-stop.'

'Understood. But did you see anyone in this part of the building?'

'No, sir. I seem to have fallen down on that aspect. This will probably be held against me in any career discussions. Pardon my frankness, but I can't afford to be snooty about work in that way you just mentioned to Dr Pinnevar.'

'Some bullshit is often required to fertilize a conversation, Keith. Forget what I said. Your devotion to your work here is exemplary.'

Quentin Youde appeared at the Raybould entrance. He looked dishevelled and sounded breathless but slaked. 'What's happening, George? I saw lights in the gallery.'

'Where were you, Quent, that you could see lights here?' Lepage replied.

'What's that on the wall?' Youde's voice approached scream pitch.

'Keith and I are trying to sort it out,' Lepage said.

'This simply appeared?' Youde asked.

'Like the message to King Belshazzar in the Bible,' Lepage said. 'Jervis found it. He deserves a pat on the back.'

Youde said: 'I suspect it's a ransom note from those people holding the El Grecos and that other work. It's how they operate: "Pay up or we'll destroy the painting." Happened with the Dulwich gallery, didn't it?' He went forward to the envelope. 'Ah, yes, as I've said: "MONEY." That's their demand.'

'Possibly,' Lepage said.

'Inside, it will say how much they want, the grasping, vandal bastards.' Youde produced a small pocket knife and reached up to prise the drawing pins clear. Pale, a little pouty, with a full head of swept-back, dark hair, Youde liked to be told he resembled Degas in a famous self-portrait. For those who might miss the similarity he had a framed print of the work hanging in his office. Simberdy reckoned, in fact, that Quentin had attempted a self-portrait himself, to point up the *doppelgänger* aspect, but had come out looking like a composite of Charles de Gaulle and Mrs Eleanor Roosevelt, so Youde had never made much of the painting.

Youde jabbed at a drawing pin.

'Shouldn't we wait for the police?' Lepage asked.

'Police? Mr Plod handling art matters? I don't think so, Director. This situation could require very subtle treatment. The fate of priceless works is on our shoulders.'

'Priceless is what we was just discussing, as a matter of fact,' Jervis said, 'but getting nowhere.'

'What? What do you mean?' Youde said, beginning to achieve leverage under the first drawing pin.

'Like, strange they're so priceless but simultaneous have a very big price,' Jervis said. 'They're priceless until the bidding stops at Sotheby's, and then these priceless objects have a price, it being what they just been knocked down for by a bid.'

Youde said irritably: 'The price is what the market in its

crude, almighty-dollar fashion, puts on something that is, in essence, unassessable.'

'Yes, I heard something like that before,' Jervis replied. 'But when they was priceless ten years ago they was priceless for a different price than they can get now. Not so many almighty dollars then.'

Youde reached the second pin. 'I don't think I follow, Jervis, though it's damned interesting and, yes, you've been very alert.'

'Thank you, sir. What I'm saying, in my own way, is this market, which is so crude, seems to change up and down in a manner that's quite—'

'Quite crude and arbitrary and grossly vulgar,' Youde replied.

'What I'm trying to get at, sir, is, say – which God forbid – them "El Grecos" turned out to be phoney—'

Youde stopped working on the pins and spun around to face Jervis and Lepage. 'I'm not taking this shit from a part-time porter,' he said.

'Or if a few eminences *said* they was phoney, in their view, which is the same thing in your game – not many facts, lots of opinions – then down would come the millions or whatever to nothing at all,' Jervis said.

'You make my point,' Youde answered, with an enormous, free-range laugh. 'The market, in its coarse fashion, is interested only in names. It thinks in labels, reacts favourably only to labels, not to the intrinsic glories of the works.'

'But aren't museums interested in labels, too? Our pictures got labels. What we must ask is are them pictures worth the millions that you paid for them, Dr Youde, *because* that's what you paid for them in the market? You, you yourself, liked them "El Grecos" all them million pounds worth so you paid it. And good luck to you. So, do we say they're worth that much never mind who painted them? You get my drift, sir?'

Youde, who was still turned half away from the wall to cope with Jervis, but had also resumed attacking the drawing pins, said: 'Oh, sod it, I've torn my thumb.'

'Don't drop blood all over the place, Quent,' Lepage said. 'They can identify from it. Genetic finger printing. Or thumb.'

'Identify? So? I'm dealing with some sort of message in my

own gallery. Is that an offence?' Youde went at the last drawing pin harder, to show entitlement. Blood flowed. 'My God!' he said. He had freed the envelope and opened it. 'Cash! Sterling!'

'Get away,' Lepage replied.

'But what does it signify?' Youde cried.

'Payment?' Lepage suggested.

'For what?' Youde said.

'Well, the envelope was in the Monet spot,' Lepage replied.

'And that indicates something?' Youde began counting the fifties on the Raybould floor, smearing many notes.

'Someone had second thoughts, maybe,' Lepage said, 'and wants to compensate for the crime.'

'Compensate? But that's mad,' Youde yelled. 'This is only chicken feed. Twenty grand! That's all, damn it. May I remind you, we're talking about a Monet, Director?'

'What I was saying,' Jervis replied.

'What? What were you saying, Jervis? We long for your analysis,' Youde said.

'That it's, like, priceless until somebody offers a price – say, twenty grand. Then an expert, such as yourself, Dr Youde, knows this is much, much too little.'

'"Beauty is truth", but beauty is also loot,' Lepage said.

'Oh, why don't you piss off back to your door-keeping, Keith,' Youde said. 'Why should I have to listen to this drivel? I have a disaster on my hands.'

'Oh, not that bad,' Jervis said. 'We'll get a sticking plaster for it.' Then, watching Youde do a recount of the money, Jervis said: 'I got an idea.'

'God, no,' Youde said.

'Maybe they have it wrong, hung it in the wrong empty space, being hurried,' Jervis explained. 'Maybe they heard me coming on my rounds. That money could be for the "El Grecos", couldn't it? They went, too.'

For a second it looked as though Youde would strike him. He was still crouched down with the notes, but his body suddenly tensed, like a sprinter on the start blocks, and he appeared about to spring up and attack Jervis. Lines of pink formed in Youde's doughy cheeks, reminding Lepage of sauce trails on a knickerbocker glory. 'You're saying the El Grecos are worth only this much – three works: that's just over six thousand each!'

'Well, if they are,' Jervis said.

'If they are what?' Youde hissed.

With a sad, diplomatic smile, Jervis said: 'There's been a bit of argument, you can't deny, Dr Youde, re authenticity. Well, look, the "but on the other hand" and "maybe this, maybe that" stuff is still here.' He pointed to the ambiguous, framed 'El Greco' caption fixed to the wall where the three paintings had been.

'What the hell do you know about arguments, or about authenticity?' Youde said. 'You're a freelance flunkey.'

Jervis smiled with lovely tolerance at him. 'You shouldn't take it to heart so much, Doctor. I worry to see you – same with Dr Simberdy when he gets into a fret. You, you goes a bit blueish. Not attractive. A warning colour. Any bugger can make mistakes. And the bigger you are, the bigger the mistakes. Just think of Adolf going into Russia. Am I, Keith Jervis – as you say, a part-time, non-staff porter – ever going to get the chance of cocking things up to the cost of millions? Ha-fucking-ha! But you're out there with the front runners, Dr Youde, and you've earned it. You got status.' He brought his hand up smartly to his forehead in a US-style, hatless salute.

'But who has done this, George?' Youde asked.

'There's been no break-in tonight. We can only guess. Obviously, someone who was involved somehow in the theft of the pictures – but the identity is a mystery. The Fatman, so-called? As I suggested, conscience money?'

From the Central Hall came the prolonged din of a fanfare by the band. Youde quickly gathered up the money, replaced it in the envelope and stood. 'It's the raffle. One ought to be present. Laura's put admirable work into it, totally unstinting, finding worthwhile prizes, persuading notable people to donate. Well, Eve Chape, for instance, a wonderful bronze. Yes, this is something of an occasion, and Lady Butler-Minton herself is making the draw. I promised I'd be there.'

'Which one?' Lepage asked.

'Which one what?'

'Which one did you promise?' Lepage replied.

Youde looked at the bloodied envelope. 'They're deriding

us,' he replied. 'And, of course, they don't offer to pay for the El Grecos, which are the real, massive loss. Anyway, what's to be done with this measly token?' He waved the envelope. 'Director, I think you should put it in your safe.'

Youde left for the raffle. Jervis said he would tour the Raybould looking for any other signs of malpractice. Lepage went first to his office and, while putting the money away, heard someone come into the room behind him. Turning, he saw Neville Falldew, who smiled with undoubted fondness. Lepage locked the safe. 'Nev,' he said, 'you're looking so smart and well. But I thought you were with Ursula.'

'I knew I should find you here, Director.' He nodded a couple of times with solemnity. 'For this is where you talk to Sir Eric, isn't it? I read about it in the newspaper: the dear platypus.' He stroked the exhibit. 'It's very moving.'

'That was Press garbage, Neville.' God, Nev must be in a bad way to start sentences with 'For'. He poured them a couple of brandies.

'He's such a presence still,' Falldew remarked.

'Flounce? We don't need him.'

'I expect you've heard.'

'What?'

'I believe I saw Sir Eric very recently.' Falldew sat down and gazed about, as if terrified. 'Look, George, is that conceivable, or am I going—'

'We all enjoyed your words from the balcony just now.'

'I meant to speak of Sir Eric there. An affirmation.'

'Yes?'

'Not meaning to be rude, George, but with Sir Eric, the Hulliborn has a future.'

'Well, a past, anyway.'

'But in a museum who can distinguish?' Falldew replied, wagging his head like a slack, pale flag in a tiny breeze.

'Me, now and then,' Lepage said.

'Ah – "now", "then" – you see, so hard to separate. After all, Director, what is Time?'

'Ask the band.'

Lepage's door was thrust open, and Julia, entering at almost a run, said: 'George, I hoped you'd be here. You should come at once. Quent Youde and Vincent Simberdy are openly brawling. And the shouts!'

'Are the Japanese still here? And the media?' he replied.

'Of course.'

'Hell. Fighting about what?' He gave Julia a drink.

'Simberdy won first prize in the raffle and kissed Penny Butler-Minton rather would-be meaningfully when she presented it – his fingers busying away at her behind. Quent was sure to object.'

'Penelope will never get over the loss of Sir Eric,' Falldew said. 'How could she? Such a unique leader. Still no reflection, George.'

'Sod Butler-Minton,' Lepage said.

'His return!' Falldew replied. 'She will be transformed by joy.'

'You mean those two were actually fighting on the platform after the presentation, Jule?' Lepage said.

'With the mike on – terms like "slob", "crud", "twat", "mini-cock".'

'Itagaki will know them,' Lepage said.

'Amplified everywhere,' Julia replied. 'Vince using the raffle prize to defend himself – a charming statuette of Seamus Heaney by Eve Pike Chape. The unique, unjangly sound of sculpture on skull.'

There was a knock on the door, and Ursula came in. 'Well, here you are, Neville.' She wore a racy, green silk trouser suit and diamanté white shoes. Urban Development was not the label for her tonight.

'I thought we might have a threesome,' Falldew said.

'You bloody what?' Julia replied.

'In any case, there are four of us now,' Ursula said, brightening.

'I mean I came for a three-sided conversation: the Director and myself talking to . . . well, talking to the sort of abiding presence, the memory of Sir Eric,' Falldew remarked.

Lepage sped down the spiral staircase. The music had resumed with old-fashioned waltzes, perhaps as a way of lightening the mood; or a reminder to Vince and Quent that their age group might be no longer at fighting peak. They had moved, or been moved, from the platform, and now hit out at each other sporadically in a corner of the dancing area, while people did the Veleta skilfully around them. Neither appeared hurt, except for Youde's thumb. As the two men lumbered about, Laura Youde, Olive Simberdy and Penny Butler-Minton tried to stop the violence by pleas and occasional tugs at the sleeves of a tail coat, like quality controllers on a production line removing faulty items. Simberdy's bulk put dashing footwork beyond him, and he sidled about slowly, now and then swinging a huge fist or the literary sculpture in great, imperfect arcs.

Youde crouched forward in something marginally like a boxer's stance, and threw energetic jabs at Simberdy's gut, the effort bringing Quentin's dark hair down over his ashen features, really mucking up the resemblance to Degas if it existed, and putting Lepage in mind of a drowning man's face just under the surface. Reaching the group, Lepage waited for a moment, seeking a chance to get between the two scrappers when Simberdy had the Seamus Heaney down at this side between shots.

It occurred suddenly to Lepage that the only other time he could recall a fight at the Founder's was five years ago when Flounce and the then Lord Mayor's chaplain fell out badly over something to do with Ovid or Ella Wheeler Wilcox, and Flounce had taken a fearful hammering, including several kicks in the groin and ribs from the chaplain when Flounce was down and virtually out, though admittedly only with dancing pumps.

Keith Jervis must have followed Lepage and now shouted above the music and bad language, 'Art, Asiatics, you fight like a couple of Tinkerbell's fairies. It makes me ashamed.' He stepped forward and, taking a handful of shirt-front on both, jammed them hard into wallflower chairs – Simberdy with difficulty because of his width – and then stood near, defying either to get up again. The band continued the Veleta – a triple-time waltz – and Itagaki and Kanda glided near with total proficiency, as if this style of dance had been a core subject at their schools back home. They broke off now and approached Lepage and the others. Itagaki's eyes throbbed with pleasure behind the big glasses. 'The Hulliborn is nothing but a clutch of rousing surprises,' she cried appreciatively. 'One imagines, all too fool-ishly, that one has it, as it were, deftly categorized, and then wham-bang where are we? An opening moment, delightful good fellowship, social serenity, the next, bunches of fives. This is like life itself, surely. A marvellous variability. Each mode equally valid, each contributing to the pageantry of change.'

'Thank you,' Simberdy replied. The statuette shone notably under a layer of sweat from his hand and arm. Lepage could see no fragments of Youde on it, nor blood.

'You, you particularly, Dr Simberdy, have the makings of a Japanese wrestler,' Kanda said. 'The presence. The neck. The dignity.'

'Thank you,' Vince Simberdy said.

'But we must not leave out Dr D.Q. Youde,' Itagaki immediately stated, touching Youde's hand in encouraging, international fashion. 'You, too, fought the good fight, to borrow a locution from St Paul. As Keeper of Art you deal with matters of sensitivity and taste, but what that obviously does not preclude you from having is balls.' She turned to Lepage. 'You must be very gratified, Director, to have two such all-round personnel on your staff. The day of the complete, Renaissance man has not gone.'

'True,' Lepage said.

'In those damned corny public school yarns, people always went to the gym when a fight impended, and did the thing under all the tedious paraphernalia of rules and fair play and big, soft gloves,' Itagaki sneered. 'To the devil with all that bourgeois shit, eh? Eh? A fight is hot. It's savage. It is of the people. It happens, but is not a mere "happening"– not theatre.'

Kanda said: 'We come back again and again to that same word: it is *life*.'

'My God, dot the Is and cross the Ts, won't you?' Itagaki said.

Simberdy leaned forward a little and began to throw up ostentatiously near his highly polished black patent shoes. He groaned once or twice.

Kanda's tone became extremely kind and gentle: 'Nobody says you are in tip-top condition, Dr Simberdy. How could you be – the enforced sedentary life? But these things are easily corrected. It would be alarmist in the extreme to suppose internal damage.'

'And then Dr D.Q. Youde,' Itagaki said. 'Remarkably unflustered, scarcely even breathing fast.' She stood back and put a finger to her lips coyly. 'I feel sure I'm not the only one to have noticed this, but you have a remarkable resemblance to a self-portrait by Degas. It is obvious to me, despite recent stresses in your face.'

'Really?' Youde replied. He obviously wanted to smile in thanks for such a compliment, but resisted this in case showing his famously comical teeth ruptured the moment.

'Has this never been pointed out before?' Dr Itagaki asked.

'I think, perhaps, I have heard something of the sort. One forgets these things,' Quent Youde replied, 'flattered as one might be. Occasionally also Byron, but in profile only.'

Lepage moved around the group to be nearer Simberdy and make sure he was all right. He heard Olive hiss something at her husband, not all of it clear, but along the lines of: 'You brought this on yourself. Grossness. Tonguing Penny and buttock-fondling her. Oh, you freight-train-load of miserable, pastiche lech. Don't ever forget we have secrets together. I could finish you.'

Dexterously holding up the skirt of her black gown as she and Kanda passed Simberdy and his indisposition on their way back to the dancing, Itagaki called: 'Oh, no, I'm afraid that in Japanese museums these stimulating, untimetabled events are just not bloody on. Such a dreary crew over there, folks. We've got more rectitude than Toyotas.'

'So, finally, why museums, ladies and gentlemen? Why, indeed, the Hulliborn?' Lepage was concluding his speech, standing at the microphone on the platform where Youde and Simberdy had recently started their conflict. People were packed around, listening. Looking out, he could see at their various spots in the crowd, Ursula, Nev, the archbishop and his wife, a couple of the editors and *their* wives or partners, Angus Beresford, Pirie the Museum Secretary, Pinnevar, Itagaki and Kanda, the BBC contingent, and Kate and her hired man, Adrian – he would be required by the agency to enjoy whatever she enjoyed, which would cover a fair range. Lepage thought they all looked passably interested. 'After all,' he continued, 'we live in a period which sets much store on modernity, and rightly sets much store on being up-to-date and at the forefront of development and knowledge. This, we are told, and are frequently told, are the prerequisites of survival. One would find it difficult to argue.' He strengthened his voice, got it into rebuttal state. 'And yet one has to ask, is there no place in this gospel for recognition of the wonders of the past – indeed, for cherishing, for learning from such wonders?'

'Yes,' Falldew cried, giving a kind of Black Power salute without the power or the blackness. It might have been an error for Nev to pinpoint himself like that. Lepage saw Angus Beresford home in on Falldew and begin to move purposefully through the audience, his face contorted by fury, towards where Neville and Ursula stood.

'There is a living spirit in the Hulliborn,' Lepage continued.

'Oh, yes, yes,' Falldew cried. 'I bear witness to that. Gladly bear witness, gratefully bear witness.'

Lepage said: 'Myself, I see the Hulliborn – as I see all this country's good museums, and, indeed, as I see the arts and humanities faculties in our universities (grand word that, "humanities") – all these I regard not as mere repositories of relics and dust-shrouded works and learning, but inspirational points of confluence, where the glories of man's history meet the equally glorious prospects for his future, in a rich union that offers fruitfulness, improvement and satisfaction. Do they, does the Hulliborn, deserve to be under governmental threat because they offer nothing measurable, graphable, visible towards Britain's gross domestic product?'

'Never!' cried Falldew.

'No, I think not,' Lepage said.

Lady Butler-Minton and Olive Simberdy were tending to Vince. He had stood up, looking very white and doddery, and both women held an arm and were bent forward to speak encouragement to each other around his great belly. Youde, still seated, watched his exit triumphantly. It might irritate him, though, that Penny Butler-Minton should help an enemy, sick or not.

Lepage continued: 'And so, ladies and gentlemen, as we have assembled happily here tonight to honour our great Founder, let us resolve to safeguard the fine traditions of the Hulliborn.' Beresford had reached Nev, but to Lepage's relief did not attack him, at least not yet. Instead, he stood close behind Falldew in the press of people, and seemed content to listen to Lepage's concluding words. Perhaps, after all, things were beginning to come right, and the best really could be brought out of people with patience. 'It is my task, and perhaps the task of all of us, to convince sceptics and doubters outside, at whatever level, that, in fact, far from being moribund, or even already extinct, the Hulliborn is alive with promising activity, and has its own positive, throbbing vigour.'

'True! How true!' Falldew yelled.

Kate Avis nodded and smiled beautifully.

'We must act together – a team, sinking absurd, petty enmities,' Lepage declared. 'I am confident the Hulliborn can count on you, as I hope and trust it can count on me, to carry everywhere this message of faith in the institution and the values it represents. And to convince those who decide policy for our nation that this museum is a symbol of much that is fine and indispensable; that its continuance as a centre of excellence is not merely merited but will be a boon and splendid asset. Thank you.'

Applause broke in full, thrilling volume. James Pirie, beaming in the front row, reached up to shake Lepage's hand. 'Grand, Director,' he said. 'Words of a true leader, and disregard any who say you're not. Words of vision.'

Others pressed forward to congratulate Lepage. Itagaki exclaimed: 'Top bracket! None of this can be gainsaid.'

Although Lepage shook many more hands, he made sure he kept a watch on Angus Beresford and Nev, especially on Beresford. But Beresford moved away from Falldew now. Yes, he might indeed have been affected by Lepage's words calling for an end to foolish rifts, despite Beresford's reasonable anger. Angus was clapping very heartily as he walked and, from his lip movements, Lepage judged he might also have been shouting, 'Bravo! Well said!'

As Nev turned to leave with Ursula, though, Lepage became aware of another kind of rift. He saw now that the back seam of Falldew's smart tux had been cleanly severed for its entire length, so as he edged towards the exit, the jacket opened at the rear and flapped gently, trailing cotton strands and some dreary segments of lining. Falldew appeared not to notice, and Ursula, walking ahead, had not seen it. Lepage realized that the damage could have been done by some exceptionally sharp instrument, standard in Beresford's trade for dissecting. When Nev took the suit back from hire he would have some considerable talking and, most likely, paying to do, unless Urse was hot stuff with a needle. Lepage felt suddenly very down. He had spoken of unity, yet here was glaring division.

Julia came to the edge of the platform. Half-automatically, he put out his hand for her to shake in congratulation, too. She ignored it. 'I'm going to help Olive get Vince Simberdy home. Penny thinks it will annoy Quentin if she seems too concerned about Vincent. This will be some of that selfless teamwork you were rabbiting about. I can call in at the kiosk, too, and see that Rowena's managing. Will you be all right alone?'

He dearly hoped it would not come to that: this had been a damn rough and wearing night, and Lepage felt the need of consolation. As the Ball came to an end, he went to the medieval breakfast room, in case Kate had meant what she said about rendezvousing there. He was surprised to find the door unlocked and, half opening it very quietly, became aware of two people on the floor, using the mock straw as mattress, as he had himself. There were no lights on, and for a nonsensical moment he thought the male figure, fully dressed in dark clothes, was the defaced patriarch. Then he saw that the jacket hung open because of its slashed back, and he heard a voice that could be Ursula's purr from beneath, 'Just like the old times, Nev.'

'But what *is* Time?' Falldew replied, thrashing about to get his clothes off. 'What the fuck's happened to this jacket?'

'Decide later,' Ursula answered, 'about the jacket and Time.'

Lepage thought he could make out on the primitive table, alongside the basic old feast, a diamanté shoe and a pair of rumpled green silk trousers. He closed the door and, just then, saw Kate approaching the tableau room in her fine gown. 'It's engaged,' he said. 'What happened to Adrian? You seemed very matey.'

'I paid him off. We can go to your room instead, can't we, George?'

'That interfering bloody platypus is there.'

'Put a cloth over it,' she replied.

Fifteen

Simberdy recovered pretty fast from his tussle with D.Q. Youde, and so managed to get to this meeting with Wayne Passow – 'Nothing Known' – at Wayne's club, the Blague, late next night. There'd been a phone call to Vince at home first. Wayne said the topic would be money, but wanted a full, detailed discussion face-to-face. 'This requires mutual presence in discreet surroundings, Fatman.'

Olive came with Vince to the Blague. The three took a table in the bar. 'You'll soon see why this isn't something to be said on the phone. No, no, no,' Wayne told them. 'We've entered the world of art. It's a world worth giving respect and attention to. This is not your chicken shit.' He put his hand through his short, blond hair, a bit bottle-aided, and gave one of those tragic, small smiles he specialized in. As Olive sometimes said, Passow had the face of a saint: long, ungenial, made for suffering, stronger than sin. If he ever did get charged, she reckoned a jury would be won by his looks and not just acquit but award huge costs against the police, then ask Wayne for personal blessings. He whispered: 'We're talking millions.'

'We're talking what?' Simberdy screeched.

'Please, keep the noise down, Fatman,' Wayne said. 'Don't advertise. This club – well, if all the jail time done by members was laid end to end and pointed backwards we'd be with the Pharaohs or that Clementine Attlee.'

Olive said: 'But how sure of this are you, Wayne?'

'There's a great career here for all of us, doubt me not,' Passow replied. 'A real load of heavy noughts. I been wasting my time. It's obvious now. All that mini-activity when this art realm was just asking for yours truly. Well, I'm grateful, so grateful, to you two for pointing me that way and, as you already got evidence of, when he's grateful Wayne Passow shows it.' He leaned across the purple, mock-onyx table and squeezed first Olive's arm, then Simberdy's. 'Still partners, still a premier division team.'

Glancing around the glossy, frenziedly décored interior of the Blague, Simberdy could see what Wayne meant about the clientele. There were faces here that Ronnie Acton-Sher might have jibbed at as being too savage and frightening for public display in his Zoology (Mammals) gallery. A couple of men seated not far from them, and exhaustively eye-inventorying Olive's body, moved their lips in great convulsive surges when chatting, as if taking bites out of a roast. Passow waved to them. 'Crispin, Redvers, lovely to see you both. I'm with friends prominent in Asian Antiquities, or I'd join you.'

'I heard they got a lot of antiquities Asia way,' one of the men said.

'Unconfirmed, but very, very possible,' the other said. 'If Redvers here believes it, it got to be very, very possible.'

'The thing about antiquities is their age,' Redvers said. 'You can't have antiquities without age. Asia's been there quite a time.'

'This is a fact,' Crispin said.

'If there hadn't been an Asia, what would have been in its place?' Redvers asked. 'I'll tell you: the sea, ocean. But oceans already cover one fifth of the world's surface. So, if there hadn't been an Asia there, the amount of sea would really be over the top, in my opinion. Right out of proportion. I don't know if your friends ever considered that.'

'We go in for the smaller Asian items, not Asia itself, in bulk,' Simberdy said.

'Exhibits,' Passow said.

'That's fair enough,' Crispin said. 'But if there'd only been sea where Asia is there wouldn't be no exhibits, so it's great that Asia is definitely in that area known as Asia. All right, you might get flotsam and jetsam washed up, but this is not the same as exhibits.'

'And what would the flotsam and jetsam be washed up on if there wasn't no Asia?' Redvers said.

'The thing about exhibits is they go back centuries and centuries,' Passow answered, 'therefore proving Asia must of been there.'

Crispin and Redvers nodded. Wayne Passow's remark seemed to have brought a satisfactory end to this conversation.

Simberdy turned to Wayne and lowered his voice. This was not for Crispin and Redvers: 'I don't want to sound hostile, Nothing Known,' Simberdy said, 'but to be frank, Olive and I would prefer no further involvement in the Hulliborn paintings episode. This is how we see it – an episode. An episode that's over, as far as we are concerned. We'll put ourselves in the clear and stay in the clear.'

'"In the clear"? How, Fatman? We're a unit. Everybody knows it.'

'Everybody doesn't fucking know it,' Simberdy replied.

'No, but everybody could,' Passow said.

Simberdy hadn't wanted to come to the club, and particularly so late at night. The Blague lay very close to Julia Chakely's jacket potato kiosk in Bray Square. Vince wouldn't like the Director's partner to spot them entering a villainous dump like the Blague at near midnight. But Wayne had insisted the telephone wouldn't do, and said he couldn't make it earlier owing to commitments. So, now, they sat in the club, drinking surprisingly excellent champagne and doing their best to get a hold on what Nothing Known might tell them. Simberdy and Olive had arrived by taxi and scuttled fast into the club's grimy, faded-red, bouncer-dense doorway. Simberdy recognized that his scuttling might be distinctive, but had tried to blur this image by holding his waist in through breath control and quietly repeating to himself over and over a line from a Cary Grant film, 'Think thin.'

Sighing modestly, Passow leaned across the foul table again and murmured: 'I got to say this to start – cards on the table; that's always my way. All right, then: I think maybe I didn't get the greatest price available for that first sales object.'

'The Monet?' Simberdy asked.

'Values are very subjective,' Olive said.

'I listen around,' Passow replied. He lowered his lowered voice. 'Thirty grand is very uplifting, but is it uplifting enough? You get what I'm saying?'

'You've had an eye-opener somehow, have you, Wayne?' Simberdy said.

'You've hit it, Fatman. I was taken for a bit of a ride. Never mind: the lad who advised me – that London dealer – he's not going to be doing nothing similar for a long time, I can tell you.'

'What?' Olive said, obviously troubled. 'Why not?'

'I heard he took very sick,' Wayne said. 'Not terminal, but disabling for a while. How can he visit customers or galleries in that state?'

'Oh, God,' Simberdy said.

'But don't you worry, Fatman. I found somebody so much better for us.'

'Yes?' Simberdy said. 'You sure?'

'This is a different dealer, also from London way, but straight, so straight. Well, he soon gave me inside stuff on that previous one, I can tell you,' Passow said.

'How do you know?' Olive said.

'Know what?' Nothing Known replied.

'That he's straight,' Olive said.

'This one, he's not just in London. He's been to Paris, Florence, Madrid, the whole scene,' Wayne said.

'Oh, God,' Simberdy said. 'Didn't you say the other one had been to Paris as well?'

Redvers said: 'Do you know what I hate, Wayne?'

'Well, you'd hate an ocean if it was where Asia ought to be,' Passow replied.

'Yes, but more than that,' Redvers said.

'This opens up a big field,' Wayne said.

'But it's obvious,' Redvers said. 'I hate to see a party of three – like you and your two friends. It don't seem to balance right, like things wouldn't be balanced if we had too much sea because of no Asia. It's a couple, plus one, and that one is you – a bit spare.'

'I'm all right with it,' Wayne said.

'How to put it right is if that nice piece from the kiosk you're in here with some nights came in now,' Redvers said.

'Red means it would even things out,' Crispin said.

'From the kiosk?' Simberdy said. 'Which kiosk?'

'No, she won't be here tonight,' Nothing Known said. 'This is just business. It don't matter only three.'

'If you say so,' Redvers replied.

'The spud kiosk in Bray Square?' Simberdy asked. Could this be? Did women move from someone like Lepage to someone like Passow? To that, Simberdy knew the answer was very much yes: women transferred from here to there and maybe back again, or elsewhere. Nobody could tell why, not even other women; maybe not even the woman doing the transferring herself. But, all the same, to Nothing Known, for God's sake? Mind, he was younger and a lot more refined looking than Lepage.

Passow switched back to the main topic, speaking quietly again, to exclude Redvers and Crispin. 'What I got to tell you both is gloriously re them other paintings.'

'The "El Grecos"?' Olive asked.

'Now, I hear from the way you say it, Olive, like "El Grecos", not just El Grecos –' he got suspicion and sarcasm into his voice for the 'El Grecos' – 'yes, the way you say it makes it clear you think there could be something wrong with them, that right?'

'Me, I love them,' Olive answered.

'No, not much wrong with them,' Simberdy said, 'just they're phoney through and through, and the man who bought them for the Hulliborn is the jerk of jerks, that's all. You're hawking a load of rubbish, Wayne.'

Passow gave that pained, saintly smile again. 'Of course, I knew there was a bit of uncertainty.'

'A ton,' Simberdy said.

'I didn't try to hide this rumour from the new contact of mine – the second dealer,' Passow said. 'In any case, he'd heard it. Something like that gets all round the art world, only natural.'

'But?' Olive asked, excited.

'Yes, "but",' Nothing Known said, chuckling. '*But* we – that's you, Olive, you, Fatman, my dealer and me – yes, we got a buyer. That's the message. Why we're here tonight. Fruitful talks are in progress.'

'Who? Where?' Simberdy asked.

Another patient smile. 'Always questions, Fatman. But why not? Who? Someone with the real stuff. Where? Let's say abroad, shall we? Who, again? Someone who knows about art and money and who knows about El Greco, and who is sure these are real with what's known in the art game as "provenance", meaning OKness, and to hell with what anybody says against. Someone who knows it so strong and who is into that provenance so deep, he's willing to pay a very jolly price. He thinks they're worth millions and will come across.'

'Yes, Wayne?' Olive said. 'How many millions?'

'Under particular discussion, as you'd expect,' Passow replied. 'Detail. *The Vision* is smaller than the other two, but that don't necessarily mean cheaper. It's not the amount of paint or the space on a wall it could fill. Other matters to consider in the price. Of course. This is the mystery of art.'

'That ponce Youde got it right?' Simberdy cried. 'Is this what you're asking us to believe, Wayne? How the hell do you know this middleman, this dealer, is straighter than the last?'

'Quieter, Fatman. They'll think you're a headbanger and have you chucked out. This place got a reputation to think of now and then.' Passow looked about slowly, smiling non-stop to signal everything was serenity despite appearances and the din moments. The man behind the gilt and glass bar seemed to accept Passow's unspoken assurance. Wayne gave Redvers and Crispin a thumbs-up and special, personal smile. 'How do I know he's better, straighter, and that the El Grecos are for real? I feel it, that's all. Wayne Passow feels it.'

'Oh, God,' Simberdy replied.

'You're poisoned by jealousy of Quentin Youde, Vincent,' Olive said. 'Haven't I told you this whole value thing is so arbitrary?'

'Now *you've* hit it, Olive,' Passow said. 'Exactly. Arbitrary. Does that mean millions? And then that other word you came out with, "subjective". What's that one about?'

'It can mean anything,' Olive said. 'That's the whole point.'

'A word and a half, yes?' Passow replied.

In the taxi on their way home, Olive said: 'Wayne is banging George Lepage's Julia?'

'There might be other kiosks,' Simberdy said.

'Yes?'

Sixteen

In the house this time, rather than the gym, Penelope was having one of her talks to Butler-Minton. Kneeling on a seedy old bit of Persian rug, her head stretched forward, Penny chatted into a cupboard under the stairs. A photograph of Eric hung on its rear wall, and whenever she opened the doors and switched on the little interior light, she chewed over a Hulliborn topic or two: the kind of things she knew would have interested him. She felt a kind of duty to keep a photo of Eric, but didn't want it in an open, prominent part of the house where she'd have to see it every day; see it perhaps unintentionally, and with an unpleasant shock at times, when looking for something else. She liked to make a conscious, planned decision to gaze at the photograph, and to have in mind a very precise duration. By keeping the snap in this hidden-away recess she could carry out her obligations to the memory of Eric, without making over much of them. The other advantage was that people calling would not see the photo in one of the rooms and feel obliged to talk about him. She would have gone to the cupboard occasionally anyway, because it was where she stored old copies of *Sporting Life*. She worked a horse-race betting system that required a lot of reference back. On account of Eric in there, though, she went to the cupboard more often than her punter research demanded.

The picture showed Butler-Minton receiving an honorary doctorate at Ibadan University, Nigeria, in about 1982, and trying his hardest to look wholesome under that big, academic pancake hat, the mark of a bite she'd given him lately very evident high on the cheek, like a mange patch. Rainbow-robed black professors surrounded him, most of them offering warm, brotherly smiles, though a few gave signs of galloping panic, as if just starting to wonder what the hell they were doing letting someone like Flounce get more deeply associated with the institution.

Except for the bite scar, it was a photograph Penelope loathed, the only one of him she'd kept when disposing of his stuff after

the funeral; and even so it stayed out of sight most of the time.
She knew she could not bear to have anything around that recalled
Eric at his best, and might force her to realize in full again what
had gone from her life. For instance, she had systematically burned
all the pictures which caught Butler-Minton in situations where
his normal, cheerful arrogance and loud, bullying and bullshitting
dynamism screamed out at her. This meant nearly all. Likewise,
she destroyed every photo where he figured wearing one of those
seven or eight gloriously lopsided, loony-stitch, Dominican
Republic lounge suits. He'd brought them back solely to cause
affront, or, at the very least, bowel-troubling edginess to H. de
T. Timberlake and other people from the Museums Board in
London. The suits themselves finished in the incinerator, having
been turned down huffily by both Oxfam and the Salvation
Army. So, this starchy Ibadan photograph and the Egyptian boatman's paddle in the sauna were about the only mementoes she
allowed herself. Although now and then she regretted having got
rid of so much, and could feel quaintly starved of Flounce, she
would tell herself, OK, she *ought* to feel starved: he was dead.
Yes, she did tell herself that, but didn't always listen.

'I had my doubts about Lepage, as you know, Eric, but
second thoughts: he might be able to handle matters after all.
Perhaps he's tougher than he seems. At the Founder's he gave
a speech fizzing with fuck-all, but brilliantly the right kind of
fuck-all – not the sort of self-advancing, flesh-creep stuff *you*
might have given, getting everyone's goat and prosing about
the agonies of your retread soul. The two Japanese seem to
like him. That's important. And, of course, he doesn't carry
any of that potentially awkward stuff from the Wall period –
the haversack straps and Mrs Cray.'

She heard a car draw up sharply on the drive outside and
then stand with its engine turning over. Headlight beams had
swung swiftly across the hall ceiling as it arrived. 'Oh, shit,
Eric,' she said, 'this will be poor Falldew again, looking for
you and the past. Well, I must help, up to a point. Things are
at crisis level with Nev at present. One must be supremely
caring.' She stood, switched off the cupboard light and closed
its doors. The motor outside had been cut. A car door was
slammed, and quick footsteps came towards the house. The

bell rang. She opened up. It was D.Q. Youde, agitated and purposeful in a cloak. 'Quentin,' she said. 'You know I don't like you coming to the house to see me.'

'You're a single woman now. It's not as when *he* was alive.'

'I still find it strange.'

'I think of you as a friend, and, naturally as more than friend,' he replied.

'Yes, yes, of course.' She closed the door and took him into the living room.

'Penny,' he said, in a terse, *fait accompli* tone, 'we must go away at once.'

'Quent, dear, what is it?'

'For good,' he said.

'What for good?'

'Go away for good.'

'Go away? What about the Hulliborn and Art?'

'*Because* of the Hulliborn and Art.'

'I'm baffled.'

'I can't take any more. Please, Penny.'

'Relax, Quent. You look terrible, love.' She knew this would get him concerned and perhaps more controlled. She watched him glance in the mirror and then ferociously try to reassemble his features into the Degas face, not taking his eyes off the process for more than a minute.

'Forgive,' he said. 'But you were the only one I could think of.'

'We'll sort something out.'

'You're looking at a laughing-stock.'

'Who is laughing?'

'Many. Some unrestrainedly, viciously.'

'Why?'

'The El Grecos. The fucking "El Grecos". I've brought contumely on the Hulliborn at a time of its greatest need. Only flight is left.'

'Let's sit down, shall we? I'll bring drinks.'

He took her arm. 'Yes, but first tell me you'll do it. Please, tell me, Penny.'

She hated being gripped in that desperate way, as if a banister in an eventide home, but generously killed off the urge to throw him against the living room wall. Like Falldew, he seemed in true want, and she must let him talk his troubles.

'I long to go somewhere abroad, a place where you lived with *him*. Say, Africa. The Middle East. Anywhere they knew Flounce Butler-Minton and you.'

'To where Eric and I lived? Diourbel? Jimma? Some rich memories there. But why? And then there's the cat.'

'Places where Flounce did his best archaeological work. I'm finished here, you see. The Hulliborn fights for its well-being, even for its life, and I make it a worldwide joke. But if people at one of those sites of his former triumph could see – actually see in the flesh – that I'd displaced the adored Butler-Minton, and had been chosen by you, a wonderful consort, to take over . . . oh, don't you glimpse what I mean, Penny? I might be finished here, but *there* I would be 1990s man. We would walk those foreign streets as the day cooled, contented, fulfilled, and people watching us would observe our happiness and share in it. They would know nothing of the "El Greco" farce.' Swivelling his head slowly he stared into all corners of the room. 'You talk to him in this house, don't you? I feel it, and I entirely comprehend.'

'There *is* regular communion,' she replied.

'I don't object.'

'Good, D.Q.'

He did release her now, and she guided him gently to a settee. 'It's charming of you, Quent – the way you always lust to be someone else. So humble, so literally self-effacing. Why don't you take your cloak off?' She undid the big metal clasp at his neck and put the garment on a chair. Without it, he seemed considerably less, like one of those joke parcels that is all wrapping paper. 'First you wanted to be Degas. Now Eric. Did you see *Zelig*? Despite Eric, I'm into Woody Allen at present. It's about a character who changes to match his surroundings: if he goes into a Greek restaurant he turns Greek, and at a Nazi rally he becomes a Hitler crony, although Jewish. You have similar chameleon qualities. It's fascinating.'

'Penny, of course I want to be somebody else. Why? Because as I am I am nobody,' he bellowed. 'I don't want to be some-body *else*, I want to be *somebody*!'

'What makes you so sure the "El Grecos" are wrong? You were confident about them when talking to the Press: not the voice of a nobody. And then the fight with Vince Simberdy because of the kiss and arse-crack clutch – again not the behaviour of a nobody, but the behaviour of someone brave and sensitive and gallant.'

'It was necessary,' Youde said. 'But, as to the "El Grecos" – a mounting certainty, a feeling about them. Of course, I hide it, keep up a bonny, fraudulent front, like any responsible professional, but the doubt grows all the time. Penny, I trust my feelings. Now, Lepage tells me the insurers are niggling, too. I've thought of suicide – inevitably. But then, timeless exile seemed more appropriate, with you.'

'Darling, you could still be right about those works. Forget the "experts". Eric always said they—'

'You see what I mean, Penny? He pervades. He is your eternal point of reference. I want that role! Oh, to walk alongside you, acknowledged by the populace, just as he used to walk alongside you! Yes, in the dusty, faraway streets of Ethiopia. That sounds perfect. You would look at me, as you used to look at him, not adoration, necessarily, but simple, calm wonderment. This would end all my troubles.'

'But Quentin, you're Art, not Archaeology.'

'He's still a part of this house, isn't he?' Youde replied. 'In the structure. In the ambience. In the very decor. Damn. Damn. Damn. That's why I want to take you away. But, so complex, so baffling – I still would like to keep contact with him, and I could bear your keeping contact with him, also. I *have* to bear it, because I know that will not change. Look, I don't really mind that you put out for Jimmy Pirie now and then. I know it means nothing, is just a kind of charity to an unfortunate. It's Flounce who is really between us, isn't it? And between us in a positive as well as an obstructive way. Why I said "complex". His memory and reputation swell, even without confirmation of that Mrs Cray business and the air-sock, while my status plunges into the abyss.'

Penelope feared he might begin to howl. There were no close neighbours, but she would still prefer he didn't. Sounds from an abyss were always going to be unsettling, probably with

echo upon echo. He might be right to see the 'Mrs Cray business' as a plus for Eric. Not everyone thought like that. Youde
sat far back on the settee, his neck, legs and whole body very
stiff, as though dead a decent while. Ethiopia? Jimma? It had
been really fine there. By then, all the children were away at
school, and she had felt wonderfully liberated. The recollections
warmed her very centre and, for a while, she indulged those
inspiring memories and found herself beginning to consider
seriously Quentin's proposition. My God, perhaps it was not
so crazy after all. She'd had some great and hilarious times there
with Eric, and the people were a delight. Could something of
that era be recovered? She yearned to think so. And wouldn't
it be a supreme relief to get away from everything here, including
that fucking dictatorial cat, Enteritis, and the research girl
working on Eric's biography, with her questions and – worse
– bits of knowledge; plus the worrying troubles of Nev Falldew
and the overall dangers to the Hulliborn? True, D.Q. Youde
could be – and almost definitely would be – a screaming aesthetic
agony for a while wherever they went: Jimma, Diourbel or
Southend. She would be able to work a few changes on him,
though, once they reached fresh ground. And D.Q. had sweet
things about him, above and beyond the impressive looks. 'Tell
me more, Quent,' she said. 'I begin to like the sound of it.'

He stirred a little. 'You do?'

'I think we might be able to make a go of this, yes. We've
only been playing around here, haven't we? It's time we matured.'

'Yes,' he said. 'Yes?'

'In Jimma there'd probably still be people I know. They
could fix us up with somewhere reasonably cheap. I'd miss the
gym, but there are other ways of keeping fit.'

He sat forward and said gratefully: 'You take things damn calmly.'

'We'll have a drink and think a bit more. Then, if things
still look good, I can pack in half an hour. Less. Don't need
a hell of a lot for Jimma. Passport's OK, and jabs. Currency
later. But what about Laura?'

'I'll definitely ring her and explain – from Heathrow or
Addis Ababa.'

She went into the kitchen to fetch the whiskey, feeling
almost totally rejuvenated. This was the kind of thrilling project,

bursting out of nowhere, that had always been on the cards with Eric, especially in the long-ago past, before the damn Director job took charge. Penelope would have liked to chat over this startling idea with him now in the cupboard, but felt that Quent might see and become upset, given his present mixed-up mood. In any case, she felt sure Eric would approve. He had loved Jimma, too – had been made a real towering fuss of there, as D.Q. suggested. Of course they would remember him and her. 'I have this flair for making those who scarcely know me in real terms love me,' Eric had said.

'It's a prerequisite,' she'd replied. That was untrue, but you could not let the bugger get away with too much delight in himself.

Musing happily as she poured the whiskeys, Lady Butler-Minton thought suddenly that she saw through the kitchen window a man crossing the lawn towards the gym. He moved very swiftly among the bushes and trees and, in the darkness, she could not be certain whether it had actually been someone; perhaps nothing but shifting shadows as the foliage flapped in the wind, making deceptive patterns from the scraps of moonlight. She was about to decide it had been imagination, but then told herself that this was slackness, evasiveness. The figure had seemed to be making for the gym. Could it really be Falldew this time? Penny felt her anxieties about pitiful, ruined Nev rush back. Deserting him for Ethiopia might be difficult – cruel. Yet she could not bind her life to his, surely. She took Quentin his whiskey and told him she would have to make certain everything in the grounds was secured, in case they set out tonight. He seemed dazed.

She ran down the garden and, pulling open the gym door, found Falldew in his usual ragtag-and-bobtail garb, standing near the sauna, though it was not switched on this evening. 'Why, Neville,' she cried, 'how grand to see you!'

'I had to come with the news. Ursula and I are to be married.'

She clapped her hands. 'That's wonderful.'

'And I—'

'You came up here to announce it. How nice!'

'Yes, to announce it.' He stared into the cold, dead sauna, as if searching.

'I felt I couldn't go ahead without consulting.'

'I'm touched,' she said. But, of course, she realized now that it wasn't herself he wanted to consult, it was Eric: part of that lasting, unhinging esteem for one who had tried against the governmental odds to keep him in post. 'It's lovely news,' she said and leaned forward to kiss Nev on the cheek.

He smiled, but a little tragically. 'Ursula will be so pleased to have your blessing.' He leaned into the sauna and stretched a hand out towards the Egyptian boatman's paddle, then quickly drew back, as if afraid of being presumptuous. In a few moments he went through the same procedure again. 'No,' he whispered, 'not for Neville Falldew.'

Penny reached over, lifted the paddle and made him take it. For a few important seconds he gazed blissfully at the rough slice of wood. Then he made a few, slow strokes in the air with it, at about his knee level, very softly chanting another pigeon-Arabic, old rope, non-song. In a while, he put the oar reverently back. 'Thank you,' he stated, into the sauna, and to the leader who had striven to protect him and his job. Correcting, he turned to Penny: 'Thank you.'

'Married when?' she asked.

'Soon. We hope you can come.'

'I might be going away.'

'Oh, Ursula will be disappointed.'

'I need a change, Nev.'

'I saw Quent Youde's car outside the house, so, naturally, I didn't want to interrupt. Why I came direct to the gym.'

'Yes.'

'It was a pity you stopped me saying my piece at the Founder's, Penny.'

'Showing off, as a weightlifter, I just wanted to see if I could carry you. Nothing more.'

They went out of the gym, and she locked the door.

Falldew watched with big horror on his face. 'Oh,' he said, 'it's usually left open.'

'In case I go away,' she said.

'At once?'

'But I'll certainly keep in touch, Nev.'

When she returned to the house, D.Q. and his cloak and the car had gone. His whiskey did not seem to have been touched. For a while, Penny sat waiting, savouring her own drink and then knocking off his. She went back into the hall, opened the stair cupboard, switched on the light and resumed her talk to Butler-Minton. 'Yes, the matter of Lepage. Let's suppose he doesn't go down with terminal shaggers' blight. In that case, I think he'll win this one for the Hulliborn. People take to him. Not people like you, perhaps, but people really like you are dead. Of course, he's got troubles. I had Quent Youde here not long ago romanticizing about an elopement to Jimma. He'll be safely back home now, but his wish to run is symptom of turmoil in the Hulliborn and—'

The phone rang. 'Oh, perhaps D.Q. did mean it after all, Lip. Has he been home for his Ethiopian phrase book? He's ringing to tell me to pack?' She went to answer, leaving the cupboard open. It was Vincent Simberdy.

'Penny,' he said, 'I'm in something of a stew.' He tried to keep his tone clipped, but she heard poorly suppressed panic. 'That bloody Youde.'

'What?'

'You're close to him. Has he seemed triumphal lately? It's why I'm calling.'

'Haven't noticed anything like that, Vince.'

'A smugness?'

'No, I don't think so.'

'He could turn out right.'

'Right about what?'

'In a major way.'

'Do you mean right about the "El Grecos"?' she asked.

'Not "El Grecos". El Grecos. That's my info now. He'll be vindicated and emerge as a star of the Hulliborn. I'm speaking absolutely frankly, perhaps foolishly revealing my dreads. I can't bear it, Penny. He'll be lauded. He will be the new Flounce. It's why I asked you about possible smugness in him. I need to prepare, while I'm still free.'

'Free? Free how?'

He was silent for half a minute. 'Not in jail.'

'Vince, what is this about, for God's sake?'

'You read the Press, do you, Penny? Follow the news?'

'Which?'

'The whole thing.'

'Which?' she said.

'The one touching us all.'

'That opens quite a number of possibilities, Vince.'

'The Fatman. I am he, Penny.'

For a moment she did not understand. Vincent was certainly *a* fatman. The weight had hampered him badly in that encounter with Quent. But then she said: 'You took the paintings – the Monet and the "El Grecos"?'

'El Grecos.'

'Lord, Vince.'

'You must promise never to tell.'

'Of course. Would I betray you? And Olive? Is she in on it?'

'In some ways more so than myself.'

'How?'

'A contact of hers, through the law practice.'

'One of her crook clients?'

'It was a mistake. Well, as you can imagine. Obviously, Olive didn't take them herself, nor I. An accidental involvement. And now things are getting worse.'

'In which way?'

'Many. I hoped you might have heard from Youde or Jimmy Pirie of any developments I'm not *au fait* with. No reflection at all on you, Penny, but you do have something more than a friendly connection with these two.'

Penelope was talking on the phone in the living room. The curtains had not been drawn. Glancing up, she saw a pale, almost spectral face at the window, aglow with tears. It was Falldew. He made a slight, desperate beckoning movement with one hand, then withdrew hurriedly into the darkness. 'Are you there?' she asked Simberdy. But he wasn't. He'd rung off. She went out and joined Falldew near the gym.

'Couldn't you leave me a key when you go, Penny?' he asked. 'I need to be able to get in to see. I need to be able to visit the gym. The point is, I don't think I'll be able to go through with all this – I mean, the wedding, Ursula, everything, if I haven't got . . . well, if I can't rely on – I must have support, you see, particularly at a time of extreme stress.'

'I probably won't be—'

'I'd always lock up when leaving.'

'I don't think I'll be going away after all,' she replied. 'These things change.'

'Not going!' He gave a little leap of joy, like thin-cut bread popping up out of a toaster. 'Oh, Penny, Penny, I'm so glad. And you'll open the gym door?'

'Of course.'

'Perhaps put the sauna on again tomorrow?'

'Yes, Nev.'

This time it was he who leaned forward and kissed her on the cheek. It reminded her of walking into a cobweb, not too awful, but also not something you would want a lot of. She went back alone into the house and, at the cupboard again, said: 'Where were we then, Lip? Look, I hope you won't get ratty about this, but too bad if you do. The fact is, I'm pissed off with being regarded only as a bit of Sir Eric. I've just heard the word "consort". So, am I a female Prince Albert? Stuff that. Talk about spare rib! I think I'm on my way to one of those identity crises you've heard about, though never suffered from yourself, of course. What an absurd notion – Eric Butler-Minton assailed by self-doubt, uncertain who he was. But, as for Lady Butler-Minton, people see me as the route to you – even as the way to *becoming* you, a sort of Visa card. And not just people – a lover! I ask you, Eric, is that on? If I'm ever going to get out from under your unsleeping, colonizing bloody aura, I'm afraid there's no other way but to destroy you. Yes, most regrettably, the only answer.

'All right, you were burned in the box, and most of your gear's gone, too. It makes damn all difference, though, doesn't it, dear? Some way, I have to get rid of this corny veneration of you – all the fearful admiration, the reluctant, besotted worship. I must take a lesson from what they did to Stalin after death: wipe out the mystique or show its grisliness. My mind's on this research girl, you see. I draw nearer to deciding to help her, nothing held back. I mean, if people knew not just the outline, standard, misty, magnificently flattering rumours about the haversack straps and the tennis ball and Mrs Cray and the Wall, but the whole scene. You see what I'm getting at, Lip? You're a threat. You're too much for me. In life I could just about cope with you. Not now.'

Seventeen

Dear Dr Lepage,

I guess if you were to ask ten people of a certain age what they know about the town of Kalamazoo, Michigan, nine would strike up with that crazy old song, 'A, B, C, D, E, F, G, H, I – I got a girl in Kalamazoo.' And the other one of the ten would say, 'Not a thing.' We ought to be grateful for just any publicity, perhaps – even that wacky tune! I suppose the same could be said about Chattanooga and the famous musical choo-choo!

Well, that's by way of introducing Kalamazoo. But I want you to believe, Dr Lepage, that there is much more to our town than a 1942 popular song. Yes, here in Kalamazoo we have a really thriving Archaeological Society, well known not only in Michigan but in Wisconsin and Ohio and even up into Canada. As an extremely flourishing section of the AS, there is, too, the Eric Butler-Minton Guild, of which I have the honour this year to be vice-president (Memorial). As you would expect, we concern ourselves particularly with Sir Eric's work through readings and photographic exhibitions, not to mention the occasional clambake at lighter moments!! My personal duties are devoted to ensuring that your predecessor in post is accorded due lasting, posthumous recognition, not simply here in the USA but worldwide.

It is in this respect that I have been mandated by the Society and Guild to write to you. There is strong feeling here that Sir Eric should be commemorated in some tangible form, and at our last gathering it was unanimously agreed that I should approach you and propose that, at the AC's expense, naturally, a bust of him should be commissioned forthwith by a sculptor of repute. The names of Amy Jessica Pill and of Raymond Norville, well known to you, I'm sure, were vigorously mooted by two rival factions within the Society, which, I expect you can imagine, added a stimulating portion of pleasantly contentious spirit to our routine October meeting of the Society, subsuming the Guild. No final decision was arrived at on this, however. The finished work would stand, of course, if you agree, in some prominent part of the Hulliborn, acknowledged internationally as Sir Eric's 'home' for so many years. There would be an explanatory plaque (ideally in Welsh slate, to remind people of his unique work on the Beaker people of the Vale of Glamorgan), and the wording would be a matter of amicable discussion between the Society and the museum. We are not a notably wealthy Society, but neither are we poor, and I am confident we would be able to meet the cost of a really first-class, wholly worthy memorial. I know you will feel, like the Society, that Sir Eric deserves some such enduring testament to his work and life.

Naturally, Director, the Society possesses many photographs of Sir Eric, and the chosen sculptor would be able to work from these. The only question concerns the age at which we should show him in the bust. Some of the later photographs, such as one of a degree ceremony at Ibadan university, Nigeria, with which I imagine you're familiar, clearly display the famous duelling scar, high on the cheek, sustained, I believe, a little before abolition of the Berlin Wall and the Mrs Cray and the whippet episode. We do feel that this scar should be represented in any memorial, as it seems to say so much about the adventurous, unquenchable personality of Sir Eric. I do hope you and your colleagues agree.

We would be very interested to hear your response to our proposal, and I sincerely trust it will be a favourable one. The AS has been very saddened to hear of the financial troubles afflicting British museums, including the Hulliborn, but we are confident that, mindful of the heritage handed down by such 'giants' of learning and achievement as Butler-Minton, you will fight to preserve all that is great in the Hulliborn's traditions. Possibly, Dr Lepage, you have an authoritative explanation of the facial scar, for our biographical records? We possess only rumour and hearsay to date, I'm afraid, and I feel this is not quite consonant with the demands of a learned Society.

With all good wishes,
Sally Jill Ash
(Vice-President EBM Guild)

Dear Ms Ash,

Thank you so much for your letter. It is heartening to discover that Sir Eric's memory is cherished in Kalamazoo. Your proposal is a generous and interesting one, and I shall circulate colleagues with copies of the letter for discussion at one of our Hebdomadal Conclaves, after which I shall be in touch with you again. I won't take it before the Conclave at once, in case you have further observations to make, arising from this letter.

As to Sir Eric's scar, I'm afraid I cannot help you in the authoritative manner you rightly require. I, too, have heard it described as result of a duelling wound, though never by Sir Eric himself. He, in fact, has said it followed a bad pecking by a seagull on the municipal refuse tip, the bird enraged because Butler-Minton was considered by the bird to be stealing its food. My feeling is that this is probably a joke by Sir Eric, in the well-known British tradition of self-mockery and understatement. Although it is true that gulls can be quite fierce, we have to ask what would Sir Eric be doing on a tip and apparently handling discarded eatables? Sir Eric was, of course, renowned for his dry sense of humour.

Yours sincerely,
George Lepage
(Director Hulliborn Regional Museum and Gallery)

Dear Dr Lepage,

I expect you can imagine the great excitement engendered when I read out your gracious letter at the last meeting of the Guild. Rumours that I had been in touch with you and would be reporting back had already spread, resulting in the fullest of full houses! It seemed like everyone wanted to hear at as near first-hand as possible about contact with the Hulliborn, an institution so irrevocably associated with Sir Eric. People were thrilled by your encouraging reaction to our proposal about the memorial, and it was widely agreed that the Hulliborn seemed in supremely capable hands, despite the departure of Sir Eric. We wait with confidence upon the deliberations of your Conclave.

I showed your remarks about the face scar to our Archivist, the historian Professor Bernard Indippe of Chover's University. He is what you British would call 'a stickler' for accuracy. He is inclined to agree that Sir Eric probably spoke tongue-in-cheek about the seagull and thinks it would be wisest to leave the origin of the scar moot in our records unless definite, reliable facts come to light.

I'm very excited to say that my husband, Frank W. Ash, and I will probably be visiting the UK in connection with his business – hair-loss treatment – in the next few weeks. Although Frank has no interest in archaeology or the Society and Guild – his own passion is baseball and specifically the Dodgers! – I, myself, of course, would make it a priority of the visit to call at the Hulliborn, and I would regard it as a very considerable privilege if I could have just a little of your time on that happy occasion. I can tell you, Dr Lepage, that this prospect has already caused great, though utterly good-natured, envy in the Society and Guild, and several members have said to me how wonderful to be actually sitting in what was once Sir Eric's own room, discussing him with his worthy successor in the presence of the famous duck-billed platypus.

Personal greetings from,

Sally Jill (if I may)

Dear Sally Jill,

I fear I have run into certain difficulties over your Society's kind offer to fund a bust of Sir Eric Butler-Minton for the museum. In seeking the kind of definite and reliable information about Sir Eric's facial scar for you, I asked Lady Butler-Minton about it during a call at her home. She was not at all forthcoming on this matter, saying it would be better if it remained private. In the circumstances

I felt I should not press the point. I did, however, mention your Society's proposal for a memorial bust, and I have to tell you that she is wholly opposed to this idea, though she would not say why. While hers is not necessarily the final word, it is a point of view the Conclave and I will have to take into account when we come to consider your proposal formally. It seemed to me important that I should acquaint her with the Society's offer and ask for her view. This was the reason for my visit to her home, with the scar question as an additional topic.

Best wishes,
George

Dear George,

But isn't it obvious? This sour bitch is jealous of him and doesn't want to be overshadowed now he's dead, as she must have been when he was alive. She's trying to suppress memories of him, so no bust. It's contemptible, evil. Do we let her stand in our way? Like hell we do! I'll be able to discuss such aspects of the situation when I am in the UK soon. And I would hope for a meeting with Lady Butler-Minton at the same time. For several years I have helped my husband with his business, and I think I can say, without vainglory, that, as a result, I know the world. Our phrase over here is, I possess 'street savvy'. I have come into contact with all kinds of uncooperative and even malevolent people and have learned to cope with such. Fear not, George, I'll be able to deal with Lady B-M in her turn. It matters nothing to me that she has a title – a title brought to her by her distinguished husband, of course. We take an unsycophantic view of such supposed distinctions in this part of the world, I'm pleased to say.

George, so much looking forward to our meeting face-to-face at last.

Sally

With this correspondence in his briefcase, Lepage hurried through the main door of the Hulliborn, making for a Hebdomadal durbar in the Octagon Room. Coming in especially late from the

Spud-O'-My-Life, Julia had badly broken Lepage's rest, and he'd overslept this morning. He felt stressed, what with the paintings, the Japanese, Kate, Kalamazoo, and always the ungovernable shadow of Nev Falldew. On top, he thought he detected some kind of change in Julia. There had been a string of these very late nights, which she said were the result of increased business, but he wondered, and the wondering had kept him awake for hours. Julia seemed strangely excited most of the time, almost frenetic, and very remote from him. He didn't like it. Was the quality of his life on the slide? Recently, his mind had turned again to thoughts of early retirement. Might things be so arranged that it could be earlier than early? Now and then he fancied just throwing a couple of things into a holdall and taking off for – oh, almost anywhere. Brazil? Jamaica?

James Pirie, Hulliborn Secretary, hailed Lepage as he hurried towards the spiral staircase. 'Director, what I have to disclose is very much for your ears only, at this stage, but I feel you should know.' He spoke at not much more than a whisper.

'Is it bad, Jimmy?'

'It's a development.'

'It's bad. Fucking bad?'

'I have certain contacts, Director.'

Well, yes, one of his contacts appeared to be Penny Butler-Minton, shared with D.Q. Youde, Art. Were they relevant?

'You wouldn't expect me to be more specific, as of now,' Pirie continued.

'Certainly not.'

Pirie was small, desperately whey-faced, with a sharp chin that Youde said had once been used for opening cans of lager when a faulty batch lacked the ring-pull. His hair was good: thick and fair and wavy, and he had very blue eyes. Youde also alleged that Pirie was a throwback to some Herrenvolk racial experiment in which all the effort had gone into producing blondness and blue eyes, but with length of leg hopelessly economized on. However, Lady Butler-Minton found him tolerable. This was what pissed Youde off, of course.

'It's the "El Grecos",' Pirie said.

God. 'Shouldn't we be in the Conclave, James?' Lepage replied.

'The police have not been sleeping. My understanding is that they're getting damn close: the "El Grecos", and possibly the Monet, too. You see the reason for my hesitation when you asked if it was bad? One can't be sure what's best for the Hulliborn in this situation.'

No, one couldn't be. 'On the face of it this is great news, surely, James.'

'What the police have done is to mount an undercover operation – known, I believe, as a "sting". One of their people has masqueraded as a dealer – as a fence, in fact. The "El Grecos" were brought to him by someone connected with the theft and, to keep things going, the undercover man gave a hugely inflated estimate of what they would fetch – many millions, I believe. Not bad for three probable fakes. Obviously, the fuzz don't want to pounce too early. They're playing things along by pretending the negotiations are complex so they can net the whole gang, including Mr Big. Or perhaps it should be Mr Gross.' Pirie sniggered.

'The Fatman?'

'Exactly. And his woman sidekick, of course.'

'This is fine work – to have discovered so much, Jimmy.'

Pirie touched his waves with one hand. 'One cultivates contacts in all walks, Director. Eventually, this pays off. It's something I learned from Flounce.'

'Sod Flounce,' Lepage said. 'Sorry, but I seem to be hearing so much of him. Can't we function on our own now?'

'If we can, it is because of what he taught us,' Pirie said. 'I see no point in denying that, Director. He left us a heritage, and a duty to look after it well. I think, incidentally, it is a reproach to the Hulliborn that the suggestion for some kind of memorial should have had to come from such a distant, nothing place, as I read in my Heb papers. Kalamazoo! Hell, we've been remiss, abjectly neglectful, even casual. I don't at all single you out for blame on this, although Director. We are all at fault.'

'Would you want the bust with or without?'

'Director?'

'The scar.'

'I heard Penny bites, you know,' Pirie said.

He'd *heard*? Or did he have some evidence of it on a

non-facial, possibly more tender part of his body? 'We should go in now, James,' Lepage replied.

When the Conclave reached 'Kalamazoo Sir Eric Butler-Minton Society' at the end of the agenda, Pirie did his bit again about the slowness of the Hulliborn in organizing something tasteful and enduring, but didn't actually endorse the Kalamazoo offer.

Lepage said: 'As you'll see from your papers, Lady Butler-Minton is against, and I've told Kalamazoo of her reaction. You'll also see that Kalamazoo is not prepared to take this as the final word.'

'Nothing by bloody Amy Jessica Pill or bloody Raymond Norville stands in this museum while I'm Keeper of Art,' Youde said.

'Director, nobody would dispute what the Secretary has eloquently and, if I may say, movingly put to us,' Angus Beresford said. 'Flounce is a presence, a formidable presence. We all acknowledge this. We do not follow Nev Falldew into his loony excesses, but we do recognize the previous Director's influence. But who wants the bugger on a plinth where we'd have to see him every working day, and where it would appear he was back to watching us? That's another thing altogether. We should listen to Her Ladyship on this.'

'Right!' Ronnie Acton-Sher said.

Others nodded and kept nodding.

Simberdy said: 'We're shot of him, more or less. Let's keep it like that.'

There was little further discussion, most of it vehemently negative. At the vote, nobody but Ursula was for the Kalamazoo proposal; she clearly felt that this was how Neville would have reacted if still in the Conclave. Pirie had seemed in general favour of a memorial, though not provided by somewhere as far off as Kalamazoo. In any case, he probably wouldn't dare to come out too definitely in support for fear Lady Butler-Minton should find out and withdraw privileges from him. He abstained.

Lepage said he would write to Kalamazoo declining the offer but heartily thanking the Society and Guild for their interest in Butler-Minton's work.

Eighteen

'Jubilation!' Dr Kanda said.

'I tell you this, you could have felled me with a feather,' Dr Itagaki said.

'We decided to come in person to bring the good news,' Kanda said. 'Or should it be "in persons"? Two.'

'Oh, heavens, it's Syntax Day,' she said. 'The Hulliborn has almost certainly won the medical exhibition. That's the full long and short of it. Yours on a damn plate.'

'This is wonderful,' Lepage said. 'It calls for a drink.'

'Something to lubricate the tonsils, mine being as yet unremoved, regardless of the exhibition,' she said.

Lepage went to his cupboard and brought out the decent brandy. 'I'll ask Vincent Simberdy to join us in a minute, if I may. Asiatics.'

'You called?' Itagaki replied, laughing considerably.

Lepage poured, using some fine, antique brandy balloons.

'Somehow, by means not intimated to us, of course, the Hulliborn seems to have avoided all the usual Tokyo red tape,' Kanda said. 'One had better term the development a miracle, I believe, for, as we understand it, you are more or less sure to be chosen, and without a final selection procedure. As I think I explained, there was to have been our visits, ahead of a further inspection by the Embassy heavy mob. Well, that second stage has been declared superfluous by someone in Tokyo – and someone mega powerful, I'd guess, so the victory is yours, as long as we encounter no last-minute hitch. The most lavish congratters, Dr Director.' He drank some brandy.

Lepage said: 'I feel vastly in your debt, and that the Hulliborn is. The report from the two of you must have been very favourable and very effective.'

'We love this place, that's the straight fact,' Itagaki said, 'and we did make this damn clear in our recommendation. OK, there's a flasher in the Folk, and old Falldew doing his nut in public – maybe the flashing, too, and I don't say this for the sake of alliteration – plus the "El Greco" thing, and the simmering Youde, Pirie, Lady Butler-Minton *pot pourri*—'

'Not to mention the mysterious haversack straps,' Kanda said.

'So you mention them!' Itagaki said. 'Paralipsis! But so fucking what? These are superficialities. These are, indeed, in some ways endearing quirks, and for all we know at this point the haversack straps, Mrs Cray and the windsock might be pluses, positives. An error to find them off-putting.'

'Returning on the train after one of our earlier visits, we both came up, independently, with this phrase to describe some of the goings on at the Hulliborn – endearing quirks,' Kanda declared. 'It was a remarkable moment in the carriage when we leaned across to each other, as if governed by the same impulse and said "endearing quirks". Other passengers were mystified. "Strange people these Asians, what, Bessy!" One can imagine that kind of Blimpish remark from a passenger to his wife.' He laughed, too, now.

'These factors are nothing but the marks of a lively and possibly sometimes outré individuality,' Itagaki suggested. 'Swipe me, Lepage; if an ex-Keeper can't use a bit of body language in his own former museum, where the hell can he? We stressed such points forcefully in our findings. Hulliborn *uber alles*!'

'You've been very kind,' Lepage said. He rang Simberdy and asked him to look in.

'But there are other hidden factors, not the smallest doubt,' Itagaki said. 'I can tell you, Director, it would be stark-staring idiocy to posit that Tokyo has acted solely on the say-so of a couple of travelling nobodies.'

'I think you are too self-disparaging,' Lepage rushed to say. 'After all—'

'Oh, somebody in Tokyo has a feeling for Lady Butler-Minton, I would hazard,' she replied, 'and that has been extended to the Hulliborn, with which her name is still identified, of course. I always say, "Cherchez la nooky," when matters as totally inexplicable as—'

'*Seemingly* as totally inexplicable,' Kanda stated.

'When well-established, previously slavishly followed procedures are skipped,' Itagaki continued. 'Butler-Minton and his wife were in Japan quite often, Flounce helping several of our museums with priceless advice, and Penelope – well, Penny radiating in that glorious, questing way of hers. There'd be a lot of time to fill in. And to get filled in.'

'Forgive us if we seem to be carelessly impugning Lady Butler-Minton's character, Director. But it can safely be said, I think, that she appreciates life.'

'Zounds! Back to British understatement,' Itagaki said. 'The fact is, Lady B-M shags like a rattlesnake, but, fair-e-bloody-nough, "appreciates life" will cover it.' Brandy balloon in hand, she did a little tour of the room, giving a nice, formal bow to the platypus, so that her large blue spectacles shifted on her nose and had to be adjusted. 'I don't make these remarks out of absolutely nowhere, Director. There are signs that Flounce and therefore Penny had some bearing on this decision.'

'Tokyo feels quite powerfully that there should be a permanent memorial to Sir Eric,' Kanda said. 'This is an additional reason for our coming to see you today. We have a proposal to put.'

'It entails a sort of package,' Itagaki explained. 'The Arts and Culture Council had instructions from the stratosphere level of the embassy to let you know about the probable Hulliborn success—'

'*Very* probable,' Kanda said.

'And to suggest at the same time that Tokyo wants to show recognition of Butler-Minton's status and help to Japanese institutions by commissioning a bust to stand in the Hulliborn, with a suitable plaque as to its donors,' Itagaki said. 'Now, please don't puke. I know it's the corniest of notions, but those stuffy old sods in Tokyo can think only in cliché: stone-fucking-memorials in this day and age! I ask you! Any time now, they're going to emerge into the nineteenth century. We're lucky they don't want him on a horse, I suppose.'

'"A sort of package"?' Lepage asked.

'They seem to have rolled the two things together – exhibition and bust,' Kanda replied. 'The plaque would be in stone taken from near Mount Fuji where all the rubble is supposed to have holy significance, you know. It would speak briefly of Sir Eric's vivid career, while also recording permanently the visit of the medical exhibition. I suppose it's a natural thing with museum people that they do seek the enduring, the lasting.'

'A couple of sculptors have been mooted, as I hear,' Itagaki said, 'one American, the other a Scot, probably both out-and-out dullards and frights or Tokyo would never have picked them: Amy Jessica Pill and Raymond Norville.'

'This is *so* interesting,' Lepage said.

Simberdy arrived. He was looking terribly bad these last few days, his cheeks and jowls that worrying grey shade of old mackerel, his great gut no longer assertive and buoyant, but carried laboriously, like a curse. Could such grim damage have been done by the incompetent blows from Quent Youde?

'We're on course to get the exhibition, Vince,' Lepage trilled. 'Come and join us in a celebratory drink.'

'This is grand,' Simberdy replied. 'It will ensure a fine future for the Hulliborn.' He smiled, but this didn't do much for him.

Lepage waited until Simberdy had sat down, with the brandy balloon safely placed, before adding: 'Dr Itagaki and Dr Kanda bring a fascinating suggestion from their embassy. Tokyo would like to commission a bust of Flounce for the Hulliborn.'

For someone who'd been at the Conclave where the idea of a memorial sculpture was treated like shit, Simberdy reacted magnificently, regardless of his appearance. 'But this is, as you say, well, fascinating, Director,' he replied at once. He took a good mouthful of the brandy.

'It's what could be described, and *has* been described, as a package,' Lepage said. 'We owe a double debt of gratitude, don't we? Oh, yes.' He answered the question himself so as not to put further strain on Simberdy's nerves. The Keeper of Asiatics would need time to get fully used to the idea that, having rejected the Kalamazoo bust, the Hulliborn must now enthusiastically welcome an identical proposal from the Japanese. The simple, ghastly equation went like this: Hulliborn needed the prestige of winning the exhibition if the museum were to be sure of flourishing and expanding, sure of surviving, in a harsh commercial climate; and, in that harsh commercial climate, the exhibition would come only if Lepage, Simberdy and the rest of the management agreed to terms stipulated by Tokyo.

'The exhibition could be in place before your tiresome Board of Museums inspection and grading rigmarole,' Kanda pointed out. 'An advantage, possibly?'

'Your government has become damn choosy in where it places its largest grants. Hulliborn, with the exhibition, will look a grand place for maximum investment. This will be to support success – the gospel of Mrs Thatcher,' Itagaki said. 'Snatch the chance, do.' She nodded definitively. 'Yes, this is how Tokyo would like things to go. We pass the message, as per instruction. But I do sympathize with you. I mean, who the devil wants the head of some old supremo stuck on a stand, as if he'd come back to cast his bullying eye over everything?'

'My colleagues will be intrigued,' Lepage remarked, with ample joyfulness in his voice. 'Don't you think so, Vincent?' By now he considered it safe to invite another comment, another slice of acting, from Simberdy.

'Extremely intrigued,' he said.

Nineteen

'Oh! Oh! Oh! Oh!' Olive Simberdy yelled. Then: 'Yes! Yes!
Yes! Oh, my God, YES! Vince, come now! Now!'

Simberdy opened one eye slightly and saw that Olive was
no longer in bed with him. She must be shouting from downstairs. Resentment at being disturbed throbbed in his head. He
had been enjoying an inspired dream in which D.Q. Youde's
coffin, en route to burial on a purple-draped gun-carriage,
preceded by a gazooka girls' band, suddenly tumbled off, burst
open, and the body hit the ground with a gloriously rounded
but splatty sound, rolled into a ditch and was fed on by lemurs.
He did a swift count and decided there were at least eighty-
eight of them. The hungriest seemed to go for Youde's balls.
In the surreal way of dreams, the words 'A Right Goodly
Number' appeared in red and green neon on what looked like
the new electronic scoreboard at Lord's cricket ground, but
stood now in the middle of a cemetery that had been serenely
awaiting Youde. Simberdy didn't really have much reason to
want the worst for Youde – he was not, like Pirie, a rival for
love from Penny Butler-Minton – but dreams didn't require
reasons.

This one had another sizeable plus. The girls' band wore
very tight, short, silver lamé shorts and pushed out their chests
and behinds unstintingly with the effort of playing their instruments. As Olive's bellowing intruded, Simberdy tried fiercely
to hang on to the totality of his vision. He began to count
the lemurs again, while also urgently seeking to redeploy more
sets of animal teeth towards that arrogant, would-be Degas
phiz. Slowly, though, despite this resistance, he was tugged into
almost full wakefulness, not only because of Olive's noise, but
also by the stupid pedantry of that bit of his brain already
conscious which said lemurs were nocturnal, whereas funerals
weren't. 'What the hell's up, Ol?' he growled.

'Oh, Vince,' she cried excitedly again. 'Come.'

'What do you mean, for God's sake, "Come." People don't say "Come" except in plays by Terence Rattigan. It's "Come here" or "Come and see" or "Come into the garden, Maud".'

'Oh, do come, Vincent,' she replied, her voice ecstatic still.

For a moment he slid half back into sleep again and, to his delight, the dream seemed to resume at once as before, but reverting to the start, with the body still on a gun-carriage. Then, as he waited for that crux moment when it was pitched off, he realized that the shape in the shroud looked much bulkier this time, and he saw that the uncovered face was not D.Q. Youde's, or even Degas's, but his own. Horrified, he simultaneously felt himself rolling towards the ditch. He screamed as an infinite number of punitive, sharp pains began in his genitals and elsewhere, but especially his genitals. He reckoned that at least eighty-eight sets of teeth were having a go at him.

'Vince, what is it?' Olive said.

He opened his eyes and found himself on the bedroom carpet, both hands clasping his crotch.

'I heard you call and fall out of bed,' Olive said, standing over him. 'The impact brought down the light in the kitchen.'

'What were you making a din about?' Simberdy asked from the floor. 'It's those fucking paintings again, isn't it? Nothing Known's dumped them as before, yes?' He managed to stop himself giving a long, voluminous, crazed groan.

She nodded, obviously wanting to look grave, but – *more* obviously – entirely thrilled. 'Why are you holding yourself like that? Did you fall awkwardly?' She held out a hand and, after a moment, he took it and she helped him to his feet.

'I was asleep, but I'm sure I counted four "Oh!"s. Or was it eighty-eight?'

'Vincent, what are you saying?'

'Let's get it clear. There were four "Oh!"s from you, weren't there?'

'Were there? What's the odds?'

'There are only three "El Grecos".'

'Yes, that's true.' She seemed to be smirking.

'What do you mean?'

She still held his hand. 'Come.' She drew him towards the door.

He pulled on a shirt and his jeans. 'I wish I had a black tie handy.'

'What?'

'My dream. And the way I feel.'

Downstairs, the three 'El Grecos' stood as previously around the dresser. On a chair was *L'Isolement*, the Monet, isolated, alone. Nearby, the extensive wreckage of their British Home Stores light fitting lay scattered interestingly on the tiles, as though someone had mounted a small exhibition in their kitchen, part conventional – the paintings – part modernistic with artefacts.

'I don't know which I like best now,' Olive said.

'How the hell did he get the Monet back? Is it real? Should it be "Monet"?'

Olive cleared some of the debris and went closer. 'Well, I think genuine.'

Simberdy sat down. 'What's his game this time?'

'Darling, do you feel all right?' she replied.

'Of course I don't bloody well feel all right. Would you?'

'If?'

'If somebody left paintings that might be worth millions in your kitchen.'

'Somebody has.'

'Yes, well.'

Gazing lovingly in turn at the works, she said: 'He's a very complex laddy.'

'Which? El Greco or Monet?'

'Wayne Passow. The paintings do brighten the room wonderfully.'

'We'll still need to get the light repaired. Did he phone? Has he called at your office to explain? Nothing?'

'Nothing. The Monet could be shown off better, I feel.'

'We don't want to show the fucker off. We want to hide it. We're not a gallery.'

She went to the chair and lifted *L'Isolement*, ready to transfer it to a clear shelf high on the dresser. Then she said: 'Wait a minute,' and fiddled with something on the back of the picture.

'There's an envelope stuck here with tape, Vince.' She pulled it off and replaced the Monet on the chair. 'It's addressed to you. Well, to "F. Man Esq".'

'Oh, God, do I want to know, Olly?'

She tore the buff envelope open and handed him the letter. Olive read it with him over his shoulder for a moment but then moved off.

> *Dear Old Fatman,*
> *When you get this and the choice items with it, I'm going to be a long way away and God knows about the phones out there, so I thought I better write even though I hate putting certain matters on paper you can bet. Eat this as soon as you've read it. You got the digestion.*

'Here,' Olive said. She'd done a tour of the kitchen, looking for signs of Nothing Known's entry, and was now calling from the living room. 'It's very neat, almost imperceptible, but that's what we'd expect from Wayne boy, isn't it?'

'I never know what to expect from the sod.'

Olive came back and resumed reading with him.

> *This will be a bit of a shock to you I know and most special, this Monet, called* L'Isolement, *which if you puts it into Anglospeak becomes* Lonesome, *or something like that they tell me.*

Simberdy felt his heart start fighting its moorings.

> *I'll be telling you concerning the Monet in a minute, worry not. There been some very big snags, Fatman, and maybe I don't know so much about the art game as I thought. This would give a new fucking meaning to 'Nothing Known', wouldn't it, meaning I don't know much, not the courts? Look then, the nice dealer who is doing so nice by me and slagging off the others turns out to be a cop. Yes, you heard right, a cop. This sweetheart is just stringing me along. So, ten mill today, twelve tomorrow, and twenty next week, just so I'll keep in touch. No real loot anywhere in sight, just words. What this is called is 'a sting'. How did I*

find out? This 'dealer' keeps saying he got to meet the rest of the
team before he can clinch things proper. I say why is that, and
he says because he's afraid I might of pinched the paintings from
other members of the team, who would come after him. He said
he needed all my mates to be with me giving the orders to sell,
and most important he wanted to meet the man in charge. That
was going to be needed defenight before any money could come
my way.

Well, that gave me a shock, as you can understand, and I
nearly said, 'All right,' and I would of brought him round to
your house, Fatman—

'God,' Simberdy said.

—but then one day when I'm out on the town with a bird I
notice him tailing me. He's very good at it, but not good enough.
I seen that kind of thing before, it might not surprise you to know.
And not just him. He got other lads on it, too, some with very
short hair and trainers. This is an operation, Fatman. This baby
– Wayne Passow – puts two and two together, don't he?

Glowing happiness as well as scorching fear took hold of
Simberdy. 'So the "El Grecos" could still be phoney,' he chortled to Olive. 'Well, of course they could. Quent Youde's
involved, isn't he, for God's sake? It follows. This "expert" who
said they were real and worth super millions is actually only a
snoop from Scotland Yard's Arts and Antiques brigade setting
up a bit of entrapment. Youde – he should be eaten by lemurs.'
    'Should be what?'
    'It's a robust but jokey saying among zoologists.'
    'Lovely.'
They read the last page of Passow's letter.

So I'm unloading to you, F.M., and giving myself a nice bit
of travel for a while. You are still right in the clear, worry not,
and I am returning these bits and peices. This Monet – well,
I was really ratty about what happened, yes, only thirty grand.
I was ripped off, and if there is one thing I hate it is for someone
to make a monkie of Wayne Passow. So, I done a little bit of

*traceing and a little bit of travel out Europe way, which is when
I got a taste for new countreys, I should think. Anyway, as you
can see, I had a bit of luck and I was able to find the guy who
had the lonesome painting and I got it back somehow. Yes,
somehow. I don't think I'll say too much about how I done
this, in case Olive is reading this letter, too, and it might upset
her. Let's just menshun there was a lot of broken glass and some
damage to clothes and a neck but he is not going to be kicking
up about it to the law, is he, because he should not of had the
pic in the first place, this is obvius? I done a little bit of spraying
at his place, too. And a signatur – like to say who done it.
But not obvius, obviusly. Like a code. You'll see it at the bottom
of this letter.*

'What the hell does he mean, "spraying"?' Olive said.

'Who knows?'

'What signature? Whose?'

'His?'

'What code at the bottom of the letter?'

'Good question,' Simberdy said.

*Yes, so these four little peices should see you all right. When I
comes back some time in the far off future, maybe you will have
something nice and juicey for me with lots of norts on the end
in a locked box at the bank. I trust you, F.M. That's how a
team should be.*

*This girl what Redvers and Crispin menshunned in the
Blague the other night is going to be upset because I'm not
around no more. You think I sound like a big-head, but I know
she will be. This is how things are with love and partings. I
did not have no time to explane to her. It was very quick do-a-
bunk time, which I am sure you'll understand. I might of asked
you to go and tell her face to face, so she could see why I had
to do a runner, but then I decided, No, I got to keep things
privut for her. Anyway, I only know her first name and where
she works. She would not tell me more. She's a carefull one, I
expect with a hubby. Maybe she would of told me more later
but there can't be no later. It would not be fair to get her too
mixed up in all this in case this letter went the wrong way*

somehow. Letters do sometimes. I am sorry to be loosing her because we had something real nice going and maybe long-distance. But in this sort of line you got to be ready to make sacrifisses, yes. We got to suffer for the job, like all the great did.

So, keep happy and clean and try not to spend it all.

Till some day then,

Fatman's Best Mate

'He means Julia Lepage?' Olive said.

'Seems so.'

'Wayne's got gallantry. Wayne's got a special way.'

'Yes, Wayne's got away.'

Olive said: '"Fatman's Best Mate" – strange way to sign off.'

'In line with his usual insolence and presumption.'

Twenty

'Forgive the hour, Director, but we must go to the Hulliborn at once,' D.Q. Youde said. 'I came over to your house because I didn't want to discuss on the telephone certain information I've just received. Too many ears.' He had on a beautiful but very severe dark suit with a gleaming white shirt and thin-striped tie. Did he sit around like this at home in the middle of the night, or had he got up and put the gear on especially for this visit?

'The Hulliborn now?' Lepage said. 'At after midnight? What information? How did it come to you, if not by—'

'Well, yes, by telephone. Only half an hour ago. But I feared yours might be tapped, so I'm here in person.'

'My private phone tapped, for God's sake? Why?'

'As Director. Simply that. Things are moving. I don't say I understand all aspects. It seemed to me a matter for immediate personal contact.'

'Yes? I'm sorry, Quentin, I'm keeping you on the doorstep. You'd better come in.'

'Thank you. This development – I'm suffering from shock.'

They went into the living room. Lepage said: 'What is it, Quent? Who's ringing you so late?'

'One has certain contacts, Director, international in scope, built up over the years. Art and its followers keep a communications network which never closes down. We are unceasing devotees, unceasing guardians.'

Lepage had on his jeans and 'Keep The Hulliborn On Top' sweatshirt. 'I sit up late some nights waiting for Julia,' he said. 'She has to stay on at the Spud-O'-My-Life kiosk. The potato is a nocturnal vegetable, you know.'

Youde shook his head slowly and sadly a couple of times and frowned, as if Julia's timetable sounded a worry.

'These last few nights she's been getting in rather earlier,' Lepage said. It was true.

'Good,' Youde said. 'She surely owes you that, George.'

'Owes me what?'

'And it's kindly of you to wait up for her.'

'A husbandly thing, that's all.'

'To your credit, Director.'

Lepage brought a pack of beer cans and some tankards from the kitchen. They sat opposite each other in easy chairs. 'I had a call from the South of France,' Youde said. 'It's about the Monet. Well, certainly about the Monet, but perhaps the El Grecos as well.'

'A call from?'

'You'll forgive me if— Shall we say an acquaintance who knows what's what and keeps his ear to the ground?'

Lepage wondered how the French would say 'ear to the ground'. He poured.

Youde drank deeply, like someone who had been through a lot lately and who expected to go through a hell of a lot more, but would be ready to fight back. 'Near Antibes. Considerable money around there, as you probably know, George.'

'A call from near Antibes saying what?'

'That French police were very close to the Monet. *Really* close.'

'Well, this is surely grand,' Lepage cried, beaming with surprised delight: as long as it was no more than the Monet. 'They can be damned efficient, the French police.'

'*Were* very close.'

'Something went wrong? Bloody French.'

'They thought they'd traced it to a well-known collector-dealer in those parts, someone loaded and not too fussy about the law. So, they visit his villa and find a window forced, the alarms doctored, a glass door smashed as in a struggle, the collector half strangled, and no Monet. Of course, when the collector's interviewed he says there never was a Monet on the premises, claims he doesn't know what the police are talking about – he's not even *seen* a Monet lately – and states the intruder only wanted cash. That's the advantage of stealing from a crook, isn't it: he can't complain to the flics even if it's about millions? Just the same, the police are sure it was there.'

'How? How can they know?'

'Director, there's another factor,' Youde said, drinking again, and holding out the tankard for more. He looked both scared and volcanically prophetic, and his extended arm, seeking more booze, seemed at the same time to be pointing out to some intriguing unknown. 'Words were written on an inside wall of the villa, sprayed from an aerosol can, like in a tower block.'

'In French? But what has this to do with going to the Hulliborn now?' Lepage heard Julia's car draw up and then her footsteps on the drive.

Youde had heard, too, and spoke hurriedly, so he could finish before Julia entered the room. 'The message was simple, Director. It said, "Gotcha."'

'"Gotcha"? Like that headline in the Falklands war?'

'A signature after it.'

'What — claiming credit, telling the police who did it? Is this credible?'

'Initials only.'

'Even so.'

'And as a clue, not very helpful.'

'Why not?'

'Some would call it a dead-end.'

'Why?'

'The initials are FBM,' Youde replied.

'FBM?'

'Yes.'

'A person? An organization?' Lepage asked.

'Nobody's sure.'

'The M standing for the Monet?'

'That's one line of thought, yes.'

'And what about the F and the B?'

'These are problematical, Director.'

'"Fetch Back the Monet"?' Lepage said. 'More or less the equivalent of "Gotcha", if the "Gotcha" means the painting.'

'Yes, that's a theory doing the rounds, apparently.'

'But what others?' Lepage asked.

Youde took a drink. 'My informant suggests — and says it's a police thought, too — he absurdly suggests . . . well, can you see it, George?'

'What?'

'FBM.'

'What?'

'The BM.'

'What?'

'Butler-Minton,' Youde replied.

'What?' Lepage gasped.

'And the F, Flounce,' Youde said.

'Flounce?' Lepage yelled.

'As I say, a fanciful guess, and a very strange bit of theorizing by the police,' Youde replied. 'Flounce Butler-Minton.'

Julia appeared and glanced about the room. 'What's happening, George. I thought I heard you calling Flounce?'

'Calling Flounce?' Lepage replied with a fair old laugh. 'Have you forgotten he's dead, love? I've got his job. Remember? Think I've caught delusions fever from Nev?'

'That's what it sounded like,' Julia said. 'His name, though as a sort of question.'

'I expect you've had a trying night. But you're quite early,' Lepage said.

'Not much doing,' she said.

He felt she sounded very down and upset. 'Maybe things will be better tomorrow, Julia,' he told her.

'Yes, maybe.' It didn't sound as if she thought so, and for a second Lepage feared she might weep. A bad night's business could do that to her? He doubted it. She behaved as though she'd been deserted. But who by? After half a minute, she made an effort and smiled towards Youde. 'You're out late, Quent. You look very full of . . . very full of import. And so smart!'

'Thank you.' He straightened his shoulders inside the suit. 'Just over for a gossip: the usual Hulliborn tittle-tattle.'

'But not about Flounce?' she asked.

'Ah, Flounce. It's certainly a name that can still ring bells, as it were. But what would there be to discuss, Julia? We have to think forward, even in museums.'

'Yes, well, look, you won't mind if I don't stay, will you? Failing to sell is just as tiring as selling.' She made for the door. 'Try not to be too late coming up, George.'

'Soon,' he said.

'You're very lucky, Director,' Youde said, when she'd gone.
'Sometimes.'

Youde went back to his story. Yes, 'Gotcha. FBM. GOTCHA
– the *Sun*'s front page screamer when we sank the Argentine
battleship *Belgrano*. The French police have put two and two
together.'

'Which two and two?'

'They've discovered that Flounce was Butler-Minton's
nickname.'

'Oh, great. Real detective work.'

'But, George, can you see the implications? That's why I
came straight over.'

'They thought they'd located the Monet, but they've lost it,'
Lepage replied. 'Someone's lifted it – "Gotcha" – i.e., as I said,
the painting. Someone or some gang.'

'The FBM gang?'

'Perhaps.'

Youde leaned forward, his eyes brilliant with tension and
ale: 'George, there are people on the art circuit, especially
abroad, who think Butler-Minton might still be alive.' He held
up a hand, before Lepage could respond. 'Obviously, it cannot
be, but that is the rumour, and this has become a vital, new
factor.'

Lepage said, wearily: 'This is mad, Quentin. There was a
funeral. Interpol can view the death certificate, for heaven's
sake.'

'Well, Director, there are funerals and funerals. There are
certificates and certificates.'

'Hell, what are you saying?'

'George, I don't necessarily go along with it, of course not,
but the French seem to know about that mysterious, clandes-
tine, spooky side of Butler-Minton's life – the Wall, Mrs Cray,
the whippet. In such a world the wrong body can end up in the
coffin. Oh, yes, it's been known.'

'Are we rerunning *The Third Man*? Someone else buried in
place of the villain, Harry Lime? Quent, we—'

'And, in any case, it's not just the police. The collector is a
big-time underworld operator, of course. The story about
Butler-Minton has spread among all that fraternity. It doesn't

need to be one hundred per cent verifiable fact to have its impact on them.'

'Which story? That someone does a robbery of an item worth millions, inscribes a triumphant "Gotcha" and then signs his name – the someone being officially dead.'

'"Officially", yes.'

'*Actually.*'

'I know the tale is hard to swallow, George, but—'

'And what do they think: that Butler-Minton's taken it on himself to protect the Hulliborn and pop over to France for one of the museum's treasures, so—?'

'Or perhaps more than one,' Youde said, his voice singing with brief hope.

'Having first located it, or them, on his own,' Lepage went on, 'he's then able to snatch it, or them, back, after knocking out the alarms like a pro, at the same time giving the house-holder a nice bit of strong-arm? And, in any case, Quent, what's it all to do with an emergency trip to the Hulliborn now?'

Youde got his thoughts together. 'I don't necessarily endorse what I'm about to say, George, but apparently the talk there is that Butler-Minton learned all sorts of dirty tricks in his East Germany era. Yes, they've heard of Mrs Cray and the haversack straps and that shooting from the Wall. According to my informant there's also been mention in Antibes of the windsock and tennis ball. But listen, Director, OK, even given all this, I'll concede that the whole thing could be regarded as far-fetched.'

'Oh, no, really?'

'Not all claim it was Eric himself. Some are saying this was a fanatical admirer acting as he thought Butler-Minton might have acted, if he were still around: using the memory of Flounce as guide and inspiration.'

'Would someone like that use his nickname – the F. It's not respectful, is it, let alone reverential?'

'Perhaps so as not to make things over-obvious. Or aerosol writing is often less than perfect and the F might have been intended as an E, with the bottom horizontal somehow missed: *Eric* Butler-Minton.'

'You're saying Nev did it, are you, Quentin?'

'Apparently, his name has come up very strongly in Antibes as a suspect. He hasn't tried to keep his obsession with Flounce secret, has he?'

'Is Neville in danger?' Lepage replied.

Youde shrugged. 'But there are other suspects. Flounce is a presence, George. An active influence. There's no denying that. Why, I've felt it myself, I admit.'

'Like the "Elvis Lives" societies.'

'Unfair, Director. May I remind you of your duck-billed platypus? I don't think you should pretend to feel indifferent to this aura. Nev is exceptionally affected: gratitude for Flounce's struggle to keep him, though doomed.'

'To hell with the platypus. So what is this spirit or this disciple or this aura supposed to have done with the picture?'

'Possibly *pictures*. This is the whole point, Director, and why I'm here now. My voice from near Antibes says it's believed there that somehow or another the works have been reclaimed for the Hulliborn, so as to restore the museum's reputation in time to qualify for the medical relics exhibition. To be very blunt, George, the pictures might be hanging in the Hulliborn gallery now – reinstalled on the quiet in their proper places.'

'Oh, God, Quent, this is—'

'Let's hurry there, Director.' Youde set his tankard down very emphatically and stared with challenging eyes at Lepage. 'I suppose I might have gone alone, but I wanted . . . I wanted support, and a witness.'

'Quent, for God's sake—'

'Time could be crucial, George. By dawn—'

'There might be Interpol or a vengeance posse from Antibes here? You really think so?'

'Not impossible, George. This crooked collector and his outfit have just had millions ripped from them. They're as hard as you might expect and won't smile long-sufferingly and mutter, "C'est la fucking vie." They'll want to make up the loss. Director, I must see the Raybould Gallery. I shan't sleep until I do.'

'Is that why you're dressed up, Quent? The occasion?'

Youde glanced down a little sheepishly at the excellent suit.

'Flounce always hated any semblance of what he used to call in his brusque, though to some degree reassuring, way, "arty-fartiness" in the clothes of people in my department – particularly in my department.' A look of terrible, retrospective pain crossed his face. 'Well, I expect you heard that once he pissed over my beige cloak where it was hanging in a corner of the gallery. I mean literally and systematically pissed over it, holding pleats open with his free hand so the gush got everywhere. The dry cleaners were puzzled and applied a penalty charge.'

'Quent, Flounce is dead and burned.'

Youde smiled solemnly. 'I do know that, Director, as a certainty. But, I know, too, that the person who called me tonight does not speak wildly, does not exaggerate. So, please, can we go to the Hulliborn now?'

'Julia will do her nut.'

'Please, George.'

Youde drove him there. In the museum, Lepage led the way, carrying a torch, which he part hooded with his fingers, for secrecy. They turned into the Raybould, and Youde, staring at the wall, sobbed and wailed at once. There was enough light to see the spaces: 'No, they're not here. It was too much to hope. Of course it was. Of course. I really am sorry for the foolishness, George.'

'Not the "El Grecos", but the Monet's back,' Lepage replied. The shock at seeing *L'Isolement* had gutted his voice of volume and made it hard for him to frame words at all, but Youde heard very well.

'What do you mean, "El Grecos"?' he snarled.

'Sorry, Quent. El Grecos.' Lepage walked to the Monet. 'It looks intact.'

'Yes?'

Lepage swung the torch beam around the gallery. 'No imme-diate evidence of a break-in.'

'Of course not. These are accomplished people.'

From the doorway came a loud shout. 'Hold still, vile pillagers. We've had your sort previous. Game's up. "Security" is speaking.'

'Relax, Jervis,' Lepage said. 'It's your Director and the Keeper of Art. There have been developments.'

Keith Jervis came forward very warily, carrying his own torch and a lavatory brush, which might have been the best he could grab as a weapon. 'Oh, the Monet's back!' he said and put *his* beam on to it. 'Not money this time. Monet.' He lit another stretch of wall. 'But not the "El Grecos".'

'What the hell do you mean, "El Grecos", you fucking non-staff porter?' Youde howled.

'Come on now, Art. Don't get hoity-toity,' Jervis said. 'It makes your skin blotchy.'

'What? What?' Youde hurried to a Corot landscape that was under glass and tried to check his reflection in it, despite the semi-darkness, trawling for blotches.

'Anyway, although I call them "El Grecos", that's only because I'm influenced, despite personal feelings, by current talk and media blab. I really mean El Grecos,' Jervis said.

'Yes?' Youde replied, his tone at once sweet with gratitude and comradeliness.

'Oh, yes. I liked them and miss the three something rotten. They're the real thing all right, kosher absolutely,' Jervis said.

'Keith, this is wonderful,' Youde said. 'Tell me how you can be so sure.' He clearly wanted to shake the part-time porter's hand, so Jervis put the lavatory brush under his arm and responded, smiling in true, chummy style at Youde.

Jervis said: 'As to being sure, well, for one thing you bought them, didn't you, Art? Is someone in charge of that whole section of the Hulliborn going to make such a ginormous mistake?'

'Thank you, Keith.'

'And then, it's just obvious looking at them – that's when I could, of course – just looking at them it was plain they're the goods,' Jervis said. 'I mean, for example, the *Vision of Malarkey*—'

'*Malachi*,' Youde remarked gently.

'Is anybody going to tell me a picture with that sort of clout was done by some pipsqueak in a night-school class?' Jervis asked. 'OK, all sorts can have visions, I grant you. We got someone down the club who's into all that mystical carry-on. But visions like that Malachi's? It got to be done by a lad with status. Fake it? It just don't figure, Art.'

Lepage said: 'Keep alert, Keith.'

'But within reason,' Youde said.

'What are you getting at, Quent?' Lepage asked.

'Should someone want to replace the El Grecos also, we don't want him scared off,' Youde said.

'Ah, I see. Of course. Of course,' Lepage said. The repetition and emphasis were to compensate for the falsity. Yes, frighten the sod right off, finally off, Jervis. Lepage would have liked to speak this thought aloud, but didn't. 'Eyes open, Keith,' he said. Jervis had the lavatory brush back in his hand and held it out in front of himself pointing upwards like a sword or truncheon.

On the return journey to Lepage's house, Youde said: 'Perhaps the fact is I *need* to believe the rumours, the fables, about Flounce. Some part of them, anyway. If this benefactor can return the Monet, he can possibly do the same for the El Grecos.'

Not if the bugger's aim was to help the Hulliborn. But, again, Lepage stayed quiet. At home, he drank the beer dregs from the tankards used by Youde and himself earlier, and soon afterwards went to bed.

Julia grunted a bit and then asked: 'Where in God's name did you go, George?'

'The Hulliborn. Quent thought Butler-Minton had brought the missing pictures back.'

After a minute, she said: 'Sorry, I must be drifting off. I imagined you said Quentin Youde thought Flounce had returned from the fiery furnace, bringing paintings.'

'That's it,' he replied. '*Somebody* has replaced the Monet. And perhaps it was somebody clever enough and thoughtful enough about the Hulliborn's prospects not to bring the "El Grecos" with it.' He cupped his hand delicately and lovingly over the warm right cheek of her behind, but she was asleep, or pretending, which would be worse.

Twenty-One

Who would have thought that Mrs Cray herself would suddenly arrive on the Hulliborn scene in that way and bring some clarification to all those rumours about the windsock and the haversack straps and so on? Lepage certainly didn't expect it, but he was getting used to dealing with outsize, Director-type shocks. And who would have thought Her Majesty's government would all at once take a big and dictatorial interest in the proposed memorial to Flounce Butler-Minton? Lepage certainly didn't expect it, but, yes, he was getting used to dealing with outsize, Director-type shocks. These two unforeseen factors, though – Mrs Cray and the government – came more or less on top of each other, and Lepage did feel momentarily dazed, caught by the old one-two; oh, longer than momentarily. The advent of Mrs Cray, bringing with her all those glimpses of Flounce's days behind the Wall, was the bigger and more sensational surprise of the two, of course. And it seemed to hit Lepage harder because the lead up to her appearance involved what had seemed a more or less routine Hulliborn visit by the Cabinet member with responsibility for the Arts, Sam Vaux, plus his dogsbody civil servant.

As they walked swiftly through Urban Development, Vaux said: 'What I'd hate you to think, Director, is that my inability to attend your Founder's Day Ball this time was in any sense retaliation for that accident with the *vol-au-vents* last year. And I'm sure it *was* an accident, though one had to expect more or less anything from that mad, gifted bastard Butler-Minton, God rest what passed for his soul. There we stood, all blissfully munching Stain-Out! and chatting away happily as if we'd never tasted anything nicer. "Regardless of their doom," and so on. No harm done, in the long run.'

'Very regrettable, but fortunately only a very light contamination,' Lepage said.

'You'd go with the accident theory, I imagine,' Vaux said.

'Unquestionably,' Lepage said.

'*I've* heard it questioned,' Vaux replied. 'Flounce Butler-Minton liked a jape. Nobody can recall his eating one of the *vol-au-vents* himself.'

'He was fussy about diet,' Lepage said. 'More of a couscous man, from his time in the Middle East.'

'Anyway, no lasting resentment or grievance,' Vaux said.

'The Minister is always inclined to take the wider, more tolerant, point of view,' Lionel Clode, the dogsbody said.

'One was absolutely prevented from coming this year,' Vaux said. 'A further crisis with the National Theatre just about then? I think so. Something of that order. God, but don't they love themselves over there? I can never understand why they need an audience or applause: they can supply the lot in-house. Yes, as a matter of fact, I was extremely disappointed I had to miss your do. One always likes to see the Hulliborn *en fête*, as it were – just as one loves seeing it on a normal working day, like now, for that matter.'

Clode glossed: 'I remember well your saying how disappointed you were, Minister.' He was taller than Vaux, better dressed, more effectively deodorized and with a full, expressive voice, ready for any tone or mode needed to endorse the Minister's.

Lepage felt uneasy. This was Tuesday, and Kate Avis often turned up on Tuesdays, ravening tremblingly for love, and liable to be rather unthinking and peremptory in seeking it. She would sometimes ring him from near the Hulliborn, and they would make a rendezvous. But now and then she simply rolled up and sauntered around the galleries until she bumped into him, and they hurriedly and gleefully made their arrangements then. She rather liked the spontaneousness and risk of this, but it might not be a good idea for her to intrude today. Although Lepage had known Vaux was coming, he knew, too, that if he warned Kate off, she would be hurt and possibly angry. It would make things look furtive, cheapen her, as she'd see it.

The Minister wanted a formal visit to the returned Monet and would be photographed alongside it for the local Press. He thought this would provide an emblem of the triumphant durability of great art and those associated with it, such as, in this instance and snapshot, himself, at least until the next Cabinet reshuffle or election. Lepage led him and Clode towards the Raybould gallery.

'I suppose you're laughing all over your fucking chops, if the truth's known, George,' Vaux remarked. 'You've got *L'Isolement* back in good shape, but not those dodgy "El Grecos". You collect the full, as-if-non-fake insurance for them, I take it, plus that twenty grand in the envelope which I heard about, and which ended up so helpfully in Hulliborn funds.'

'Director, this is a right fucking turn-up for your book,' Clode stated.

'Youde's still wholly convinced about those three works,' Lepage counter-stated, with a firm, counter-stating intonation.

'Who's Youde?' Vaux replied.

'Oh, D.Q. Youde is Art here,' Lepage genially explained.

'Yes, I know that,' Vaux said. 'But what I mean is who the hell *is* Youde?'

'In the sense of, well, who the hell *is* Youde?' Clode said.

'Who listens to Youde?' Vaux said.

'Is he a rated voice?' Clode asked.

'D.Q. has an enviable reputation worldwide in his speciality, Minister,' Lepage said.

'Which is what, buying crap in triplicate?' Vaux chortled.

Clode had a properly rounded guffaw in support, the more definitive because of his height. 'Unerring, unique and universally recognized flair for sending good money after bad, unprovenanced art?'

'But I do admire your loyalty to him, George,' Vaux said.

'Admirable,' Clode said. 'To stand by one's troops regardless of their balls-ups is a basic of leadership. Bravo, George, if I may.'

When they arrived at the Raybould, they found Lady Butler-Minton giving *L'Isolement* a damn good stare. Near her, against the wall, were a suitcase and holdall, as if she were about to travel. 'My dear Penelope,' Vaux cried, 'a double treat, *L'Isolement* and you.'

'Eric loathed this picture,' she replied cheerily. 'He could be such a twisted idiot. He used to say the blue had the grandeur of an aniseed ball and refinement of a bruise. I felt I had to come down at once and welcome it back. It's so lovely.'

'Well, off the record, ducks, I can take Monet or leave him alone,' Vaux replied. 'See one water lily, you've seen them all. Same as pussy. Bloody Impressionists making a career out of blur. Still, J.F. Kennedy did pretty much the same. Well, if Flounce hated it we must try not to put his bust anywhere near, and possibly not in the Raybould at all. Let's all sit on the sofa over there and give *L'Isolement* some steady eyeballing until the photographer arrives, shall we? Impressionists often seem fractionally more tolerable when one's off one's feet and the arse is well-spread. Such a jumble, this gallery. All periods mixed. That Youde?'

'Quentin says Art is not a slave to sluttish Time,' Lepage replied.

'I'd love to hear him enunciating that, the trite ponce,' Vaux remarked. 'Sorry, Penelope, you and he have something nice going, haven't you?'

'But pretentiousness is so much a *bête noire* with the Minister,' Clode pointed out.

He, Sam Vaux and Lady Butler-Minton sat in a cramped, unrelaxed line, like refugees hoping their papers would eventually get them across the border. Lepage stood near.

'No,' Vaux said. 'It's hardly better from here. Still like the product of a sudden sneeze while eating blackberry pie. Would it be better if that section on the right – the fronds and other guppy-nest pool stuff – were scratched out? I think so. But, obviously, there'd be a deal of hoo-ha over any proposed improvement of that sort.'

'Knee-jerk protests from hidebound pedants,' Clode suggested.

Lady Butler-Minton turned to Vaux: 'You spoke of a bust of Eric. But I believe that notion has been decisively rejected. This is so, isn't it, George?'

'The Kalamazoo suggestion has been, yes,' Lepage said.

'But now the Japanese desperately want to sponsor a memorial of that kind,' Vaux said. 'We're very lucky. They're sentimental old biddies really, and these days nothing like *The Bridge on the River Kwai*. As you know, Penny, they thought very highly of Flounce. Perhaps quite rightly. Well, almost certainly. I feel we must not stand in their way as to the bust. You can imagine, I'm sure, that there are more matters involved in this than the Hulliborn, more even than the general museums situation. Her Majesty's government is fervently seeking to attract more Japanese industry here, and to open markets for ourselves over there, so it's very important we maintain a happy relationship on all fronts. Oh, I know the Japanese are reputed to have played the white man and ditched restrictions on imports, but they can still make things orientally sticky if they take a hate. Although the bust might seem a marginal issue, even a rather esoteric issue, Tokyo is very quick to feel a snub, or to read in an apparently small rebuff a general insult. I'm not saying it would be a hari-kari job for someone, but while we *seem* to be talking about Flounce in stone, really the subject is exports and the wooing of Honda and Sony and Nissan. You understand, Penny? They've got a couple of people coming to see me here today, as a matter of fact: on site, as it were.'

'But has the Conclave actually voted in favour of the Japanese offer, then?' Lady Butler-Minton asked.

'I feel convinced it will,' Vaux replied.

'These things take on a kind of grand inevitability,' Clode assured her.

'One deduces you are not at all in favour of this recognition for Flounce, Penny,' Vaux went on. 'I'm unclear as to why not. But presumably you feel that the old creep is already too much of a posthumous presence, infringing on your own time and space. What was that German thing meaning they had to eat up Czechoslovakia and Poland and France? *Lebensraum* – room to spread themselves and develop? You feel that? I'm not unsympathetic, believe me. I walk into the Hulliborn and the memories of Flounce hit me immediately – not just the poisoned *vol-au-vents* and subsequent choral vomiting, but his whole egomaniac, vicious, foully indomitable, enragingly jolly persona. The point is, though, Penny, as I see it at least, busts are always of very deads, so allowing this to proceed – even boosting it – is simply an affirmation that he has become a memory only.'

'It has to be the case,' Clode said. 'Think of that stone image of Marx in the London cemetery. OK, his work can still cause havoc and boredom, but not him personally.'

Vaux said: 'I imagine you might retort, Penny, there's nothing *only* about the memory of Butler-Minton. But, after all, they're going to do the thing in some scorched and shagged-out stone from a volcano, aren't they? Could any material have less of life about it? There'll be a plaque, too, and it will say very clearly when he died. We can insist on this, if you wish. I mean, much bigger figures than his birth date. The whole project will declare Flounce well and truly gone. In every sense, the bust is a plus.'

'I'm against it, Minister,' Lady Butler-Minton answered. 'Let's leave him as ashes.'

'But as I hear it, this is not at all how you behave personally, Penelope,' Vaux said. 'Would you deny feeling he is near you sometimes now?'

'I sort of talk to him,' she said. 'I can control that. I initiate these sessions, and I close them. Well, obviously. They are just an occasional lapse, a tic. I call him "Lip" not "Flounce", in tribute to his brutal mouthings. I don't want the bust. I've moved on, Perhaps we all should.'

Vaux sat back on the sofa looking ratty. He'd be approaching fifty, plumpish, mid-height, dark slightly receding hair, a small chin beard also dark, heavy horn-rimmed glasses, a suit of very good material and cut, but not cut for him, or not recently enough, though not as bad as those Dominican Republic suits Flounce used to wear in order to insult people. Behind the glasses, Vaux's eyes looked unforgiving and clever. A snub nose did its best to give him a cheeky-chappie charm, but Lepage was not a great believer in noses as character tests.

'Well, I'm distressed you feel like that, Penny, I really am,' Vaux said. 'We would have much preferred things went ahead with your approval, or, better still, encouragement. However, it must go through, either way. Once we can demonstrably establish a really sound Hulliborn–Tokyo rapport – agreement for the bust and then the medical exhibition – this museum is certain to be placed in the government's premier category, with all that implies for prestige funding. Absolutely certain, you see. I'll have a word with H. de T. Timberlake – Board of Museums chairman – and everything will assume its proper place. Timberlake – known familiarly as Gadarene, of course – can be utterly reasonable if you catch him right. He writes a kind of poetry and at present is into composing something rather longer than *The Faerie Queen* about rust, so he won't be looking for distracting aggro with me and the Cabinet. The Board's intended grading audit of the Hulliborn would be a formality, or even waived – as so much of the procedure for the medical exhibition might be. I'm sure, Penny, that Dr Lepage and the rest of the Conclave would be only too happy with that outcome, and one does hope you can see things from the Hulliborn's point of view. We must all adapt to conditions – the new, tough but bracing conditions of viability. Hulliborn cannot be an exception, nor any other institutions, however worthy.'

The newspaper photographer arrived accompanied by a reporter, and Vaux posed with the Monet. The others watched. Vaux gave some quotes about the general worthwhileness of art.

Lepage heard a woman's footsteps approaching behind him and, feeling alarmed, quickly turned: sometimes Kate would surprise him from the back and, putting her hand up between his legs, give his balls a breathtaking cosset, not greatly worried about people nearby. But it was not Kate. For a few moments, Lepage failed to recognize this young woman properly, though he knew he had seen her around the Hulliborn.

'Ah,' Penny said, 'yes, dear, I'm ready to go now.' She stood.

The woman carried a canvas holdall, something like the one lying with the suitcase against the gallery wall, and had a large shoulder bag, its wide strap across her chest.

'We're arranging a trip, and agreed to meet here first,' Lady Butler-Minton explained. 'It seemed especially appropriate somehow. We're going to spend time together in Ethiopia, starting at Jimma. In fact, we might not return.' At the word 'together' she leaned across and gripped the arm of the younger woman, who put her hand over Penny's for a moment.

'Jimma is one of Flounce's old stamping grounds, surely,' Vaux said. The photographer and reporter left.

'In the south-west. But we'll do a trek north as well and get up into the Ethiopian Highlands. Often, I need mountains,' Penny said.

'Oh, how one knows that yearning,' Vaux cried. 'At times,

I long for a topography that can make me seem small, dwarf me, remind me of my mean stature in the wide scheme of Nature.'

Clode said: 'Minister, I have heard you more than once utter a kind of plea – "Ben Nevis, Cader Idris, heights of Lammermuir, let me but appreciate your scale, cower under your grandeur!"'

'I do see myself as rather Wordsworthian,' Vaux replied, 'an insignificant, reverential figure against the majesty of landscape. I hope that to regard one's self as akin to the poet is not arrogant.'

'Arrogant?' Clode disbelievingly repeated. 'It is the very reverse. It is a resemblance based only on humility and self-effacement.'

'But have we met?' Vaux asked the young woman.

'This is Trudy Dingham,' Penny Butler-Minton said.

Now Lepage remembered. Of course, she was Butler-Minton's former research assistant, the girl whose family members had come to the Hulliborn incompetently seeking sex vengeance on Flounce, and whose bush had turned tern in the Birds cupboard.

Penny Butler-Minton said: 'Trudy and I are cooperating on a biog of Eric. I've been shooting her all the dirt. But totally bloody all! We'll publish in due course. That's what I mean about the bust – why I'm opposed. It will be mad to set up a monument after what we're going to say, like reverencing a carbuncle.'

'But this must not be,' Vaux cried.

'No way,' Clode shouted.

In the tortured circumstances, Lepage felt glad the journalists had gone, and that there was only one other person about the Raybould now – a woman, probably out of earshot at the far end of the gallery, apparently fascinated by one of the big old Italian things that hung there.

'We intend to be very frank, but also just,' Lady Butler-Minton said. 'I've told Trudy everything I know, good and bad. And there are some tapes that Eric kept under lock and key at home. I've looked those out. Haven't listened to them yet, but they're certain to provide disclosures. These might be favourable, might not.'

'The Japanese will not like uncertainty – the prospect of a possibly scurrilous book coming out, endorsed by Flounce's widow,' Vaux said.

'There could be ramifications,' Clode said.

'From things Eric let slip I have the idea that the tapes cover his time in East Germany – the Wall, Mrs Cray, the haversack straps and so on. This material might be very positive – might show Eric in an excellent light,' Penny said.

'And if not?' Vaux asked.

'Would you still publish?' Close said.

'We aim for a complete portrait of Eric, don't we, Trudy?' Penelope said.

'Research does not merit the name "research" if it suppresses or falsifies,' Trudy said.

'We're going to work on the first draft in Jimma, drinking that extraordinary tea they have there. Volume length. It will be a kind of exorcism,' Penny said. 'Friends in the town will lend us something to play the tapes on. We'll get the draft finished, take a break in the Highlands, and then come back to Jimma and polish up our work, ready for submission to a publisher.'

'But why are you doing this to Flounce?' Vaux asked.

'How, how, can you behave like this, Lady Butler-Minton?' Clode said.

'My mind is settled,' she answered. 'I've given up those talks with the spirit of Eric. A foolishness. A weakness. Obviously, I'll listen to Lip on the tapes once or twice, and then this will be at an end, too. Our book will close that book.'

The Minister said: 'I'm afraid there is only one word for what you propose, Lady Butler-Minton. It is "betrayal".'

'No other term will suffice,' Clode confirmed, with a hint in his voice that he had mentally tried a cohort of others.

'We all need to be free of Eric now,' Penny replied.

'But how can you be joint with Trudy?' Vaux said. 'Didn't I hear Flounce was banging her at one stage, or more than one?'

'A posse of your relatives hunting him, Trudy?' Clode said. 'That's the report as I remember it.'

'There was an episode,' Trudy said, 'it being the *kind* of episode that, in changed circumstances – changed ideas about love – can bring two women together, having at a previous time being, as it were, linked via one man.' She put her hand on Penny's again.

'Yes, changes have come,' Penny said. 'I, too, have had recent interludes.'

'Youde? Pirie?' Vaux said.

'Spreading it rather,' Clode said.

'Closed now,' she replied. 'Especially Pirie. He was so much in favour of a memorial to Flounce – reproaching the Hulliborn for tardiness. Yet he knew I was against. It seemed a sort of perversity considering how things were.'

'Ah,' Vaux said.

'Oh,' Clode said.

Vaux stared at the luggage beneath *L'Isolement*. 'The tapes are in one of these bags, are they?' he asked.

'And are staying there,' Penny said.

'Get up, Lionel,' Vaux snarled abruptly at Clode. 'Don't just sit there like part of the fucking Royal Academy judging panel. Find those tapes. We don't know what damage they might do. The risk of the dubious is too great. Turn out her gear. Secure them. It's our only way to hit back.'

'Of course, of course,' Clode said. He got up from the sofa and moved resolutely towards the luggage.

Lepage said: 'Minister, I don't think I can allow this kind of behaviour on Hulliborn premises. Lady Butler-Minton is entitled to—'

'"Entitled", pox,' Vaux said.

'Absolute pox as for "entitled",' Clode remarked. But he had paused when Lepage spoke.

'This is the health and future of your bloody museum we're talking about, Lepage,' Vaux said, 'plus the whole panoply of British culture, plus, more to the point, the integrity of Anglo-Japanese relations in a commercial jungle. Don't you grasp this, dickhead?'

Clode moved forward again. Over his shoulder he shouted: 'It's your well-being and the all-round well-being of Britain in a ruthless world that concerns us, Lepage, you jerk.'

'Wait!' Lepage yelled after him. 'I forbid this.'

'It's OK, George,' Penny said. 'I'll deal with that string of wind.' She took a few short, swift steps and, just as Clode bent over to unzip the holdall, got a grip on him by the seat of his fine trousers and the back of his superior dark suit jacket and, swinging him off the ground, rammed his head hard against the wall just to the right and below *L'Isolement*, then repeated this twice. It seemed to Lepage like an extended version of how she had handled Neville Falldew on the balcony. Clode's thin arms and legs trailed the ground like loose guy-ropes on a breeze-blown tent. The Raybould wall shook and, although the Monet held firm on its hook, above it, to the left, an N. Sotheby Pitcher wartime seascape, *Convoy Assembling Under Barrage Balloons, 1941*, shifted slightly, hung askew for a moment, then dropped.

Clode lay face down, very long and still, nestling into the right-angle between wall and floor, possibly conscious but making no sound. Once it had come loose, the picture of battered looking but beautiful merchant ships, with their individual single balloons, fell very straight down the wall so that the bottom horizontal of the frame struck Clode across the back of the neck, like a guillotine, or the humanitarian chop for dispatching rabbits.

Lying there, Lionel Clode took on a kind of dignity – that touching dignity of the mutely suffering, or of one who has fought the good fight, although gravely out of his class, and is unlikely to demand a return. The seascape finished face up on his back, and it occurred to Lepage that members of the public coming into the Raybould might assume the picture and Clode littering the ground like that comprised one of those significant modernistic collages, saying something new and didactic about the war at sea, or the relationship of Art to Humanity. It would be pushing it a fair deal to have Lionel represent Humanity, but his clothes were magnificent. Fortunately, though, there were not many people in the museum today, and at present the Minister's group had the Raybould to themselves but for the woman at the far end, still apparently preoccupied by one of the larger Italian daubs. She seemed so set on loitering that Lepage peered hard, wondering if it were Kate, untypically showing some tact. But this woman was too old and too garishly dressed.

Penny Butler-Minton picked up her luggage from close to Clode. He stirred now, then reached forward with one hand, vainly trying to stop her taking the holdall. He shouted from the floor in a remarkably strong voice for someone felled: 'Nothing, I say *nothing*, can stop the Tokyo Flounce bust!'

'Rest,' the Minister told him. 'Lie there, Li. Your duty is not well done, but it's fucking done. Your mother would be proud.' Vaux turned to Penelope and explained: 'She is extremely unassuming, though tall. It was such a thrill for her when Li somehow passed high into the civil service Admin class. She would think it wonderful that his work brought him close to prized art.'

Lepage was hardly listening. For several minutes he'd been watching Trudy Dingham, who seemed suddenly overcome by a strange, fiercely powerful, perhaps painful, excitement. 'What?' he asked. 'Trudy, what is it?'

'Wait!' she cried. 'Oh, please, wait.' She had a large, encompassing, privately educated voice which quivered impressively now with undefined passion.

'Wait?' he asked. 'Who, Trudy?' At first he'd thought she feared Penny might leave without her, as if the destruction of Clode had brought some kind of seminal crisis, cancelling all previous understandings and arrangements, like the 1914 assassination of Crown Prince Ferdinand at Sarajevo, igniting the Great War. How intense Trudy's feelings towards her must be, he reflected, and how odd and consoling that two women who'd been having it off with Flounce turn-and-turnabout not long ago should subsequently establish this powerful, cockless, substitute bonding, and decide they must together dossier him intimately for the attention of the world. Was this another case of the survivors controlling what history could say? Lepage would treat himself to a slice of cynicism occasionally.

But now he realized Trudy was in fact looking past Penelope, and realized, too, that the volume of her voice was meant to reach the far end of the Raybould. He turned. The woman who had been so obsessively studying one of the paintings there had now taken a few steps towards the gallery exit, but for the moment gazed fixedly towards the Vaux group with, as far as Lepage could make out from that distance, a small, hostile smile on her face: something she might have borrowed from Laughton as Captain Bligh in a movie channel showing of *Mutiny On The Bounty*.

'Trudy, who is it?' he asked.

Vaux had noticed, too. 'Yes, who?' he said.

Trudy moved towards the woman, but then halted, as though scared.

Vaux did not approach the woman either, but called out, 'Madam, have we met? Arts Council? I see you're a Carpaccio Vittore fan. Into the saintly, are you? He certainly had a way with that kind of stuff. I don't mind it too much.'

From the floor, Lionel Clode called out gamely: 'Minister, I've often heard you remark of Vittore Carpaccio that, although he might not be all plus, he certainly was not all minus. "Paints saints" you epigrammed, I recall.' He tried an appreciative laugh, but it was swallowed up by the formidable Hulliborn wainscoting.

'Leave it, Trudy,' Lady Butler-Minton whispered. Lepage had never seen her other than full of confidence and strength, but even she sounded apprehensive now.

Then, the woman abruptly turned away, and, without looking again at the Carpaccio, strode swiftly from the Raybould, her red and cream skirt and vermilion shoes flashing splendidly as she passed through a patch of sunlight from the window.

'No, no, please don't go!' Trudy cried. The woman took no notice, did not glance back. After that first small movement towards her, Trudy seemed transfixed, but then suddenly called, 'Mrs Cray!' in that meaty, well-bred tone. 'It *is* Mrs Cray, isn't it? I *must* talk to you.'

For several moments all the Vaux party were clearly dazed by her words. Then, astonished and even shaking a little, Lepage moved urgently to stand near Trudy. 'Mrs *Cray*? How can you know this? You've met her previously? Who has ever seen her? Hell, does she even exist?'

'I feel it. I know it,' Trudy replied. 'Somehow. Eric gave fragments of description – the clothes style, the untroubled brow.'

'You can see the untroubled nature of her brow from here – from this distance?' Lepage asked. 'Aren't we talking about a chimera? This is absurd.'

The Minister had joined the two of them and heard this moment of talk. 'Mere guess? Intuition?' he asked. 'It's not a subject to trifle with, you know. How foolish!'

'Totally inane,' Li bellowed from the floor.

'Please, Director, stop her leaving,' Trudy said. 'Don't let her disappear. For once, she's alone. Somehow, officials and protectors will close around her again and she'll be gone.'

Lepage said: 'But—'

'Please,' she cut in, 'somehow I know this is our chance.'

'You could go yourself, come to that, damn it,' Vaux told her.

'What's wrong with your own legs, Trudy?' Clode said. 'They look grand to me from here.'

'Somehow I can't,' she said.

'Too many sodding somehows,' the Minister replied.

'Somehows are somehow running riot,' Clode remarked.

'Very well, Trudy, I will,' Lepage said. This was a girl who had lovely breasts which, although unfeelingly divided for the moment, by the harness of her shoulder bag, would obviously soon re-form as a very sound unit; and who possessed, in addition, a wonderful, chubby, compact arse surmounting slender thighs and bonny long legs, as admired also by Clode from a different angle. Plainly, there was a case for taking her seriously, even if she did seem to have gone gay.

'Mrs Cray could give the answers to so much,' Trudy said. 'Take us beyond the speculative in some of our research.'

'Cray sounds a British name,' Lepage said. 'Does she speak English?' He did not wait for an answer, but ran down the Raybould and out on to the landing. From there he could see 'Mrs Cray' quickly descending the main staircase towards the revolving door exit, her skirt and shoes still giving occasional multi-coloured gleams. 'Mrs Cray!' he yelled. He waved. Some museum visitors turned at the noise, but she didn't. He made for the spiral staircase. With any luck he'd come out ahead of her.

He got none of that luck, though. As he descended, he met Angus Beresford coming up. There was no room to pass. 'Go back, please, Angus. It's an emergency,' he said.

'What emergency?' Beresford asked. 'Did I hear someone calling Mrs Cray? Wasn't she to do with the Wall and Flounce?'

'Go back and let me through,' Lepage replied.

'Is it concerning that flasher, Falldew, again? I thought I glimpsed him near Zoology (Mammals).'

Lepage tried to push by, but Angus was too burly.

'It *is* to do with him again, isn't it, George? Where? Let me deal with this.' Now, Beresford did turn and started to descend. 'It happened where I said I saw him, did it?'

'Yes.' Send Beresford somewhere else – *anywhere* else.

At ground level, Beresford ran off to the left, making for Ronnie Acton-Sher's department. Lepage went directly ahead, towards the revolving door and, as he arrived, saw the woman approaching across the foyer. 'Thank God,' he said.

'What, sir?' Keith Jervis said, on duty at this main entrance. 'Is it the matter of an incident?'

'No, no, I must speak to this lady, that's all,' Lepage replied. He spun around to face her.

'Who *are* you?' she said. English, but possibly not her first language.

'Is it Mrs Cray?' Lepage answered.

'Why are you pursuing me?' she said.

'But you *are* Mrs Cray, aren't you – Flounce, the Wall, the whippet, the air-sock?' Lepage asked. 'Surely, there can't be two such foreheads.' She was about sixty, medium height, elegantly thin, though her face seemed a little doughy, almost frighteningly impassive, even though she obviously had her rats up. Of course, this deadpan-ism might have been inculcated on some training course. She tried to go around Lepage to the door, but he prevented this by moving in front of her. Enraged, she took a step towards Keith Jervis.

'Are you Security?' she asked.

'Part-time only,' Jervis said.

'This man is being exceptionally offensive. He is either mad or vile,' she said. 'You must deal with him. Even call the police.'

The Minister arrived and, a little later, Angus Beresford. 'I can't find him now,' Beresford said.

'Who?' Lepage said.

'Falldew, of course. You said in Zoology (Mammals),' Beresford replied.

'Is that skinny dick-swinger part of all this?' Vaux asked. 'How the hell is *he* involved as well as "Mrs Cray" and so on? Does the Hulliborn really need such recurrent situations, Lepage?'

'Oh, I wouldn't put it as recurrent,' Lepage said.

A class of school children with their teachers came in through the revolving door and formed up in the foyer, chattering and starting on their sandwiches and Kit-Kats. The woman would have used the confusion as a chance for slipping away – another skill she might have learned in undercover training – but Jervis prevented that. 'Although I am only part-time Security, this is obviously part of that part-time, or I wouldn't be here, would I, madam? An allegation has been made by you. This cannot by any stretch be casually ignored.'

Beresford heard most of this. 'What allegation?' he demanded. 'Stretching what? Is this lady another who's been insulted by him?'

'There are children present, Entomology,' Keith Jervis warned.

'I'm willing to forget it,' the woman said. 'Simply, I would like to go.'

'No, no, madam,' Beresford replied. 'That must not be. This is how these things too often end. Creatures like Falldew trade on it. They get their filthy kicks and know they will not be brought to book because sensitive people such as your good self do not complain officially. Surely, a lady visitor to the Hulliborn should be able to enjoy the exhibits – the *museum* exhibits – unharassed.'

'You're certain it was Dr Falldew?' Jervis said.

'Who the hell else?' Beresford answered.

'I don't know names, but it was *this* man,' she said, nodding towards Lepage.

'*This* man? The Director?' Beresford howled. 'Where?'

'The Raybould Gallery. Art,' she said.

Lepage said: 'Angus, there's been a mix-up, I think. The lady doesn't mean—'

'Art? My God, George, a personal furniture show amid all those noble pieces and expensive frames? That's worse than Falldew. Consider how hurt D.Q. Youde would be. Don't you believe there can be full satisfaction in looking at great pictures? Something extra is required? Is this, then, to be the language of the modern day museum? I think back to Sir Mortimer Wheeler, that great archaeological scholar, and wonder what he would make of the changes. Call me stuffy if you like.'

Lepage noted that all-purpose term again, apparently natural to the Hulliborn – stuff, stuffed, stuffy. 'Stuffy Beresford?' It did have something.

Lady Butler-Minton and Trudy came down the main stairs. Each carried luggage in one hand and, with the other, supported Lionel Clode, the Minister's attendant, between them, their arms crossed across his back, the way trainers helped rugby players from the field when a hamstring went.

'Yes? Is it she?' Trudy called. Her grand voice seemed to contain a meld of pleasure and dread. 'I saw there was a whippet on a lead in the Venetian picture that fascinated her so. A give-away?'

'Mrs Cray, we bear you no ill-will, not in the least,' Vaux declared. 'We perfectly understand that you had your job to do, and a difficult and dangerous one.'

'Mrs Cray!' Beresford cried. 'So, I did hear that! Christ, George, you've been waving it at *her*?'

The woman de-deadpanned for a moment and allowed herself to look puzzled: 'Cray? Mrs Cray? Who is she? Why do you call me that?'

The Minister said: 'But we all had the impression you—'

'Who the devil *is* this Mrs Cray?' she replied.

Lepage felt that the phrasing indicated a foreignness, even though he couldn't detect an overseas accent. Did anyone outside prize-winning radio plays say, 'Who the devil?' these days?

'I hear names that mean nothing to me,' she went on. 'Falldew? Which dangerous job? I work in millinery. Hat pins?'

'Identification is obviously going to be of some importance here, in the circs,' Jervis said in a Security voice.

'I've a banker's card that gives my name,' the woman said, opening her bag.

'Please, why deny who you are, Mrs Cray?' Trudy said. 'Of course you have papers with another name on them, a cover name, plus others suggesting your occupation. Millinery, did you say?' Trudy laughed a while. 'We are not children.'

Jervis took the card. 'Veronica Anselm,' he read. 'Mrs or Miss? It could be to the point. Again, in the circs, such circs being an illicit display of maleness.'

'Mrs Cray, I'm sure it will interest you to learn that we are seeking to arrange a suitable memorial for Sir Eric Butler-Minton,' Vaux said. 'Perhaps you have returned in this regard – to assess progress with it, possibly. Take my word, it goes ahead very well, very well. If I may say, we do not want these arrangements compromised by any . . . well, any disturbance, any outside intervention, however well-meant. The past should be regarded as the past, especially when those aspects concerning yourself and your contact with Sir Eric are so shadowy and remote.'

'Can former times not be left to slumber unprovoked?' Clode said.

'Come, Trudy, we really must get to the airport,' Penny said. They had released Clode, who now seemed quite able to stand. On one side of his head his fair hair was matted with blood.

'Have you really nothing to say to us, Mrs Cray?' Trudy asked plaintively.

The party of school children began to move off towards Urban Development. Lepage saw Falldew feverishly pushing his way through the line, calling and waving both arms. Even by his own standards he looked unkempt. 'Penelope!' he cried. 'Wait, please.'

'The cheek of the bastard!' Beresford said. 'Are you sure this isn't the man, madam?'

'Which man?' she replied. 'I've never seen him before.'

Falldew, bright with sweat and weeping badly, muttered: 'Penelope, they told me – your neighbours – that you were leaving for Ethiopia and had come here before flying out.'

'Why do you pester this place, Falldew, indeed pollute it?' Beresford said. 'We don't want your sort.'

'You will still be able to have your sessions with the memory of Sir Eric, Neville,' Penny said. 'I've put a key in the post to you today. The electricity is on for the sauna. Just lock up and switch off when you leave.'

'Is this really true?' Falldew said. He began to beam and tugged with nervous joy at that sad beard. 'The Egyptian paddle?'

'It's there. You can sing your boatmen's song while plying it, as ever. In return, all I ask is that you occasionally put out some food and milk for the cat. He's near feral, but will sometimes come when called: "Enteritis", or just "Tis". Try not to get too close to him, especially at night.'

Falldew quietened. He glanced about at the others, as if ashamed of the panic he'd shown. 'A little ritual, to help the days go by, that's all,' he said.

'It's your other little rituals we don't like,' Beresford said.

The revolving door spun. Dr Itagaki and Dr Kanda appeared, Itagaki ahead and looking very eager.

But Kanda spoke first: 'Why, Lady Butler-Minton, isn't it? This is a privilege little expected.'

Lepage went forward to make introductions.

'Ah, my Japanese contacts, I think. I'm glad we've met you here at the entrance,' Vaux said. 'You might need reassurance that the elks in the mammal display present no hazard!'

Kanda was very swift to laugh: 'If there is one thing I bloody love, it's a joke,' he said

'But this must be Mrs Cray,' Itagaki said. 'The clothes and brow.'

'A day of remarkable significance,' Kanda remarked.

Vaux said: 'We thought somewhere central for the bust, possibly this foyer.'

'Admirable,' Itagaki replied.

'It would strike an instant note,' the Minister said. 'A party of children were here just now. If the Butler-Minton bust were central they would make a beeline for it and ask their teacher who it was and why he had been carved in Japanese stone. This would truly be an education from the moment of entering the Hulliborn.'

'If there's one thing children react to instantly it is Japanese larva,' Lionel Clode said. He seemed much less groggy now, and Lepage felt glad. Lepage had moved to the edge of the group, and he leaned against a large, brown Celtic cross. After a moment, from behind, he felt a hand move swiftly up his inside leg and then expertly and lingeringly finger him. Because he had been half ready for it he was able to contain his reactions and did not turn or speak to Kate, in case of drawing attention to her. He continued to register polite interest while the Minister and others talked. The hand slipped down Lepage's leg and withdrew.

Itagaki and Kanda came over to speak to him by the cross. 'Are those two a loving couple all of a sudden, Lady Butler-Minton and her friend?' Itagaki asked. 'Isn't that Trudy Something, the doctoral thesis and research assistant Flounce was belting every ten days or so towards the end, and all credit to him?'

Kanda said: 'But scholarship and sexual desire are by no means antipathetic bedfellows.'

'Is that copyright or could any sententious fucking creep use it?' Itagaki replied.

Lady Butler-Minton and Trudy went for their taxi. Vaux, Clode and the two Japanese began to examine possible spots in the foyer for Sir Eric's memorial. 'I'm leaving, too, now,' the woman told Lepage.

'Mrs or Miss Anselm, my objection is still extant in that respect,' Jervis told her. 'Your charge is as yet unanswered. We part-timers have to be even more careful than staffers, since we have no *job* security, despite being, on a temporary, *ad hocish* basis, Security.'

'Goodbye,' she replied.

To Lepage she suddenly seemed irresistibly authoritative and even, to pick up the Minister's word, dangerous. Jervis evidently came to feel this, too. Despite his last statement, he stood back now, making no real attempt to detain her. She did not seem to be the sort who'd have a name like Anselm.

Lepage said: 'I'm sorry you've been troubled. It was one of those errors that begins as something slight – a sudden impression, no more than a whim – and then expands out of control.'

She gave a small, tolerant nod, her brow utterly unlined. 'Like Hitler and the Jews,' she said. 'But it's meant my visit here has not been a total success.'

'Regrettable,' Lepage said. 'Perhaps you will return. I promise there will be no interference next time.'

'No, I don't think I shall come to the Hulliborn again. This, too, was – what did you call it? – a whim. I wanted to see Youde.'

'Quentin? Some query about that Venetian work? I'm sure a meeting could be very easily arranged, Veronica – if I may. We do owe you something.'

She held up a hand, rather wearily. Lepage thought he felt

some approaching change in her thinking, in her tactics. Jervis went to answer a visitor's query at the other end of the Reception counter. 'There are certain rumours,' the woman told Lepage.

'About?'

'Paintings were stolen from the Hulliborn, weren't they?'

'That's a fact, not rumour,' he said.

'A Monet and three "El Grecos", as I understand it.'

'Quentin would refer to them as El Grecos, not "El Grecos".'

'Yes, well . . . It's unimportant.'

'He believes otherwise.' Lepage knew now that his guess at a shift in her had been correct. He couldn't specify to himself yet what that alteration was, but undoubtedly something had happened. This was not the same woman who had noisily accused him of pestering her in the Raybould and after.

'France,' she said.

'France what?'

'That's where they start, apparently.'

'What do? Where?'

'The rumours. Antibes. You've heard about all that, I expect. "Gotcha" emblazoned on the wall.'

Yes, yes, he'd heard about all that from Quentin. Lepage began to sense now why she wanted to see Youde. And he began to sense, also, that first suspicions had been right and this was not Mrs or Miss Veronica Anselm, milliner, but, maybe, Mrs Cray.

'Simply, there were these reports, channelled via him, I gather, that Butler-Minton might still be alive.'

Lepage did his startled bit. 'What! Flounce alive?'

'Ridiculous, of course,' she said at once. 'But I and my people on the other side of where the Wall used to be were naturally given rather a fright by these stories. We are trying to settle down to a happy, ordinary, tranquil sort of life since reunification of East and West. We don't want any trouble from a closed era. People will believe almost anything of that brilliant bastard, Flounce, including a falsified death. We think of that Graham Greene tale, *The Third Man*. The switched corpse.'

Yes, Lepage had recalled the tale, too, when listening to Youde – and had suggested the comparison was preposterous.

She said: 'These things – the haversack straps, the tennis

ball, the dog, even the white windsock, are far in the past,
from another time. Unnerving to see a whippet in the Italian
picture, yes, but that was entirely fortuitous.'

'The meaning of these items – never anywhere near clear,'
Lepage said.

'Oh, best leave them lie. And, you know, Director, I'll do
what I can to persuade others this is so – Flounce significant
only as a monument? I will try, really try, to accept that, and
to get others to accept it. It's good to hear about the bust.
Perhaps my visit to the Hulliborn was not entirely in vain.'

Jervis rejoined them. 'We have no address for you, Ms, in
case of subsequent repercussions arising from this incident,' he
said. 'The hat shop would do, as a matter of fact. We could
be in touch "care of".'

'Yes, we ought to have some means of contact,' Lepage
added. 'Vital. Quite vital.'

'Well, I'll be away now,' she replied and went swiftly through
the revolving door, her shoes fiery in the sunshine.

Vaux, Clode, Itagaki and Kanda returned to Reception.
'Good,' Vaux said. 'We have a kind of working shortlist.'

'The Minister likes to consider all aspects of a proposal or
commitment before making a decision,' Clode said.

'Time spent on reconnaissance is never wasted,' Kanda
remarked.

'Oh, God, a maxim,' Itagaki said.

Lepage wondered how long it would take to get free from
them and find Kate about the place.

Twenty-Two

Dear Lepage,

I thought I should drop you a formal note to say how much I enjoyed my recent visit to the Hulliborn. I speak also for Lionel Clode, despite the rather unexpected set-to involving Lady Butler-Minton (a bonny fighter, as she would have needed to be cooped up with that maniac, Flounce). Lionel was as right as he ever is only a day after, even smiling at the memory of that tussle (his unrecriminating word). I am sure that my meeting with the charming Japanese pair can have done only good, as to the bust and the medical exhibition. I am sure, too, that you and your Conclave will not wish to stand in the way of continued good relations with Tokyo.

Have you, by the way, had any dealings with an American citizen named Frank Weygand Ash? I'm handling some rather garbled correspondence concerning him, which makes unhelpful reference to the Hulliborn, though I'm not altogether clear in what regard.

Thanks again for an excellent day,

Sam Vaux

Dear Minister,

I had to think hard to place Frank Weygand Ash, but I consulted the files and see he is the husband of Sally Jill Ash, who runs a society in Kalamazoo, Mich., devoted to the work of Sir Eric Butler-Minton, and whose offer to sponsor a bust of him we declined. According to my records, Ash himself is not interested in archaeology or Butler-Minton but is concerned with hair-loss treatment.

We are all very pleased that you enjoyed your day

with us at the Hulliborn, and that Lionel bears no ill will
for the wound.

    Yours,

    G. Lepage

'The Minister on the line, Director.'

'Look here, Lepage, this bugger, Ash.'

'I know nothing beyond what I told you in my letter,
Minister.'

'I've had Trade and Industry badgering me about him and
his business. He's apparently got some pull in the States.'

'He's a hair expert.'

'Yes, I know that.'

'Perhaps he fixed up Reagan.'

'Their Embassy are involved.'

'Involved, Minister?'

'This bust of Flounce.'

'Which one? The Japanese proposal?'

'No, for God's sake. America's.'

'Kalamazoo's?'

'Kalamazoo's. We're going to have to rethink this one.'

'But—'

Vaux said: 'Kalamazoo is important.'

'There's a famous song about the place,' Lepage said.

'Fuck songs.'

'They're certainly enthusiastic in Kalamazoo.'

'This Ash was planning to establish a manufacturing plant
here in time for the European trade free-for-all in 1992. The
company to be called Hair Apparent. He'd base the firm in
GB, but also trade with countries like France, Belgium, Italy
and so on. I don't know whether this is news to you, but one
Western European country – I forget which – has point nought
nought three per cent more baldness than the world average
for men, and point nought nought five for women. If it's
Belgian-, Flemish- or French-speaking makes no odds. And
Holland's a big market, too: amazingly, baldness could be related
to canals – some special atmospheric thing associated with
slow-moving or still water affects the scalp. Queen Juliana
always looked OK, but she might have had a wig, I suppose.

Frank Ash's factory here would be hi-tech and labour intensive. That means jobs and no noise, smoke or dirt nuisance. It's the sort of place Trade and Industry regard as the grail – gongs in it for all associated with securing him. But now Ash is saying he doesn't think he'll come after all.'

'He's offended over rejection of their bust?'

'His wife's been at him, that's plain. You know what their women are like. The Kalamazoo "Let's Slobber Over Flounce" society somehow got wind of my meeting with the two Japanese in the Hulliborn and worked out what might be happening.'

'Tricky,' Lepage replied.

'Ash himself has been on the phone to T and I, talking about the "special relationship" and all that shit. I gather he and his wife were due to come over for a pre-look-around.'

'Yes, she said so.'

'What age, the wife?'

'Nothing on that I'm afraid.'

'"Sally Jill". I mean, it sounds potentially interesting.'

'That's possible. I don't know what to suggest about the busts, Minister.'

'We must keep Frank Weygand Ash on the side of Britain,' Vaux stated.

'Clearly.'

'Apart from all this, someone high up at T and I is apparently scared Ash is going to find out about some very successful English book called *Baldness Be My Friend*, by implication knocking his product. Was it some kind of early Brynner cult?'

'I think it was *Boldness*.'

'What?'

'*Boldness* not *Baldness*.'

'Ah, this would make a hell of a difference. Thanks, Lepage, I'll tell them. That's half the battle, then. As to the other, there's no reason why you shouldn't have *two* busts of Flounce at the Hulliborn. They wouldn't need much space. He can take the double exposure. He has the prestige, somehow.'

'Identical?'

'Haven't thought.'

'By the same sculptor?'

'Stop nit-picking, for God's sake.'

'Two? But the Conclave has already said we don't want *one*. I'm afraid my colleagues—'

'Sod the Conclave. This is major, Lepage. Nothing must disturb the present state of balance. I've sent Lionel to Jimma to get those tapes, and no muck-up this time. He'll do a fair job. His defeat in the Raybould wasn't typical. Politically, one of Clode's great assets is that he looks a prat but isn't, not altogether. Like Crossman or de Gaulle. Those two women – Lady Flounce and Trudy – could upset not just Tokyo but Washington-stroke-Kalamazoo as well. If that happens, where do you think the Hulliborn is? No-bloody-where, cock. We've all got to learn that culture in this country certainly has a place in government thinking, but it is a place that needs to be earned, day in, day out.'

'Would Tokyo and Washington-stroke-Kalamazoo wear it – each providing a bust? Sharing the honours?'

'They both have to realize that Butler-Minton was, indeed *is*, the prized property of the whole world, the princely shit. Everyone's entitled to do obeisance to him.'

Twenty-Three

'I'm driving past, see the light on, thought I'd come and find how you doing, Fatman. Why up so late?'

'I don't sleep too well recently, Wayne,' Vince Simberdy said. 'I have some worries.'

'The art?'

'That kind of thing.' It was just after three a.m. Simberdy rolled out of bed half an hour ago and had been doing a bit of pacing in the living room. The curtains on one window weren't properly drawn together and, on one of his little journeys, he'd become aware of a saintly-type, elongated face outside in the gap, and the gleam of unnaturally blond hair. Oh, God. But he'd gone and let Nothing Known in. 'I thought you were abroad in hiding, Wayne,' he said. 'Your letter said so. To me, that seemed very wise.'

'And you're worrying about how you can get my share to me and can't sleep? It's OK. I'm in this country again.'

'What share?'

'"What share?" he says! Oh, nice. Brilliant!'

'Not so loud.'

'Cool, Fatman.'

'There isn't any share.'

'Is that so? No share for Wayne, you mean. Just one big fat share for the big fat man. Through and through is what you are, Fatman. I'll give you that. Crooked through-and-through. A true professional.'

'Why are you out at this hour?' Simberdy replied.

'I've gone back to that timetable I told you about in the Blague. I see a friend late, after her work. We're thinking of doing a runner. So, I need the funds.'

A runner with George Lepage's Julia? But Simberdy didn't ask. No more complications, please. They sat in easy chairs. Simberdy poured a couple of whiskeys. 'Wayne, I don't think you understand.'

'You sure about that, Fatman? I think I understand pretty good. I seen some life, you know, and watched what money can do to people. It's not always very lovely.'

Simberdy turned to face him square-on and gave him the special smile he liked to think of as brave and frank, the one he usually kept for members of the Museums Inspectorate. 'There aren't any funds,' he said. 'We returned the Monet and the cash. Yes, hung them back on the wall of the Raybould. I put them there myself. It seemed an inescapable decision. We'd have done the same with the other paintings, too – the "El Grecos" – but we knew the Hulliborn didn't really want them. This is the kind of people we are, Olive and I – always conscious of duty, and always terrified of the law, which Olive, of course, knows quite a whack about.'

For a second, Passow was quiet. Then he had a big, admiring giggle. 'Yes, you're real through-and-through, Fatman. You can lie like you done a varsity degree in it, face wide open and sunny, like a field of wheat.'

'What I'm telling you is true. The return of *L'Isolement* has been in the Press. A photograph with the Arts Minister.'

Passow thought about this. 'So, the museum people bought it back from us, did they – paid a ransom without knowing who to? Like Nothing Known, you could say. You let them have a bit of a discount, did you, for old-time's sake and your love of the Hulliborn? It goes far, far back that love, doesn't it, when the other Bossman was there? I heard he's dead and the widow's gone gay and emigrated or something. But, anyway, you adore that museum. This is all right. I'd expect that. Life can't just be about business and making a packet. But there should still be plenty for a good team split. I found out about the real price of that painting, didn't I?'

'No, Wayne. We put it back secretly. No deal. No ransom.'

Again Passow considered. The skin of his face had begun to shine almost as much as his hair. Simberdy couldn't be certain whether it was sweat or rage. 'You put it back – you mean for free, and it's worth millions?' he said. 'You made it a gift?'

'Please don't shout. You'll wake the household. No, not a gift. It belonged to the Hulliborn, didn't it? As I said, we felt a mixture of fear and duty.'

Wayne sat hunched up in the armchair, hands gripping his face and head. He'd put the empty glass on the floor. Simberdy saw Passow's fingers spasmodically kneading his scalp as he tried to cope with this new concept, duty. It would be like trying to learn Mandarin Chinese in a day. For a few moments Simberdy thought Nothing Known might attack him physically. But then it looked as if the shock had drained Passow, disabled him, at least temporarily. They both stayed quiet for a time.

In a while, Passow began to straighten out his body in the chair. 'Well, that's how it is,' he said. 'Wayne don't believe in making a song about what can't be changed.' His long, saintly face seemed to get longer and registered appalling pain, yet pain that he accepted must be borne. 'Is that fucking blue water-lily thing hanging in the same place again near the window? If you put it back personal, you'll know. The exact spot like before?'

'What? Yes. But listen, Wayne, you can't.' Simberdy was almost yelling himself. 'You'd be mad to try it again. They've got extra security electronics on the windows and all round. Trying to crack the Hulliborn now is hopeless. It would be the end of nothing known about Nothing Known.'

Wayne nodded slowly in grief, like someone hearing of the death of a fine friend. 'Yes, you could be spot-on, Fatman. And, of course, you'd worry that if they got me it might lead to you and Olive.'

'That's not a consideration.'

'Not much it isn't.'

'I don't believe you'd ever squeal.'

'You think I'd be like that *omerta* thing in the Mafia, do you?'

'Absolutely.'

'Thanks, Fatman.' Wayne touched his hair in a bit of a preen. 'Really, thanks. What about the others?'

'The "El Grecos"? We've kept them, naturally. The Hulliborn doesn't want those three. They'd be a damn nuisance – upset their account books. Olive likes them, so everyone's content.'

'Not quite everyone,' Passow said.

'I'm sorry, Wayne.'

Passow punched the air warmly. 'I trust you and Olive implicit, Fatman. If you say that's how it is, that's how it is. This is still a team, yes?'

'True. So, what about your plans, Wayne – doing a runner with your late-night companion?'

'Plans got to be fluid, haven't they? This is a setback, no denying. I mean, to come expecting millions and find only your busy conscience. That got to be upsetting. Crucial? Maybe.' He stood and went out into the hall. Simberdy followed. Passow turned and shook his hand. 'Look, Vince, this Lady Butler-Minton I mentioned – her house got nobody in it now, that correct? I mean, if she's abroad.'

'Well, yes, the house must be empty.'

'They'd have some fair stuff, I expect, her and sir – all the collecting their sort do, foreign and home, and I don't mean beer mats.'

'Passow, she's a friend of mine.'

'Fatman, I can't be doing all this travel and taking risks for nix can I? There got to be earnings. Wayne's not a museum, don't cop no grant. Wayne's not duty. Wayne is catch-as-catch-can. Wayne is what built the British Empire so them others could give it away owing to conscience. I done a bit of art work myself, you know.'

'What? How?'

'Antibes way. France? Work called a mural, I believe, meaning walls. I signed it, like artists should.'

'You what?'

'Initials only. Don't worry.'

'Which initials?'

'FBM – Fatman's Best Mate.'

Twenty-Four

'Why, Quentin!' Lepage cried as Youde rushed unannounced and radiantly angst-flecked into the room. Lepage was conducting an interview with Keith Jervis, who'd requested the meeting, and, until interrupted by Youde's arrival, had been exhaustively describing how undervalued he felt by the Hulliborn.

'I'm sorry, Director, but I had to see you at once,' Youde said. 'An extremely private and urgent matter.'

'Now, you relax, old Art, and just say whatever you got to say,' Jervis told him. 'Don't worry about me in the tiniest bit. I have problems, too, and also extremely private and urgent likewise, but if you think you've got exec troubles of a priority nature so you need to push in first with the Director, that's OK by me, never fear. Just you talk as if I wasn't even here. Whatever is said, it will be like I never even heard it, a total blank. Count on me. All right, for controversial and deeply hurtful reasons I'm still only part-time, not staff, which I been mentioning today to the Director, but one thing I'm familiar with is loyalty, and mum's the word. With me, this is a well-known feature.'

'Director, could we be alone briefly?' Youde replied.

'It will be like you were just that,' Jervis said. 'I know how to self-obliterate when the big boys and girls are talking on the larger topics.' He began to gaze about Lepage's office, as though out on a country walk delightedly taking in the scenery, his mind seemingly miles away, and enjoying some of the over-ample leisure he had, through being only part-time at the Hulliborn.

'What is it, Quentin, so pressing and acute?' Lepage asked. This was turning out to be a rotten morning.

Youde hesitated for a moment, but then seemed to ditch his objections to Jervis's presence. 'Director, I must have time off, at once. I believe I'm entitled to several sabbatical months. I need to take them.'

'Yes, you might be, Quent. I'll check. Starting when?'

'Soonest,' Youde said.

Jervis gave a long and resounding intake of breath, wagged his head twice and stared gravely at Youde.

'I see,' Lepage said. 'This is some sudden, scholarly opening, opportunity, perhaps? I know that can happen, and one must take one's chance. Is there, perhaps, new material, requiring further work, to show the authenticity of the El Grecos? This is understandably a topic close to your heart.'

'Oh, stuff the "El Grecos",' Youde answered. 'They're rubbish and they're gone. All say, "Good riddance!" I'm wholly aware of that, Director. No need to play about any longer, pretending to cater for my feelings, when everyone's laughing at me *sotto voce*.' His body twitched, and he closed his eyes for a long moment, like someone who craved merciful sedation.

'Never, Art,' Jervis cried. 'Never a *sotto* or, indeed, other *voce* giggle to my knowledge. This is a foul slur on colleagues, who wish you only the very best – with the one or two obvious exceptions. I'm surprised and hurt to see you lose spirit. To be frank, Youdey, you never struck me as someone who would crack that way. Oh, you're pale, yes, very pale, but not sick pale, not feeble pale, you know what I mean? More calm pale, no hypertension, no panics. Maybe even above and beyond calm. Maybe serenity itself. All right, there's your teeth, admitted, but you can't help that, can you, not unless the cost of implants? In any case, they don't really come into it, do they – not part of that interesting paleness?'

'Well, yes, it's true, I am calm, I am,' Youde replied.

Lepage could hear the bonny fight for calmness in his voice.

'It's perceptive of you to notice my serenity, Jervis,' Youde said. 'You're entirely right. People can probably read in my features that I do not panic.' He looked about instinctively, as he often did when in Lepage's room, seeking a mirror, this time to reflect congenital non-panic. Then he seemed to remember again that there was no mirror here. 'My current opinion of the "El Grecos" is not, after all, some sudden collapse, is it? Hasn't it been forced on me over months by the weight of outside expert opinion?'

Lepage wanted some concreteness. 'If not the "El Grecos", what then, Quentin? Why the urgency?'

Youde trembled, almost catastrophically, for a moment. To Lepage it appeared as though Quentin had been shocked to hear him – Lepage – apply the tone of doubt to the paintings, even though Youde had just applied it himself. 'I'm afraid this goes much deeper, George,' he said. 'Much deeper than dead relics from the past, false or genuine. This is a vivid, breathing, alive matter. That is why I burst in on you so untypically like this, and why I must go immediately.'

'But go where, Art?' Jervis replied. 'Whither away?'

'Yes, where, D.Q.?'

Youde had not sat down and now took a couple of agitated, significant paces, his lips fiercely set. Lepage had once seen the Degas portrait that Youde was supposed to resemble, but today he looked more like President of the Supreme Soviet, Leonid Brezhnev, really quite late on. 'I've hurt a woman,' he said, 'hurt her beyond bearing.'

'This can happen in life,' Jervis said consolingly. 'You go ahead, Art, and tell us. You'll find a mature and tolerant hearing, I know. Women? The Director and I have seen some of that, I think, one way and the other.'

'Perhaps irreparably,' Youde said.

'Well, irreparably's big,' Jervis commented. 'But this sort of thing is bound to occur to someone like you: your looks and so on are always going to bring complications. Like I said, forget the teeth. You'll never be without chicks ogling, flashing the inner thigh and licking their brilliant lips, suggestive.'

'I must try to put matters right,' Youde declared. 'The obligation is inescapable, George. It is in the last resort a matter of maleness.'

'You sound great, Art, you know that?' Jervis replied. 'Strong, true to yourself, yes, even noble.'

'No, no, no,' Youde said. Lepage realized it was a humble protest. 'I'm afraid I cannot allow that. Nothing so worthy, I fear. Simply, I cannot see a choice.'

'Many would give themselves one, regardless,' Jervis said. 'They would shut their eyes to the situation and shut their ears to the cries for compassion. Isn't that the eternal tale of men and women? Do I hear someone mention *Tess of the d'Urbervilles*, made by Roman Polanski, if you please?'

'The woman would be Lady B-M?' Lepage said. 'Away now in Jimma.'

'Who else but Penny?' Jervis asked sadly.

'My failure has forced her to amend her sexuality,' Youde stated. 'We were to have gone away together – escaped – sought to banish the memory and hold of Flounce by meeting them squarely on his own ground, you might say. Yet it was I who reneged. How could she recover?'

'Deep water,' Jervis told him.

'I must go to her at once. Already, I have delayed too long,' Youde replied.

Jervis did some mulling. Then he said: 'Yes, Art, this is a truly high-calibre impulse, but what about Mrs Youde, and there are kids, aren't there? How's she going to cope with them on her own? Have you thought about this enough? In your present steamy, though certainly important, condition, these might seem only details, but—'

'Yes, details. Nothing but details,' Youde snapped. 'I really can't be expected to give my mind to them now. And listen, Jervis, why don't you keep your fucking prole nose out? Haven't you heard of the right to remain silent?'

'Oh, thank you, Art,' Jervis replied. 'Thank you *so* much. That your attitude, you'll get nothing more from me.' He turned his face away. 'I tried to give only help, of full, *bona fide* quality. But from now on it will be like I'm not even here.'

'You said that before,' Youde answered. 'But listen to you.'

'Your sodding loss, Dr Youde,' Jervis pointed out. He faced Youde again.

'Lionel is already out in Jimma,' Lepage said.

'Lionel? Who the hell's Lionel?' Youde asked. 'How many has she been giving a welcome to, for God's sake? Pirie there, too?'

Jervis said: 'Now you *do* look like high-voltage panic, Art. That dribble swinging from your chin? I'd deal with it good, if I was you. What you definitely want to keep out of is an African loony bin.'

When Youde had gone, Jervis said: 'This is what I mean, you see, Director – a hardly suspected spectrum of duties comes my way: one day Security, the next giving Art familial and sex advice.'

Lepage's phone rang. Calls had been switched through direct because his secretary was out buying a Hulliborn wedding present for Ursula and Falldew. When Lepage answered a man's voice said: 'Tip, here.'

'What?' Lepage replied. There was a famous and influential US politician called Tip O'Neill, wasn't there? God, had Kalamazoo got him involved somehow? 'Tip?' Lepage said.

'City,' the voice replied.

'I don't—'

'City Tip, Benediction Street.'

'Rubbish?'

'Right. And you are Dr Lepage, Museum Director?'

'Yes.'

'Someone here says he knows you. Gave your name as reference.'

'Yes? For what?' Lepage asked.

'Trouble, Director?' Jervis whispered. 'Anything I can do? I'm used to all sorts in this post, you know.'

Lepage mouthed: 'It's all right, Keith.' Then into the phone he said: 'I'm not sure I understand.'

'Entirely forgivable, sir. It's a strange situation. A Mr Indippe?'

Lepage heard stern muttering in the background.

'Sorry,' the tip said, *'Professor* Indippe. Bernard?'

More muttering.

'Ber*nard.* From the States. Kalamazoo, Michigan.'

The name came back to Lepage slowly, part of the Sally Jill Ash correspondence. Wasn't he their thoroughgoing archivist and researcher? 'Professor Indippe? Yes,' Lepage replied. 'Is there a woman with him, name of Ash?'

'You do know this man, sir?'

'Well, I know *of* him.'

'Do you think you could come down, sir?'

'To the tip?' Lepage said.

'He's being obstructive. We don't want to call the police.'

'Police?' Lepage replied.

Jervis frowned and squared his shoulders. 'Can you handle this, Director?' he said in another whisper.

'This man's making an exhibition, Dr Lepage – professor or not.'

'An exhibition?' Lepage asked. 'What kind of exhibition on a tip, for God's sake? Is the woman with him – a Mrs Ash?'

'A nuisance exhibition. No, we've come across no woman. He's been taunting seagulls, waving sandwiches far up on the tip. Are there usually two of them, then? You've come across this sort of thing before? So, what's the game? Something to do with the Green Party?'

'Is it an offence?' Lepage replied.

'What, sir?'

'Well, to make a show of sandwiches on a tip,' Lepage answered.

'He shouldn't be up there.'

'Can't you summon him back? Haven't you a megaphone for shouting warnings and so on?'

'He ignores instructions. We really don't want to resort to physical force. That's not in our remit.'

'Very well, I'll be there,' Lepage said. He put down the phone.

'I deduce a crisis, Director,' Jervis remarked. 'There's something in my make-up that can sense such challenges. Whatever and wherever, I must obviously accompany you.'

'No, no, Keith. It's something entirely routine, as a matter of fact. You're needed here. Dr Youde, very stressed; and, now, myself absent for a while.'

Jervis followed him to the door of his room. 'But what I have to come back to as a topic, Director, is, is it fair to ask me to fill the breach like that, take over the bridge, when I'm only—?'

'I'm going to think about full-time and staff status, Keith, think very seriously,' Lepage promised over his shoulder as they hurriedly went down the spiral stairs.

At the bottom, Jervis shook Lepage's hand. 'I ask no more, Director. I am content. For leaving this matter with you is like leaving it with the very spirit of the Hulliborn itself, and that's enough for me.'

'God,' Lepage groaned to himself in the car, 'but who or what *is* the spirit of the Hulliborn, and do I bloody care? Roll on early retirement. No, quicker than roll on, and earlier than early. Much. Both.'

A few minutes later, as he climbed the gentle, uneven slope of Benediction Street tip towards the solitary, arms-twirling figure of Indippe, he saw a gull swoop majestically and snatch a piece of sandwich from the professor's grip, then a second bird, then a third, all screaming at him on their downward plunge. Others circled noisily, and Indippe looked very spattered. And yet, because of the enormously wild, but disciplined, vigour of his movements, played out so starkly against a grey-sky background, it looked as if Indippe were the attacker, not the birds. Near his feet he had a large, closed, black tin box, the kind of container people left in bank depositories, presumably loaded with more sandwiches.

'You Lepage?' Indippe yelled when they were still quite a distance from each other. 'A name native to the Auvergne region of France originally, I believe. Fine to make your acquaintance, Director. Grateful you've shown up. I'm only just starting here. Negative results to date, but well worth the trouble, I think.'

Pausing with his brogues on a sealed plastic bag of something disturbingly soft and slippery, Lepage replied with a shout, into which he put some fine affability of tone – probably, he thought, the most affable tone ever heard at this height on a tip: 'Yes, lovely to see you, Professor Indippe.'

'Oh, please,' he yelled back, while freeing himself from a sheet of old greaseproof paper which had been blown against his face, 'could we, perhaps, become less formal? Call me Bernard.'

'Well then, I'm George.'

'OK, George.'

'And is Sally Jill—?'

'Ah, Sally Jill,' he cried, smiling very warmly. 'Come on, then, you fucker, come on then! Wound me! Rip me! Come on, PUNK!'

Lepage saw he was shouting at a black-headed gull that remained hovering, instead of diving in for the food Indippe held. Lepage began to climb towards him over well-compacted vegetable matter, old foam rubber and paint pots.

'I thought you'd ask about Sally Jill,' Indippe said. 'People do.'

'What age is she?'

'She's up in London with Frank W. Not true it stands for wanker, but I don't know why not. You have that word, "wanker"? But maybe this is presumptuous of me and it's Brit to start with: infinitely the more mature culture, after all. Sally Jill and Frank W. have some business-enhancing talks on – Ministers involved, the whole big rigmarole. Ah, so you've made it!'

Lepage was close now.

'Great,' Indippe said. 'Sort of Sherpa Tensing of the shit-heap. I won't shake hands. Mine are not too spruce, I guess. About twenty-nine, Sally Jill. Maybe less. They make trouble down below – the functionaries? I told them it was merely scholarship and to do with someone immensely distinguished who had been based locally – Sir Eric – but I think they feared I'd run off with their best treasures. I believe there's a word for it in Britain – recovering stuff from tips?'

'Totting.'

'Let me note that,' Indippe said. He put the remains of a sandwich down at his feet and pulled a pad and a pencil from the inside pocket of his magnificent long green leather overcoat, streaked badly front and back over the left shoulder area, but easily cleanable. He wrote the word and a definition, smearing the page with matter from the sandwiches. He put the writing materials away, and as he bent to pick up the food, a gull swung in at him, yellow beak open and menacing, seemingly set on an infuriated rip at his head, face or neck. Delighted, Indippe held the position, turning his profile provocatively towards the creature, while nibbling ecstatically at the sandwich and making loud noises of satisfaction to enrage the bird more. But, suddenly, the seagull obviously realized this was a tease, maybe a trap, and pulled out of the dive without touching the food or Indippe. 'That was heartening,' he said. 'Almost a success. Perhaps it *is* possible then.'

'You're checking on Butler-Minton's face scar – the origin of?'

'If he says he was attacked on a tip, one has to consider that he might have been speaking seriously. Did he have a reputation for irony? Well, it is the British disease, I'm told, so perhaps it's wrong to read too much in. But to do the actual field work is the only way I know of digging out truth. I don't have to tell you, do I, someone so experienced in reading the past? Oh, sure, there are reeks here, sure there is ugliness, but who said truth was going to be sweet? Not St Augustine. It looks as though the sculpture project might be on for Kalamazoo again, doesn't it, Director, so I need to get my research in place? I'll give it another couple of hours. First, I've got to get these birds to think only "sandwich, sandwich, sandwich" when they see me, so I make a big show of coming from the States especially to give them treats – cheese and pickle, tuna, sweetcorn in a range of goodies. Then, I'll start disappointing them, hiding the snacks, maybe eating some of it myself in full view, just like now. That's going to turn them malevolent, if anything can, and so we might mimic the circumstances when Flounce got savaged – if he ever did.' He gazed down. 'We're at quite a height here. Nice view of the town.'

Far below some men were shouting and waving, ordering them back, but Indippe ignored all that. 'Of course, there are other theories about the scar to be checked: Enteritis, the cat, Lady Butler-Minton, or a duelling wound. I favour Enteritis. I've heard good, confirmatory information of its savagery.'

In a while, he stopped wielding the sandwiches high above himself like semaphore flags and, instead, pushed them very slowly and ostentatiously into the outer pockets of his gorgeous overcoat. Immediately, the gulls in the sky grew confused, even bitter, and their din became fierce. Indippe stared up at them and started haranguing again: 'What's keeping you, then? You yellow? You all noise, you wheeling, drifting, squitting nothings? George, pity it isn't steeper. From below I'd look like Prometheus.'

'You must have a lot of research on Flounce,' Lepage replied.

'You said it, George. I'm going to be writing up my notes for a long time. There's been a great deal of travel, I can tell you. That Mrs Cray material! And the killing at the Wall. So much. She Satan, you think?'

'You're into Mrs Cray?'

'What else? Once I started I had to go on. The haversack straps. It all falls into place, you see.'

'Yes?'

'Oh, sure.'

The men below seemed to think Indippe had been shouting to them, not at the gulls, and were yelling back, asking what he wanted to say.

'I brought this black box for my notes,' Indippe remarked. 'And the notes of one other. They're going to have to be under strict lock and key. "Sensitive" is not the word!'

So, not more sandwiches.

For a little while, Indippe gave up the bellowing and switched to a gentle, wooing voice to entice the birds, the way people talked to babies or kittens. 'Here we are then, my sweeties, see what Ber*nard* has brought for you. Come on, my little chicks, come, come, come.' Then he spoke to Lepage, ordinary voice. 'Of course, Sally Jill and the whole Butler-Minton Society in Kalamazoo were very upset when they heard Her Ladyship and Trudy, the researcher, might get together to destroy his image. Some countering had to be arranged. Well, you can see why Sally Jill and the rest of the Society, myself included, grew disturbed: here they were, striving for the right to sponsor a monument to him, really working on your government after that initial refusal by the museum's Conclave, and then, suddenly, they hear somebody is going to say he was nothing, or worse. No, not just *some*body. *Two* bodies, both of which he had known extremely well. Incidentally, the Bible belt in the States is going to find it very difficult to understand how two women join together like this, when the husband of one of them was adulterously fucking the other. Anyway, it became even more imperative to discover the real facts, and to protect Eric Butler-Minton's name.'

Around the base of the tip men seemed to be gathering in a posse.

Indippe looked up at the gulls, though. 'I guess I feel a kind of connection with Flounce out here,' he said. 'It's a thrill. Do you get that feeling, too, George? As if we were sort of linked to him by the sandwiches? Well, not just linked. For myself, I have the sensation now and then that I actually *am* Flounce, an *alter ego* able to engage in aspects of his very life. It's as if I have been, oh, sort of *flooded* by him, like a blood transfusion. But perhaps you wouldn't regard that as very scientific. I'd have to concede the point.'

The birds seemed to have lost interest. They still circled, but further off now, and their cries were less frequent and not so committed: there might be a general objection to being used willy-nilly in an experiment. Indippe had taken one of the sandwiches from his pocket and was displaying it again. The gulls gave it the big ignoral. 'Bastards,' he muttered. 'Ungrateful horde. Think of Flounce, you jerks.'

Lepage felt startled. '"Think of Flounce"? Why should they? Who or what is Flounce to them? These wouldn't be the same birds who attacked him, if any did.'

'They're so damn choosy. So damn pampered.'

'Whereas?'

'Whereas Flounce – try to imagine, George, what he'd have given for a sandwich like this – even a fragment of a sandwich – at the worst moments in the Mrs Cray sequence. Oh, yes.'

'I don't think I follow this, Bernard. Are you saying Butler-Minton was in some ways a *victim* of Mrs Cray?'

'Oh, sure, eventually – for a while.'

'We've heard rumours, of course, but there's never been any suggestion of that sort. Is this what you meant when you asked whether she was Satan? Most of us have thought that if there was any villainy it most probably came from Flounce, though everything remained terribly vague – some involvement of a whippet, and haversack straps, but no detail of what this involvement was.'

'And the air-sock. Did you hear of that?'

'The air-sock, yes. Flounce apparently muttered about these things on his death bed. A nurse heard him. Lady Butler-Minton had slipped away to the betting shop. The stuff is garbled.'

'I think they're coming, George,' Indippe replied.

In a wide arc the men who'd been waving and shouting from the base of the tip began to climb towards them. It was late afternoon, and in the dwindling winter light they looked sinister, threatening. But for the absence of baying bloodhounds it might have been a manhunt scene from one of those old Devil's Island movies.

'They don't understand,' Indippe said. 'I tried to explain to

them, but they'd never even heard of Butler-Minton. Doesn't
that of itself plead the cause for the monument, George? This
was a man who, on his own, without the help of your MI6
or the CIA, attempted to rescue from behind the Wall one of
the greatest . . . Of course, suddenly, months ago, the Wall
came down – is only a memory. It's increasingly difficult for
people to recall its appalling effects, and the dangers it brought
to those deemed to be disloyal and rebellious, even the most
distinguished scholars. But . . .' Spinning around he confronted
a gaggle of gulls who were lying off behind him, obviously
interested in the food, yet remaining at a distance. 'Come on,
come on, you craven crew,' he called. He'd given up the soft
approach. He glared at the birds, and his chubby, lined face
with its tight little NCO's grey moustache had grown sombre,
even vindictive.

'Flounce attempted to rescue a great scholar?' Lepage asked.
'A great and unforgivably subversive scholar, as the East
German regime saw him.'

Lepage's memory got to work. 'You're talking about Uwe
Koller, are you? But I'd always thought—'

'Shot by guards on the Wall when he tried to make a dash
to the West. Koller had been in hiding in East Berlin. Flounce
knew him well – camaraderie of scholars – and was trying to
get him out. The East German authorities rightly suspected
Butler-Minton had secret knowledge about Koller, including
his hideaway. They took Flounce in for interrogation, sometimes in East Berlin, sometimes in Rostock, up on the Baltic.
Koller seems to have thought that Sir Eric would betray him.
Koller panicked and had a go at escape himself. It failed.'

'Koller? But, look, I thought—'

'You believed Koller was given away by Flounce and elimin-
ated in a deliberately fixed incident? I'm very familiar with
the disgusting rumour, obviously, though I haven't found where
it started – not yet. Would Mrs Cray deliberately spread disin-
formation? It's possible. She's a Brit, a widow, but very fond
of the old East German regime – employed by it in some high
secret-police post. I gather Flounce would never talk about
what actually happened. He hated failure, even a failure brought
on by the errors of others. It's possible this biog by Penny

Butler-Minton and the researcher will use the same old misinformation.'

Indippe bent down and picked up the iron box. 'I think we have done as much as we can here, George. I guess there has to be a large question mark over the seagull as cause of Flounce's face scar. We will have to look for other explanations. But that's scholarship, isn't it?' He flung the remains of the sandwiches on to the tip and the birds hurled themselves down at the food.

Indippe and Lepage began to run over the rubbish in the opposite direction from the advancing men and towards a skimpy, fog-shrouded copse. The main group of birds, seeming to sense that all chance of the food might be leaving with Indippe, zoomed in close again and increased their din. The men approaching seemed satisfied to have shifted Lepage and Indippe off the high point of the tip and towards the trees and exit. The platoon turned back and began to descend.

Lepage found it hard work running over the old washing machines and discarded carpets and infinitely stained mattresses. Indippe, carrying the box, and hampered by his long coat, began to gasp.

'Take care here,' Lepage said. They had come to some dumped, rusted coils of old barbed wire.

Looking at them, Indippe said: 'It seems so damn appropriate for this tale – reminiscent of the Wall.'

Lepage put out a hand to help him. Indippe would not have that, or not at first. He staggered slightly, and strands of the wire fixed dedicatedly on to the leg of his drill trousers. Lepage had to crouch down and slowly unhook him. Indippe stood there, like some trapped animal, proud and defiant, but grown sloppy with age. Lepage freed him. They resumed their trek. At a slight downward slope on the very edge of the tip Lepage found what remained of a blue, two-seater Utility settee. 'We can rest here,' he said. 'The pursuit is off, and, in any case, they can't see us because of the dip.' They both sat down, Indippe with the box at his feet. His grey hair had been cut ruthlessly *en brosse,* perhaps to suggest virility and youthful spirit. It wasn't too bad a try, but the wheezing messed it up.

For a while he was silent, amassing some breath. Then he

said: 'It was Mrs Cray, in her professional security role, who
devised that foully cruel, parody banquet.'

'Banquet? I don't know of this.'

'Yes, the banquet: simple and barbaric. After Flounce had
been starved and questioned for two days in an abortive attempt
to make him disclose Koller's whereabouts, Mrs Cray put on
a banquet-stroke-picnic, as if in his honour, but a sardonic,
malevolent meal, sort of *Dérision sur l'herbe*. You never heard
of this, and the menu, George?'

'No.'

'Really? Fricassee of haversack straps in thick Melba sauce,
followed by braised whippet, with a tennis ball in its mouth,
all served in a field at Rostock on a vast, brilliant, mocking
tablecloth cut from an airfield windsock. Genuine antique fish
knives and forks for Flounce, travesty acknowledgements of his
top-notch country house breeding.' An aged but still sticky
fly-trap paper covered with corpses that must have lain between
the settee cushions fixed itself to the professor's leather coat
and Lepage's jacket, and, for a time, they fought to unlink
themselves, and then to get the remains off their fingers.

'One thing I love is the fucking ivory tower of research,'
Indippe said. 'Flounce devoured those straps and the whippet,
though leaving the tennis ball, and then told Cray to send out
for more, especially of the straps. Yes, *especially* of the straps,
my source says. B-M was too much for them, George. I can
understand why people want to be like him – why people
even imagine they are part of him. As I said, I do myself now
and then. The Hulliborn and Britain should be proud, and
yet there is argument about a measly commemorative bust.
Cray and the others gave up. Flounce was released, but not in
time to save Koller.'

They strolled on again and reached the trees. Lepage found
a track and went ahead, looking back occasionally to check
that Indippe and the box kept up. The professor waved him
forward each time, and seemed to be recovered, though it was
hard to see him properly in the gathering shadows. He appeared
to grow ghostly, insubstantial, his grey hair merging eerily with
the foliage. A piece of the fly-paper still clung to the breast
of his coat and caught the occasional, very low sunbeam that

made it through the trees, glowing like a distant navigation buoy in harsh seas.

When they had been traipsing for about ten minutes, Lepage glanced behind again and could not spot Bernard at all. Lepage listened and then called, but there was no sight of him and no sound of footsteps on soil. The fly-paper's gleam had passed away. For a tiny part of a second, and for no reason he could pinpoint, Lepage recalled that line in a radio broadcast just before the war: 'The lights are going out over Europe.' As he emerged from the little wood and made for the road, the gulls clustered above him, perhaps thinking that on his own he could be bullied more efficiently. They restarted their hullabaloo, and a few swooped down towards him, beaks fierce-looking, their brilliant white bellies plump with tip spoils, almost certainly in some cases Indippe's sandwiches. 'Get lost,' he yelled. 'Not me, you sods, not me. Do you hear? I'm not the one who wants to be the new Flounce.'

In the night at home, Lepage had another phone call, this time from the police. He was sleeping well and, for a few seconds, had difficulty taking in the message. When he could, he did not feel much happier. 'Director, we wondered whether you'd mind going up to Lady Butler-Minton's property. One of our patrols has run into a situation there.'

'Situation?'

'Yes, sir, what does seem to amount to a situation.'

'Now? What time is it?' He saw Julia was not home yet, but that didn't tell him much.

'It's one fifty a.m., sir.'

'What's happened?'

'People acting in suspicious fashion, Director. Two have mentioned your name as a sort of reference.'

'Two? Who? How many are there altogether, then?'

'We don't like giving personal details over the telephone, sir. But I see no harm in telling you that at least three people are involved. That's our present knowledge. The patrol is still dealing with the matter, sir. It can't leave at this stage. This is why we'd be so grateful if you could go. It might be of great assistance in clearing things up.'

'I'm thinking of getting right out of this fucking job, you know.'

'Sir?'

'OK, I'll go.' He dressed and drove out to Penelope's. A uniformed constable met him at the gates of the drive. Indippe stood near him, looking delighted.

'This American gentleman gave your name, sir,' the constable said, when Lepage came from the car.

'What the hell's been happening to him? Have you people roughed him up?' Lepage replied. 'This is a professor and distinguished archivist from a country which is one of our closest allies. Do you realize that?'

'He was attacked by a cat in the dark, sir.'

'George, look at it,' Indippe cried, pushing his wounded head rapturously towards Lepage. 'Enteritis did this.'

'Pardon me, sir,' the constable said, 'but you don't get a deep facial cut like that from enteritis.'

'You see the significance, George?' Indippe demanded joyfully. 'I simply tried to befriend that cat in the garden, and it flew at me, entirely unprovoked. As one scholar to another, do you think we can say after this we have a workable hypothesis − I put it no stronger for now − we have a workable hypothesis that Flounce's scar was, indeed, the—'

'Your headquarters said two people had given my name, constable,' Lepage replied.

'Yes, sir. Perhaps you could accompany me.'

The three of them walked across the lawn, Lepage and Indippe following the officer. 'This will about wrap up my researches, George. Closed book.'

'Where did you disappear to after the tip?' Lepage asked. 'I was worried.'

'I had an experience.'

'Yes? What kind, Bernard?' Lepage had the feeling it would turn out to be at least mystical, and possibly magical.

'I thought I saw someone ahead.'

'You did. Me.'

'No, I don't think so, George. It wasn't like you.'

'Oh? Who *was* it like?' He knew the answer. Yes, mystical or magical or hogwash.

'George, it could have been Flounce, dressed in the robes and large academic hat of the degree ceremony in Africa. It's so crazy, I know – so disgracefully irrational, so occult.'

'How did he manage with that headgear among all the branches?' Lepage replied.

'I wanted to get close to him. I left the path.'

'And?'

'No, I didn't get close. Well, no, of course not. A delusion, obviously. And I found I'm very unfit and failed to keep up – I mean, if he'd actually been there to keep up with.'

'Carrying the box would slow you.'

'I have to look after it. I've left it in my hotel's safe for now.'

'Your notes?'

'Mine, and some from my sources and contacts.'

'Which?'

'Here we are, gentlemen,' the constable said. They entered the gymnasium. A couple of police sergeants were talking through a steam cloud to Nev Falldew, seated naked in the sauna, a piece of wood that looked like a rough, improvised paddle in his hands. As Lepage and Indippe went nearer, the conversation with the two sergeants ended and Falldew began to sing, or rather chant, an extremely high-pitched number, its words unintelligible and probably not English, or any known language.

'Ah,' Indippe declared ecstatically. 'Communion with Flounce.'

'Dr Falldew said you could vouch for him,' the constable told Lepage.

'Certainly,' he answered.

Falldew broke off from the music for a second: 'Now, altogether in the chorus!' he shouted at the police and resumed his anti-melody. The officers didn't seem to respond, but Indippe, quickly taking off his clothes, joined Falldew on the sauna bench and, smiling blissfully, tried to pick up what there was of the tune. For a while, the steam aggravated Indippe's wound, and the sauna, already a bit bloody, became extra bloody. But then clotting stopped the flow.

'Flounce brought back ditties from Egyptian boatmen, didn't he?' Indippe said. 'I've heard of this, but never expected to be able to participate. Such good fortune!'

'We understand Dr Falldew has a key to the gym while Her Ladyship is away,' a sergeant said.

'Quite possibly,' Lepage said. 'So there'll be no evidence of a break-in – no crime involved.'

'Not at the gymnasium. It's the house. Someone's in there. Through a forced window, we think.'

'A burglar? Did he give my name, too?'

'No, sir. We haven't got him yet. But we will. We think it's someone we've been waiting for for years. Known as Nothing Known, to date. It would not be proper for me to give his true name at this juncture. We've got a cordon all round. He can't do a bunk this time.'

Indippe seemed to resent that Lepage had switched his interest from the professor to the sergeant. Indippe stopped singing and turned to Lepage. 'George,' he said. 'The box.'

'The one you were carrying?' Lepage asked. He felt guilty about being clothed, like someone in a suit on a nudist beach.

'As you'd expect, I've been in touch with friends and colleagues of Uwe Koller, as crucial to my researches,' Indippe said.

'Absolutely.'

'One such colleague had been asked by Koller to look after a manuscript he was working on up until his attempted escape – too bulky to carry when he did his run. The plan was that it should be brought out to him once he'd made it to the West. It was to do with the provenance – the authenticity – of certain famous works of art.'

'Yes?' Lepage said. 'Yes?'

'I knew you'd be interested. I asked if I could photocopy the El Greco pages.'

'Yes?' Lepage said. 'Yes?'

'Of course, they were written a long time before the present controversy to do with the Youde purchases. In my view, that makes these pages more, not less, valuable as statements. Koller didn't have to take sides, put a slant on things, because at the time there were no sides.'

'No,' Lepage said. 'No.'

'On those pages, Koller, in considerable checkable detail, gives the established, verified, separate provenances of *The*

Stricken Fig Tree, Vision of Malachi and *The Awakening.* No lacunae, no guesses, no speculation, only meticulous, thorough documentation.'

'They're the real thing?' Lepage whooped.

'Nobody has ever challenged the scholarship of Koller. Certainly, I would not.'

Another constable came in hurriedly and said to Lepage: 'We've picked up a lady in the grounds, sir. She gave your name.'

'Of course she fucking did. Who?'

A policewoman came into the gymnasium with Julia. One of the sergeants closed the sauna door on the two naked men, Indippe duetting again now with Nev. Julia looked very upset and ashamed. He put an arm around her. 'What is it, darling?'

'I saw your car leaving as I came home from Spud-O'-My-Life,' she whispered in his ear. 'I couldn't understand where you could be going so late, so I followed. You know what jealousy can do, George. Out-of-hours calls at the Hulliborn, for example. I've been on edge a little. Now, I find from the police that you have enough trouble here, without my bringing extra. What the hell's that filthy screaming noise?' She stared at the sauna door.

'A little celebration. A get-together: Nev, an American professor, and Flounce. Please, Julia, don't blame yourself for tonight. It must have appeared as if I—'

The main door of the gym burst open, and a young, clearly desperate man dashed in carrying a distinguished-looking vase. He had short, peroxide-assisted blond hair and a long, sad, saintlike face. Lepage was still holding Julia and felt her grow almost unbelievably tense as she gazed at this man. And the man stared at her for a moment and stood still. He seemed on the point of speaking but then recovered himself. Glancing about wildly he saw the group of police and spun around as if contemplating retreat back into the grounds. But from out there came the sound of police whistles and snarling dogs.

The man suddenly flung himself at the sauna door, perhaps thinking this was an alternative way out. Steam and the non-music rolled forward and enveloped him. He ran ahead, apparently still unaware that this was not an exit but a cubicle. More police arrived at the gymnasium door, some with dogs. They closed around the sauna entrance. Escape for the man with the vase was impossible. Now, it was much more reminiscent of a Devil's Island chase and recapture.

'Oh my God, my God,' Julia muttered, freeing herself from Lepage's arms.

'Don't be upset, darling,' he said. 'It's a burglar, that's all. He's still carrying some of the stuff.'

One of the police sergeants entered the sauna and after a few minutes came out with the young man handcuffed to him. In his free hand, the sergeant carried the vase. A constable handcuffed himself to the man's other wrist.

Again, Lepage saw him stare at Julia, then possibly half smile and shrug. She was weeping. The sergeant said: 'You're going to have to change your nickname, Nothing Known, because something will be.'

'Will be what?' Lepage asked.

'Known,' the sergeant said.

From the sauna came the sound of the would-be song getting under way again after the interruptions, louder and less catchy than ever.

Lepage said: 'Julia, you think you know this crooked intruder? It was almost as though he and you—'

'Altogether in the chorus!' Nev and Bernard yelled as one.

Twenty-Five

The wedding of Falldew and Ursula Wex turned into nothing less than a full-scale festival, their own ceremony serving as a starting point for this general Hulliborn day of glorious jubilee. As was so often the case, Dr Kanda put things admirably. He told Lepage: 'This is like the highly meaningful end of many, if not all, Shakespearean comedies, such as *A Midsummer Night's Dream*, I would say, in which the main protagonists are married; this happy bonding also typifying restoration of general social order after prolonged chaos, with all-round reconciliation of previously antipathetic elements.'

'Ghost of F.R. Leavis, thank you,' Dr Itagaki said.

Just the same, Kanda was right. Urse and Nev held their reception in the Hulliborn main hall and everyone came, including Sam Vaux, the Minister, and his wife, and H. de T. (Gadarene) Timberlake, chairman of the Museum's Board and Mrs Timberlake. Her thin body was so plank-like that Lepage wondered sometimes whether H. de T. had married her to suit his surname. Itagaki and Kanda had some Japanese embassy people with them, eager to see how the medical exhibition would be housed, now choice of the Hulliborn had been confirmed. Most of the museum staff were also invited, plus relatives and many local dignitaries.

Lady Butler-Minton did not attend, but remained in Jimma with Trudy; apparently they were very content with each other. There'd been hints that Quent Youde might go out there to reclaim Penny, but he seemed to have abandoned that plan. Vaux told Lepage: 'You'll recall I sent my bag man, Lionel Clode, to see Penelope. He's the one who reports their rhapsodical state and good relations with the locals, although older people remember Flounce and call Penny Sir Lady Butler-Minton, which annoys her. Surprisingly effective though he might be, Clode failed to get the tapes. Perhaps anyone would have failed. But the tapes are not important any longer, are they? After all, Penny and Trudy have given up any idea of writing their scurrilous material about Flounce, in view of what everyone now knows Bernard Indippe discovered re Butler-Minton's courage and competence: the tapes, I gather, endorse this favourable version. Given the universal esteem now attaching to Flounce's name, Penny has withdrawn her objections to a memorial. Or memorials. Perhaps we should think of a bust of dear Bernard next! Maybe once in a while or less – oh, yes, less – American scholarship is not such a fart-arseing joke. Did I hear that scratch from Enteritis went septic and could affect the sight of one eye?

'Myself, I'm damn relieved to see it all buttoned up, and I assure you Gadarene is, too. He's been able to settle down to a new canto on the rust epic now this crisis is out of the way. I'm relieved, also, that your Conclave decided so wisely that it would be worth having both busts of Flounce. If a thing's worth doing, it's worth doing twice, as it were, particularly when it concerns someone as deep-down unquenchable as B-M.'

'Several of us had been hoping to see Sally Jill Ash,' Lepage replied, 'to give her the excellent news direct, Minister. As a matter of fact, Angus Beresford is always very interested in talking to people from that part of the States.'

Vaux glanced about, possibly wanting to make sure his wife was not close by. 'Probably we'd all gained the notion that she'd turn out bonny. Justified,' he said with a very wholesome smile. 'Totally justified. Something of a *tendresse* developed between Sally and me in London during the negotiations. I don't think I'm overstating her attitude. I am definitely not overstating mine, and believe I conveyed everything that needed to be conveyed. You can tell Beresford he can keep his roving hormones caged. Sally Jill's husband is a quite a w—'

'Wanker?'

'Is he? Why do you think that? No, I was going to say quite a wonderful chap, and is highly satisfied with the deal struck for distribution here and in Europe of his stop-baldness balm. Perhaps when Sally's over again I'll bring her down to see their Flounce thing in place. Oh, yes, she'd like that, and there'll be a lot of visits to Britain now, because of Frank W.'s business.

I gather the Kalamazoo bust will be done as if looking at B–M
from the left, and the Japanese one as from the right. Or vice
versa. Anyway, they complement each other nicely, a sort of
global view, which is appropriate, given Flounce's international
status. It's all turned out a treat, really. The Japanese internal
exploration and cutting gear are pulling the crowds, aren't they,
and you've got your first-class rating officially blessed by
everyone short of the Queen? This, though, I can tell you
now was little to do with the Japanese exhibition, but almost
wholly a matter of the "El Grecos" turning out to be El Grecos.
The credit for that really did make the Hulliborn look golden,
Youde standing out virtually alone against all the attacks. Of
course, you were among those few who supported him, so the
knighthood might yet come.'

To Lepage, this seemed less important now. Why had he
sweated so much about that? Julia would probably still like it,
but after the strange little display of tremors over the peroxided
burglar at Penny Butler-Minton's, Lepage could not feel certain
Julia would always be around. Such a puzzle! She had appeared
deeply jealous about him at Penelope's house that night, yet
had obviously also been obsessed by the young crook, as if
knowing him much more than very well. Women could operate
on two fronts at once, just like men, couldn't they? Naturally
– and why not?

As to Kate Avis, he thought titles would matter little to her.
Kate's tastes were basic, though not as basic as what Nev had
offered in Folk, thank you. She and Lepage had spent a happy
morning on the floor of a stores' Portakabin out at the Iron
Age village site. Maybe his future lay with her. For all sorts of
reasons, she seemed part of the Hulliborn now. He decided
he'd probably hang on in the job for a while.

'I hope you'll congratulate Quent Youde personally, Minister,'
Lepage said. 'He's surprisingly vulnerable, and sets store by
these things.'

'I have already – the eternal, posturing, Degas-wannabe twat,'
Vaux replied. His wife approached with Gadarene Timberlake
and *his* wife.

'Felicitations, felicitations, George,' Mrs Vaux cried. 'The
Hulliborn is where it should be, on top again. You've shown

how to fuse commerce and culture, a very modish skill. But, tell me, have you discovered yet how not only the Monet reappeared on its Hulliborn wall, but also the El Grecos?'

'No, but the day after their proven authenticity became known they were suddenly back, just like that. Same procedure as the Monet. Same source? Who knows? But we'll gladly do without the El Greco insurance, as long as they're here and real.'

'Inside job?' Gadarene suggested.

'What about Simberdy?' Mrs Vaux said. 'Couldn't it be him? Wasn't there a fat man involved? He fits.'

'But Simberdy is Asiatics,' Lepage said.

'Just an idea,' the Minister's wife replied. Then she stepped in among Lepage's special uncertainties and worries. 'Look here, George, I don't think Julia is looking too great. There's been a change since I last came to the Hulliborn with Sam on one of his official visits. Is the potato thing taking too much out of her? I heard she runs a late-night kiosk.'

'Something's disturbed her,' Lepage said. 'I wish I knew what. We happened to see a burglar captured in the act at Penny's place. That did bother Julia. The trouble is, the police say he's hard and won't talk to them about anything. I'm puzzled as to what the incident meant.'

Gadarene said: 'The story is around. I gather he was carrying a piece of Kangxi porcelain. Would Julia have been perturbed in case he broke it – or simply at the sight of someone's treasures being abused? I mean, a sort of symbol: vandals bearing off a revered thing of beauty. People can be so sensitive over such matters.'

'Oh, get stuffed, Gadarene,' Mrs Vaux replied. 'Why not try living in the real world? A pretty burglar, Lepage? Quite possibly local?'

Lepage thought back to the holy face. 'Well, yes, I suppose he was pretty. Local? Yes, again, the police recognized him.'

'Women can be very susceptible that way,' Mrs Timberlake pointed out. 'You've heard of "a bit of rough", I expect. Good body – I mean thighs and so on?' She grew breathless.

'And you, preoccupied in your various ways, George,' Mrs Vaux said. 'Is it any wonder, poor girl?'

There was a joyous call for silence by the master of

ceremonies. This afternoon, Falldew had on a good, properly fitting tails suit that made him look like the enlarged snapshot of a black-handled penknife. He went now with Ursula to the spot on the balcony where he had started his previous speech at the Founder's, so briskly terminated by Penny B-M. 'Friends,' he began, 'we are in a wonderful treasure palace of the past this afternoon, perhaps the most wonderful in the world, and the past will always be the creator of today, the necessary foundation of today. Thank God for the past and those who brought it to us, such as Sir Eric Butler-Minton, alas now deceased. Yes, finally deceased.' He smiled, as if freed from a burden, like the traveller in *Pilgrim's Progress.*

Keith Jervis – full-time staff at last – and standing just behind Lepage, said: 'He's pissed, of course, but not too pissed. Doesn't Keeper Wex look regal? You can't beat a blue silk suit for class.'

Falldew continued amiably: 'At this lovely wedding –' he turned and kissed Ursula on the cheek – 'at this lovely wedding we see the Then and the Now sweetly cohabiting. And that is how it should be, must be. In one way, Ursula and I are the Then – she Urban Development, myself Palaeontology (involuntarily retired). Yet, though we both have inhabited a distant past and reverence it, we are also so much part of Now, even, perhaps, if I may be permitted, *stars* of this glorious, unique Today. Yes, in this resplendent Now, we two come together, come together vividly, infinitely satisfyingly, elements of the beautiful present.'

'Is he getting crude?' Beresford asked Lepage. 'Shall I go and thump him?'

'He's fine,' Lepage replied and led the applause. Ursula shook hands with herself, hands above her head, like a victorious boxer.